GETTING PICKLED

ALLISON RAYNE

ISBN (paperback) : 979-8-9902897-2-7
ISBN (ebook) : 979-8-9902897-3-4

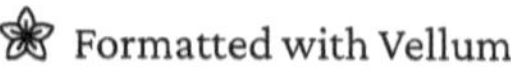 Formatted with Vellum

*To all those who feel the need to put on a
mask to get through the day.*

I see you.

Every part of you is my favorite part.

CONTENT WARNINGS

Getting Pickled is a spicy, romantic story with an HEA, but includes some things I want readers to be aware of:

- Explicit language (my editor said there were a lot of "fucks" and then I added more)
- Explicit (and consensual) sex scenes, including oral sex, edging, domination, and spanking
- Depiction of physical injury (accidental)
- Familial abandonment and emotional neglect
- Parental sickness (Alzheimer's) and death
- Toxic/manipulative relationships and emotional abuse
- Alcohol consumption
- Anxiety disorder and depression

All dogs in this story remain alive and happy at the end, as always!

pick·led | ˈpikəld |

Losing a pickleball match without scoring any points
    (typically 11-0)

1

———————

WILLOW

Sweat glides down my burning hot skin. My heart pounds wildly against my ribs as I squeeze my eyes shut, trying to control my ragged breaths. Readying myself for this. God, I'm so close.

Licking my lips, I look to my partner, whose name I don't actually remember. He isn't all that good, and I've been doing almost all the work myself here. But I really need this.

I'm so close now.

Just two more points and I will win this pickleball tournament.

"Ten nine on two!" my best friend, Angie, shouts from the other side of the court before lobbing it in my direction. I let it bounce in my square and return it easily to our other friend, Faris. As I run up to the kitchen line, Faris hits it to my left out of reach, but luckily my partner gets to it just in time. Angie returns a fast shot, the bright yellow ball flying past me on the right, definitely too far out of reach for me or my partner to hit, and it lands just inside the line before bouncing away.

And that's game.

The small crowd gathered around us erupts in cheers.

"UGH!" I yell out, turning around to my partner. "Sorry, man, I should've had that."

"No worries, Willow. That was a close one." He extends his paddle out to me, and I tap it in return. "There's always next week."

True, this wasn't a real tournament, just one of our weekly matches that determines our rankings in an app called DUPR, the standard system for ranking pickleball players based on their opponents and the outcome of matches, as well as points won and points allowed. The members here have their ranking posted on the wall for all to see, to help motivate us to be the best. So I treat every one of these matches like a tournament.

Because I seriously hate losing.

I've been trying to raise my number for weeks, but I keep slipping further and further down the ranks. Maybe if they stopped pairing me with bad players I could win a few matches once in a while.

The next round starts in about twenty minutes, so we'll see where everyone ends up after they finish.

Angie and Faris are jumping up and down, cheering as the other members of the facility begin to disperse and resume their own matches. We walk up to the net to congratulate them on their solid victory, but I silently berate myself. I should've had that last shot. I've just been so distracted all morning.

"Good game," we all say, tapping paddles.

My partner is another semi-regular here at our local indoor pickleball facility, but I cannot for the life of me ever remember his name. Is it Jim?

Possibly-Jim walks off the courts as he says, "Alright, I've gotta head out, I'll catch you all next week!"

"Bye! See you next week," I shout after him.

I really need to get better at remembering people's names. I'm not trying to be rude, I'm just not a people person.

He packs away his paddle and lifts his duffel bag over his shoulder. When he walks past the front desk and through the front doors, Angie nudges me with her elbow.

"What?"

"What's up with you today?" Angie asks with pinched brows. "You seemed distracted out there. That's not like you."

In the distance, laughter echoes off the tall concrete walls as a memory from last night flashes through my mind. I feel a prickle of heat climbing up my neck, but just as quickly, I shake it away.

"I know. Just off. I didn't sleep well." I place my paddle on the ground to tighten my high ponytail before running my hands down my face with a sigh.

"Wouldn't have anything to do with your date, would it?" Faris asks with a devilish grin.

"Oh, you mean the worst date I've *ever* been on?" I lower my hands from my face dramatically. "Yeah, that might have something to do with it."

The two of them exchange a knowing glance and roll their eyes. Traitors.

"What did you call him?" Angie puts her index finger to her chin in fake contemplation. "The asshole who killed your desire to ever date anyone, ever again?"

I raise my eyebrows and nod vigorously. "Yes. I'm done. This is what I get for listening to you two and downloading Tinder. Why can't you just let me rot in peace?"

"Okay, so you had one bad date, big deal. You'll match with someone else again," Faris says, bringing his water bottle to his lips.

"Umm, no. I deleted the app off my phone before I even left the restaurant."

"What?" Angie shrieks.

"What's the point? I hate dating apps and...you know...people in general. They're the worst."

Faris wraps a sweaty arm around my shoulders. "Aw, come on Will, isn't that a bit extreme? I'm sure the right person is just around the corner."

Here we go. Faris, the eternal optimist. The hopeless romantic. Even when it comes to a lost cause like me.

"Easy for you to say, you landed the perfect husband." I shrug off his arm. "Simon is funny, sweet, supportive...not to mention insanely hot."

"That is true," he says with a flash of his warm, brilliant smile. He adjusts his headband to hold back the wild, curly black hair that's come loose from his topknot. "He's also waiting for me at home, so I need to start heading out. Big anniversary plans today and all."

I grab his forearm. "Wait, has it been a year already?"

Angie and I attended their lavish wedding last year in the Bahamas at this incredibly fancy, all-inclusive resort, with the ceremony right on the beach. Bright, tropical flowers surrounded the twenty of us present as the grooms, in matching white tuxes, said their heart-wrenching, poetic vows with the waves crashing behind them.

It was so beautiful it almost made me believe in love again.

Almost.

"One year. Crazy, right?" He beams.

They're so cute it's obnoxious.

"Well, happy anniversary!"

Angie adds, "You two have fun. Don't do anything I wouldn't do."

"I don't even want to know what that could possibly entail, Ang," he says.

I nod in agreement. Angie has always been pretty wild, and even at twenty-six she hasn't shown any signs of slowing or settling down. She's only had one serious boyfriend in her life, and that was her high school sweetheart. It didn't end well.

"See you for open play next week?" she asks.

He leans down to hug her. "Wouldn't miss it." He turns to me and wraps me in a tight, sticky embrace. Faris is one of the only people in the entire world I would ever let hug me, let alone when we're covered in sweat.

"Love you, miss you!" he says with a grin.

"Love you more!" Angie and I say at the same time.

We both watch as our sweet Faris heads to the back wall to gather his things. The sound of hard plastic balls against paddles echoes around the enormous space as he exits through the front doors of Dink Shot.

Run by an awesome guy named Darrell Frink, this place opened two years ago and has been growing in popularity ever since. It's one of our favorite places to hang out.

The indoor space is comprised of eight courts spread out on the main floor—four on each side, with a grouping of tables and chairs down the center—separated by waist-high netting. Along the back wall are benches and shelves to store players' belongings.

Near the entrance and to one side of the reception desk are a few plush couches and a self-checkout snack bar. On the other side of the front desk is a pro shop where you can buy all kinds of merchandise and equipment.

But the best part of Dink Shot is upstairs above the lobby and pro shop: the bar. A fun place to hang out after playing or even just a casual night out. Their food is really good too.

"Singles match? Just you and me?" Angie asks, wiping the

sweat off her brow. Strands of blonde hair have fallen out of her braid, sticking to her pale, freckled skin.

I'm so off my game today I'll probably get crushed, but I say, "Let's do it." I can never say no to playing another round of pickleball.

I grab my paddle off the ground, and we walk to one of the two courts our group has reserved for open play. Taking my place back near the baseline, I pull in a deep breath to get centered.

Angie stands diagonal to me, ball in hand. She holds her hand out as she says, "Zeros on start!" before dropping the ball and serving it over to me. We go back and forth for a few rounds, getting into a decent groove. I'm still not up to the level I'd like to be, but at least I'm not embarrassing myself.

Everyone around here knows I'm ultracompetitive, but I really can't help it. I've always been this way. Ever since I was a kid and my older sister and I would turn every little thing into a competition. Cleaning our rooms, racing to the bus stop. Family game night was our Olympics and usually resulted in lots of shouting and cursing.

Plus, I love games where there's a clear winner and a clear loser. It gives me a tangible goal to focus on and work toward. It's just how my mind works.

That laugh again. Now I *know* I've heard it before. The obnoxious cackling grates on my nerves.

I look around the room to see where it's coming from, but suddenly Angie hits the ball to me, and I nearly miss her serve. I return it at the last second, but now I'm way too distracted. I try my best to ignore this person so I can focus on beating Angie and *not* throwing my paddle in a fit of rage.

I hit the ball back to her, but it goes wide, awarding Angie her seventh point.

"Fucking motherfucker!"

Okay, that's it.

I turn with a scowl, and staring back at me is a handsome, dark-haired man holding a paddle and wearing a wide, shit-eating grin.

Luca Giordano.

The worst Tinder date of all time.

2

———

LUCA

"It'll be fun, Luca. I promise," Max says as he parks at the indoor pickleball facility downtown. He presses the button to open the trunk as I climb out of his family's minivan, the sweltering late August air slapping me in the face.

I'd heard of this place before but have never actually been here. For months, Max has been trying to get me to join his group that plays pickleball twice a week. On Saturdays, they play here at the indoor courts, where members participate in ranked tournaments. Wednesdays are more casual and take place at the courts in our neighborhood, where the other players tend to be a little older, and it's more about socializing than competition.

He assures me that everyone in the group is cool, but I haven't played in over eighteen months. The memories with Dad are still too fresh in my mind.

"I might be too hungover for this." I rub my temples, willing this headache to go away. Haven't I suffered enough? I try to avoid thinking about last night, failing miserably.

"That's definitely a *you* problem," he says, grabbing his bag from the trunk. "I still can't believe you fucked up your date so badly."

I hoist my bag over my shoulder. "Can we please not talk about that? I'm trying to forget it ever happened." The reminder of it still has me cringing. I'll be replaying it in my mind for months, if not years. My brain has a special place for memories like these so it can torture me as I try to fall asleep.

"Oh, absolutely not." He clicks his key fob, closing the trunk and locking the van with a beep. "Usually, I'm the one who's making an ass out of myself. This was a welcome change."

"Screw you." I flick the hat off his head, exposing his short-cropped, graying hair.

Max is my best friend and neighbor across the street. After moving to Athens, Illinois, last year, I met him on my first day in our little neighborhood suburb of West Brook, and we got along instantly. The crippling stress that comes with moving to a new city melted away every time he and his wife, Kayla, invited me over to hang out.

The way they are so kind and affectionate with each other reminds me a lot of Mom and Dad too. I've always wanted a marriage like that.

We've become incredibly close this past year, and their two small kids call me Uncle Luca.

If it weren't for them, I would've spent my twenty-sixth birthday last month alone.

"Maybe it wasn't as bad as you remember," Max offers as we approach the front doors. A middle-aged man exits the building, saying hi to Max as he walks past.

"I appreciate you trying to make me feel better, but no. If anything, it was way, way worse than I remember. Remind me to never drink that much ever again, please."

"I'll do my best," he says with a two-finger salute, holding the door open for me.

Liar. He's a five-star instigator. He's loving this.

I can't help but laugh as we walk in. I'm glad I never told him her name or any embarrassing details about last night. He's never going to let me live this down.

"Well, the offer still stands if you want Kayla to set you up with her friend."

I shrug. "I'll think about it."

I need to get my shit together first. The way I acted last night cannot happen again.

Being a Saturday, it's pretty crowded in here, but our group has two of the courts reserved until one o'clock. Max and I are also scheduled to play in the next round of ranked matches in about twenty minutes.

"Wow, this place is awesome!" I say, following Max to the tables in the center where a few other people are gathered.

Suddenly, that familiar and distinct sound of a pickleball paddle colliding with a ball has my chest tightening.

"Hey," a man with shaggy blond hair says to us as he approaches.

"Hey, Gary," Max replies. Pointing a thumb in my direction, he says, "This is Luca, the guy I was telling you about."

I stick my hand out and we shake. "Hey, nice to meet you, Gary. Thanks for letting me join."

"Nice to meet you too. Glad you could come out. We've got courts four and five over there," he says, pointing at the side wall to his left. "Both are taken right now but one should open up soon."

I follow the direction of his hand and am struck by the sight of a tall, beautiful woman on the court. I can't see her face from this angle, but I'm immediately drawn to her.

Her long brown hair is pulled up into a high ponytail, and

she's wearing a neon orange crop top and small black running shorts. Every perfect curve on display.

She plays with the confidence of a trained athlete and, based on the way she moves, I would put money on her having a background in tennis. I simply can't look away.

I watch as she hits the ball over the net, and it lands just outside the line. She curses like a sailor, and I can't help but grin. Who is this woman?

She whips her head in my direction, and that's when my heart stops.

Oh no.

Willow Blackburn.

Someone has sliced me open, and my guts are now spilling all over the court. I think I'm going to puke. Again.

Her face is contorted in rage as she takes me in. Oh yeah, she remembers.

I quickly turn back to Max and rub the back of my sweaty neck, trying to process what the hell is happening right now.

What is she doing here?

Shit. I was hoping to never face what happened, but seeing her here now with clear eyes, I imagine you don't get a lot of chances with someone like her. She's even more beautiful than I remember. No, not just beautiful. She's gorgeous.

And I'm an asshole.

"Hey, you okay?" Max asks. "What's wrong?"

Blood is thrumming in my ears. I'm sweating profusely. What do I do with my hands?

"Um, I don't know." I fumble for an explanation that doesn't make me look like a complete idiot. "Head rush maybe? I should've eaten a better breakfast, I guess."

"Oh, I got you. There are some granola bars in my bag. Help yourself," he says, unbothered as he starts stretching and chatting with Gary.

I don't need a granola bar. I need to figure out a way to fix what I did last night. Or maybe I could just leave? Fake being sick and...run the twelve miles home? That's a normal thing people do, right?

I steal another glance at her. She's talking with the short, blonde woman she was just playing with, as they both glare at me. The way Willow is looking at me tells me everything I need to know.

So why is it really turning me on?

Averting my eyes, I start stretching alongside Max. One thing I learned early on is that this sport is notorious for injuries, so you want to take your time stretching and warming up. And I'm definitely rusty.

After a few minutes, we join Gary at the court that just opened up, next to where Willow has since continued playing. I silently praise myself for managing to avoid looking directly at her, since there's no telling what I might end up saying to her right now.

Gary turns to me as we take our places on the court with another guy he just introduced us to, but I was so distracted that I didn't catch his name. I think he just said it's his first time playing?

"You ever play before, Luca?" Gary asks.

I pause. It's an innocent enough question, but the memories with Dad still affect me more than I'd like to admit.

"Yeah, I used to play with my dad, but...it's been a little while." Every mention of him is a punch to the gut. "Just need some practice."

"Awesome, man!" Gary says. "Just a quick rundown since we have another newcomer here." He motions to the other new guy, and I give a terse nod.

"This area by the net is called the kitchen. You want to stay out of this zone, which includes the lines. First team to eleven points wins, as long as they're ahead by two. The serve has to land in the diagonal square, and the ball has to bounce on each side before it can be hit in the air. Sound good?"

Other New Guy laughs. "Sure, why not."

"We'll help you out as we go. Our group is pretty relaxed. We're just here to have fun." He waves at the surrounding courts. "Most of us anyway."

Wait. Does that mean *she* is part of this group? I can't help but look back over my shoulder at Willow. When we lock eyes again, my mind goes blank, paralyzed under her stare. Piercing light brown eyes assess me and the guys I'm playing with.

Fuck, that look.

It reminds me a little too much of Sadie.

Why am I always attracted to women who are so wrong for me?

Turning to the blonde, she whispers something in her ear and then walks off toward the back wall. Her friend looks at us with wide eyes, her mouth twisting to one side. She gives us a small wave before following Willow off the court.

I turn back to the guys. "Who was that?" I try my best to sound casual, pretending I don't already know.

"You mean Willow?" Gary says with a laugh. "Watch out for that one. She's prickly."

"She's not so bad," Max interjects. "Just competitive. She takes the game very seriously and is known around here for her…short temper. Trust me, you do not want to get on her bad side."

I swallow around the lump in my throat.

I get the feeling it might be too late for that.

3

WILLOW

Monday morning, here we go. I've got my steaming hot coffee in hand, my ninety-five-pound black Labrador, Henry, at my feet, my favorite pickleball podcast playing through my speakers, and just a few more hours left on this freelance project before I can stop and relax for the rest of the day.

Being a self-employed graphic designer, I get to set my own hours, but the work has to get done regardless of what time it is, so it's easy for that line to blur between personal time and work time. I have an official office set up in the upstairs guest room, but sometimes I just end up with my laptop on the kitchen counter or my iPad on the couch, depending on the work. Today is one of those days I need to be up in my office.

I think back to my first design job after moving here three years ago. By chance, some guy named Darrell Frink found me on social media and inquired about me making the logo for an indoor pickleball facility and bar he was opening: Dink Shot. I wrote back and told him he missed a golden opportunity to name the place Frink's Dinks, and from there, our friendship was born.

The logo I created is a pickleball sitting on the rim of a shot glass like a garnish with "Dink Shot" arched over top. It's one of my favorite designs, and it makes me smile getting to see it in person every week on the building and all the merch.

Settling into my cozy, leather chair, I stare blankly at my dual monitors and try to summon the motivation to get going. But I'm struggling.

This project I've been working on has been particularly difficult, and it has everything to do with the client. A lot of people who hire designers never know what they want until they see what you've done, and suddenly they have all sorts of ideas. Most of the time, they just want to feel like they had a hand in it so they can take credit.

I've produced three separate logo design options for this client, and so far in each round of revisions, they get ripped to shreds.

I try to be accommodating though, seeing as how these days a lot of companies will just use AI to generate something boring and soulless and call it a day. I'm grateful when a client understands the importance of humans creating art. Even if the "art" in this case is a rebranding effort for a disgusting, sugary energy drink.

But despite difficult clients, I still love my job.

ANGIE

sign-ups are live for the tournament!

ME

yes! let's go!

once the tourney starts though, you are my competition

and Faris and I will destroy you

respectfully

ANGIE

bring it on bitch

In less than two months, Dink Shot will host their annual mixed doubles tournament, the Pickle Bowl. It's a chance for everyone in the surrounding area to come together and compete for the grand prize: tickets to the US Pickleball Open in Florida.

I would give anything to go.

The Pickle Bowl is a pretty big deal here in Athens, and also my favorite time of year.

You can sign up with a partner, or by yourself, in which case Darrell will pair you up with another single player. With mixed doubles, a man and a woman have to play together, so unfortunately, I can't play with Angie. We both agreed I get to team up with Faris this year, because he partnered with her last year.

I'm still salty over last year's tournament. I made it to the final round, but ultimately my partner and I lost by three points to Jerry and Margaret Feldman, an older married couple who were new to the area and just absolutely dominated the scene. Nobody saw them coming. But I remember everything about them and their playing style. Their strengths and their weaknesses.

This is going to be my year.

I have to attend the US Open.

ANGIE

what would it take to get you to redownload Tinder and do a double date with me and Chad this weekend??

ME

...

ANGIE

come on

ME

not gonna happen

you couldn't pay me

ANGIE

we WILL pay!

ME

hard pass

why don't you ask Faris and Simon?

ANGIE

Simon has that work trip

ME

oh yeah

sorry

enjoy Chad's huge D

ANGIE

for the last time, it's not just the size

it's *perfectly proportioned* in every way

ME

I don't need to know this much

ANGIE

what if Chad brought a friend for you?

ME

not gonna happen

ANGIE

boo. you're no fun

Like I'll ever make that mistake again. I have zero interest in dating anyone ever again.

Luca, the Tinder date from Hell. What was he even doing at Dink Shot? And he's friends with Max? I don't know Max all that well, but he's a regular in our group and comes to most of the open play sessions. Maybe Angie can find out more from Max about his annoying friend. She's way better than me at socializing.

I take a sip of my coffee, trying and failing to put Luca out of my mind, as I work on this never-ending logo design. The voices from the podcast play through my speaker, but I'm barely paying attention. I'm too busy thinking about how unfairly attractive he looked the other day, which just pisses me off even more.

He was good-looking the night of our date, as well as in his profile pictures, but I was just focused on getting the hell out of there, despite his high cheekbones, chiseled jaw, and well-manicured facial hair. Then seeing him at pickleball sober, clear-eyed, and showing off his tanned, muscular arms in a tank top was like a slap in the face.

He clearly has some personal issues to work out, and I refuse to be responsible for managing someone else's emotional baggage.

Not again.

Did he know I was going to be at Dink Shot? Somehow found out I was part of Max's group and came to torture me, all because I walked out on our date?

I'm surprised he had the balls to face me again after how he left things.

The look on his face when he recognized me though, appeared to be pure shock. So maybe it really was just a coincidence that he was there.

Some twisted surprise from the universe.

Regardless, I was here first. He can go find somewhere else to play.

ME

I still can't believe Luca showed up this weekend

ANGIE

you failed to mention how he's 10x hotter than his picture

think he's free for a double date? :)

ME

go to hell

No doubt the guys in our group have already told him about my reputation. I saw them all looking my way and laughing.

That laugh. I knew I recognized it from the night before.

He sure seems like the type to put on a nice guy act and then laugh about you behind your back. If people have something to say, then they should just be up front and say it. I don't care to try to figure people out. It's better to assume people are being dishonest from the start, making it easier when they eventually stab you in the back.

I'm very particular about who I trust and let into my life. Angie, Faris, and his husband, Simon, are pretty much it. My parents haven't made much of an effort to be involved in any part of my life, and I haven't seen or talked to my sister, Holly, in almost twelve years.

Fine by me, fewer people to concern myself with.

"…has a nice topspin. I really enjoy watching him play."

I'm not even listening anymore, so I turn off the podcast.

What's with Luca's sudden and relentless appearance in my life?

I can't help but wonder if he's actually any good at pickleball. I was too pissed off to stick around and watch him play. But...I guess I could check the DUPR app to see how he did in the ranked match.

I open it and scroll through the names in our group. When I see his score, my mouth drops open.

"*Four point three*?"

Henry's head pops up.

"Are you *fucking* kidding me?"

I've been trying to claw my way back up to a four these past few weeks, but even my highest score a few months ago was only four point two.

Looking closer at the stats, I see it was his first-ever ranked match, and he and Max played against two really good players, beating them by a decent amount. That explains the high score. But one good match doesn't prove anything. Eventually, his score will drop and average out to where it should be.

Closing my eyes, I take a deep breath. I can't let him get to me. As far as I'm concerned, he's just another opponent to beat to win the tournament.

As long as he stays out of my way.

4

———

LUCA

Mondays are the worst when you work in Corporate America. The job pays well, and I enjoy the work itself most days, but it comes at a different price: my soul dying a very slow and painful death underneath sterile fluorescent lights.

It wasn't always like this. When I was brought on as a Junior Developer five years ago, I loved everything about my job. This used to be a small, progressive company with tons of perks and a great culture. That was, of course, before we were acquired by RavTech, one of the fastest-growing tech companies in the country. Half of our staff was let go within a month, along with any "unnecessary perks," which tanked morale and shifted the company's primary objective to profit.

Sipping my coffee, I try to catch up on my morning emails, but my mind keeps wandering.

I can't believe Willow is part of Max's pickleball group. What are the odds? God, she really is beautiful. I had such a strong physical reaction to seeing her on Saturday, which I don't remember happening on our date the night before.

I guess I shouldn't be surprised, considering how wasted I was.

Then, of course, there was the crying.

My cheeks flush with heat. Fuck, that was so bad. The guy who showed up that night is not who I am.

Not that it would have worked out between us anyway. Not if she is anything like Sadie. I barely made it out of that relationship alive. She's the whole reason I moved out here.

After the acquisition, a spot opened up in the Athens office, and I jumped at the opportunity to transfer. Sadie once told me how much she hated Athens and could never live here.

It was perfect.

And now that I'm finally feeling ready to move on, I go and thoroughly ruin the first date I've been on in years like a total dickhead.

Get it together.

"Morning, Luca. Happy Monday!" Kevin says a little too cheerfully.

"Hey, boss. Good weekend?" I ask in that fake corporate voice I've perfected over the years.

Typical office chatter. I die a little each time I have to say crap like this. Like in social situations where I've learned to fake confidence to mask my anxiety, I'm basically just creating an alter ego. My work personality is my least favorite, because this kind of interaction is so forced and inauthentic. I hate it.

He leans on the doorframe to my office, crossing his legs at the ankles, and I instinctively grab a stress ball off my tidy desk.

"Can't complain, can't complain. Hit the course yesterday, been working on improving my swing, sharpening my short game, you know?"

"Yeah, no, for sure."

No idea what he's talking about. I've never played or had

any interest in golf whatsoever. I'd much rather play something fast-paced with more physical activity.

I squeeze the stress ball, unable to come up with anything else to say to fill the awkward silence.

Kevin clears his throat. "Say, I came by to see if you and your team will be ready to present this week. Higher-ups want a status report on the curriculum software."

"Oh yeah, we're still on track. Let me discuss with them and I'll put something on your calendar."

"Great, great—let's circle back soon."

I nod.

"Alright, man, make it a great week," he says before pushing off the doorframe and taking a sip from his oversized *#1 Boss* coffee mug.

"You too," I say, dropping my artificial smile the moment he's out of sight.

That coffee mug is a blatant lie. My old boss quit after just six months of working for that nepo baby motherfucker. Kevin only got the job because his dear father—who comes with his own set of problematic behaviors—is the CEO of RavTech.

I take out my morning anxiety meds from my top drawer and swallow one down with a gulp of water.

Why am I still working for these people?

I was hired right out of college, back when it was still called Spark, and we focused mainly on educational software for grade schools. I pitched a product that helped teachers build comprehensive lesson plans catered to the individual needs of students. The core objective was making sure all kids could flourish within the classroom.

RavTech loved the idea and invested a bunch of money in building up the software and expanding its capabilities. We're finally set to launch by the end of the year.

A buzz from my phone pulls my attention, and I set my stress ball back down.

MAX

Sending you the link to sign up for the
Pickle Bowl

I had forgotten all about that. Max explained that this tournament is kind of a big deal around here. The winners also get a trip to Florida to watch the US Pickleball Open, which would be cool.

ME

awesome, sounds fun

Dad would've loved all this, and he would've been so happy that I found a group of friends to keep playing pickleball with, now that he's no longer here. I was worried I wouldn't be any good on Saturday, but I pushed through the ache in my chest before muscle memory kicked in, and Max and I ended up winning our match, rising to the highest rankings of our entire group. It felt like my dad was right there with me.

MAX

Signups go on for a few weeks

And we'll find out our pairs after that

ME

I don't know how I managed to land such a good friend out here. I lucked out with Max and his incredible family. Lord knows I needed to pack up and leave Greendale to start fresh last year. I'm not sure I'll ever fully recover from so much pain and heartbreak, but each day gets a little easier.

MAX

Also dinner and drinks at our house tonight

I can't help but grin. Something to look forward to and get me through the rest of this unremarkable day. Something else to think about besides boring work emails. Or Willow.

ME

wouldn't miss it

5

WILLOW

Thank Christ we're playing tonight. It has been such a shitty day. It's like everything that could possibly go wrong has gone wrong, and I've just hit my fucking limit. Between my client rejecting all of my logo designs, my air-conditioning going out, and Henry barfing in my bed at two a.m., I really need to take this frustration out on something. Or someone.

I've been hanging out at Angie's for the past hour, already dressed and ready. The AC guy can't come until tomorrow, so Henry and I are having a sleepover here tonight. I absolutely cannot sleep if it's too hot.

Not that I haven't crashed on her couch a million times before. I have a drawer here for my stuff—just as she does at my place—even though we only live a few houses down from each other. It's just easier this way, especially if one of us winds up needing something in the middle of the night.

Our dogs, being brother and sister from the same litter, chase each other around the house. They'll hardly even know we're gone.

"Ready to head down yet?" I ask Angie from her living room, setting down a bright yellow pillow on the couch. Bold colors cover every inch of her place, from the indigo couch to the rainbow area rug to the royal blue walls and everything in between.

"Yep, let's go," she says, coming out of her bedroom and putting her hair up in a tight bun. "Do we know who's coming tonight?"

"No idea. I haven't been checking the group chat."

"Me neither."

I turned off notifications for the group months ago after a bunch of drama went down. One of the older guys got so mad he threw his paddle at someone's face and subsequently got banned from playing with us. It nearly broke up the entire group.

Now sometimes I forget there even is a group chat.

We say goodbye to our pups and head out, duffel bags slung over our shoulders. Angie locks her front door, and we start walking down the street toward the clubhouse. Wednesday matches typically take place at the West Brook neighborhood courts. Thankfully, they approved the renovations to convert half the tennis courts into pickleball courts last year.

I like playing here for the convenience, but the indoor courts are where I can play more competitively and work on being a better player in our ranked matches.

"How are things going with Chad?"

"They're good," she says unconvincingly.

I narrow my eyes. "What was that?"

"What was what?"

"Come on, don't bullshit me. What did he do now?"

"Nothing! He just..." She pauses. "I don't know, he seems

distant lately. Starting to feel like if I didn't initiate conversation, it would all just fizzle out, you know?"

"Then let it. Stop texting him. If he's not pursuing you, then he's a waste of time."

"But I like him. I'm not ready to give up on him yet. Or his perfect dick."

"I know. Just don't settle, okay? You deserve to be with someone who is borderline obsessed with you and worships the ground you walk on. Regardless of his penile qualities."

She shoots me a warm smile. "You deserve that too, babe."

I shrug. Sometimes I wonder if that's even true, or if I'm too jaded for any kind of happy ending.

I take a moment to look around at our little neighborhood and appreciate how beautiful it is. Tucked away from the bustling nearby city, the entire area is surrounded by towering ash and pine trees, with a massive lake in the center. At night, if it's quiet enough, you can hear the frogs croaking in the distance.

Angie and I have lived here for three years now. The people here are mostly, sort of, okay. There are a few cool people, but a lot of them are super nosy. The Facebook page is entertaining though. Watching people with nothing better to do fight over insignificant, stupid shit. People convinced their mail is being stolen or complaining about kids walking around after dark.

Thank goodness we got townhouses on the same block so we can hang out almost every night. We've known each other for eight years, ever since our first year of college and fate matched us up as roommates. It was like magic how quickly we became best friends, almost as if we had already known each other our entire lives and were simply reuniting.

It only took us a month to decide that we would travel the world together someday. We started putting money aside so we would have to do it when the time was right. We really should get on that soon.

Although we get along so well, we honestly could not be more different. She is outgoing and loves a crowd, while I am definitely more introverted and wary of other people. She would always be the one dragging me around to parties and making friends, while I typically ended up in strangers' laundry rooms playing with their pets.

"You think Max will be there tonight?" I ask.

"I don't know, maybe. He's usually here on Wednesdays." A smile plays on her lips. "Why do you ask?"

"I thought maybe you could get some info on Luca and why he brought him on Saturday. I'd like to know if he's going to be ruining *all* of my weekends from now on."

"I see," she says with a smirk.

"What?"

"Would it be the worst thing if he started coming around to Dink Shot?"

"Yes. He's a jerk, remember?"

"If you say so. I'll see what I can find out."

Despite making the decision to associate with Luca, Max seems pretty cool. Though I haven't talked with him a whole lot outside of some friendly chatter at the courts. He runs a vet clinic just outside the city, but I only learned that fact after Angie and I started seeing the one recommended by the breeder. Angie has met his wife and kids, but again, I've been told I'm not very "approachable," therefore making it hard to make friends.

Is it even possible to make new friends once you reach a certain age?

God, I'd rather not think about my upcoming birthday. I certainly don't feel twenty-seven.

Angie wants to do a whole big thing, but I'd be fine just going to a quiet dinner with her, Faris, and Simon.

I really hate birthdays. Like it's some big accomplishment that you were born? Even worse are the people who try to make it their birthday *week*. Sorry, no, you're not special.

Besides, the memories associated with my birthday still send me into a bit of a depression, so I'd rather not think about it at all.

The plinking sounds grow louder as we approach the courts next to the clubhouse. Angie and I step onto the blue asphalt and put down our stuff along the fence before stretching. I count eight other people here, and they've already split off to start two doubles matches. We warm up, just the two of us, hitting the ball back and forth, unconcerned with where it's landing.

"Do you think anyone else is going to show up, or do you want to start a singles match?" The moment the words leave my lips, I spot them walking toward the courts.

Max...and *him*.

I let the ball bounce past me as I clench the paddle at my side. My jaw is so tight my teeth might crack.

What is he doing here?

Why is he suddenly everywhere I am?

"You wanna serve, or—" Angie follows my eye line and notices them too. "Ah, this should be interesting." A wide, mischievous smile spreads across her face.

I walk over to her, smacking her on the arm. "What the fuck?"

We both survey them coming closer, too late to make any kind of escape.

"You sure you don't want to give him another chance? Cause he's looking pretty damn good right about now."

Dammit, she's right. He's even more attractive today than

he was on Saturday. A bit of black hair peeks out from the sides of a white backwards baseball cap, giving him that charming bad-boy vibe.

He's wearing black gym shorts that stop just above the knee and a sleeveless navy-blue athletic shirt cut low under the arms, showing off the sides of his toned olive-brown torso and those strong arms I can't help but stare at. He's muscular, but not so much that it looks like he spends every waking moment in the gym. It's the body of someone who is active and takes care of himself.

The man is a walking contradiction.

Like right now, how he's smiling and carefree. Nothing like the guy who showed up to our date. This "happy" persona is probably just an act to get people to like him. Proving once again that people are always lying about something and hiding their true intentions.

He's not fooling me.

Thinking about that night just makes me angry all over again. Maybe his showing up here is actually a blessing in disguise. I need someone to take my frustration out on tonight.

6

———

LUCA

Max knocks on my door around six o'clock. I step outside and take a deep breath, appreciating the cooler weather we've been having the past few days. The faint smell of woodsmoke hangs in the air, and it finally feels like summer is coming to an end.

A perfect night for playing.

We walk the few blocks down to the clubhouse where the group plays on Wednesdays. This is my first time playing in the neighborhood, and I love that we can just walk to the courts.

I've seen people out here playing before but never got the nerve to join them. And now, after playing just once since I moved here and remembering how much I loved it, I don't want to stop.

Hopefully, it wasn't a fluke. I'm not sure I'll ever be able to play without thinking of Dad, but at least on Saturday it only brought back happy memories.

"Work going okay?" I ask as we pass by a playground teeming with small children. Their playful screams and laughter echoing around us.

"Not too bad. Pretty busy, but I wouldn't give it up for anything." Max's vet practice was just voted one of the best businesses in town. He got a plaque and everything. "What about you?"

I shrug. "Not great."

"Sorry, man. Can't help you out there, unless you want to come work with animals."

"Don't tempt me."

He shoots me a sympathetic look but doesn't pry. He's heard me vent enough about my job this past year.

Less than a block away, the courts come into view, and my stomach drops the moment I see her.

Fuck.

I haven't told Max that Willow was the woman I went on a date with. If you can even classify that as a real date. I'm still reeling from the fact that she's even friends with this group, and that if I'm going to be playing regularly again, I'll be seeing her every Saturday.

But what is she doing *here* at the West Brook courts?

Is it too late to turn around and go back home?

What am I going to say?

I clear my throat. "Hey, didn't we see those women at Dink Shot this weekend?" I ask Max as casually as possible.

"Oh yeah, they live in West Brook too. You'll probably be seeing them a lot if you keep playing. Especially Willow. She never misses open play."

Of course she lives here.

Of course she plays all the time.

The universe hasn't thoroughly punished me enough yet.

I'm not sure I can do this.

How have I never seen her in this neighborhood before tonight?

My heart picks up speed as I rub the back of my neck. "So, Willow, and...uh...who's the other one?"

"Angie Harris. They're best friends, and they both live in the other section of townhouses down the street," he says, pointing to his right.

"Awesome." I'm doing a terrible job stalling. We're almost to the courts.

He smirks. "I believe they're both single or at least not married if you want me to introduce you. I only know them a little from playing though, I've never hung out with them socially or anything."

Nausea swirls in my stomach.

As we approach the entrance to the courts, I grab Max's arm. "Wait. I need to tell you something before we go in there, because I don't think I can avoid this any longer."

He shoots me a startled glance as I let go of him. "What is it? You alright?"

No, I am most certainly not alright.

I take off my hat and run a clammy hand through my hair, looking off toward Willow and Angie as I take a deep breath. "Okay...so...about Willow? She...umm...how do I say this? We've actually met before."

"Oh, really?" He pauses and shakes his head. "Wait, then why have you been acting like you don't know who she is?"

I chew on my lip as he narrows his eyes. Putting my hat back on, I fidget with the hair sticking out on the sides.

"No..." he says, glancing toward the courts where Willow and Angie are no doubt staring at us. I don't dare follow his gaze to confirm. "Tinder date?"

I wince, nodding slightly.

"The epic failure of a date where you acted so horribly that you claim you can never speak of what happened, even to your best friend? *That* date?"

I nod again.

"Oh damn," he says, dropping his head with a laugh. "This is too good. You've pissed off Willow Blackburn. You're fucked."

I wipe my mouth and cross my arms. "I thought I would never have to face her again after that night. Now you're telling me we play in the same pickleball group *and* live in the same neighborhood?"

He claps a hand on my shoulder. "I wish you luck, my friend."

I follow Max onto the court where there are two other doubles matches going on, and then there's Willow and Angie standing in one of the open courts. I keep my gaze averted for as long as possible, but when I finally look over, I realize I really am fucked.

Tonight, she's wearing a cute little white-and-black tennis outfit. A skin-tight tank top tucked into one of the shortest skirts I've ever seen, revealing her long, tan legs. A high pony-tail pokes out from a matching visor.

Heart-shaped face and full lips. Those light brown eyes I've already committed to memory narrowed in my direction. I can practically feel the searing heat of her gaze.

It's going to take all the strength I have to focus on playing tonight and not imagining pinning her to the ground and doing unspeakable things under that skirt.

Ahead of me, Max approaches them and waves.

"Hey, Angie. Willow." He motions toward me. "I'd like you to meet my neighbor, Luca. He's joining the regular group."

I guess we're just going to pretend like we all don't know what happened?

She's almost as tall as I am, so probably about five foot ten. Now that I think of it, I do remember her being pretty tall that night, because I could not stop staring at those legs. Like an asshole.

Angie elbows Willow ever so slightly and gives her a stern look before extending her hand to me. "Hey, Luca. I'm Angie." She smiles up at me sweetly, her pale face freckled.

I shake her hand. "Nice to meet you, Angie."

We all look at Willow, who hasn't moved an inch. I shoot her my best winning smile, and she slowly, reluctantly holds her hand out.

A small, colorful tattoo on the inside of her wrist catches my attention. It's a heart with watercolors splattered around it like paint. I suddenly want to know everything about it and about her. I'm a sucker for a girl with tattoos.

I wonder if she has any other tattoos.

Stop.

I can't go there.

The images of Sadie's tattoos drift into my thoughts before I quickly block them out.

Our hands touch, and my body lights up as electricity shoots up my forearm.

No, not electricity. Fire.

I force my expression to remain neutral, but my insides feel like kindling, and she just struck a match. "Hey. I'm Luca. It's nice to meet you."

She nods once and breaks our handshake way too soon. With barely more than a second glance, she turns away.

Max silently mouths "*fucked*," before calling out, "Guess it's us four. Who wants to serve?"

"We're up," Willow says evenly as she and Angie walk around the net to the other side of the court, taking their places behind the baseline.

No turning back now.

Max said the other day that Willow is ultra competitive,

and right now she's eyeing me like she hopes I'll drop dead right here.

Time to turn on the charm and pretend I have more confidence than I actually do.

I may still be a little out of practice, but after Saturday I was pleased to find I could still play a decent game. By now she's probably seen my ranking on DUPR, so I won't insult her by playing down my skills and letting her win. I get the feeling she would see right through it.

So instead, I'm going to have some fun and mop the floor with her and her little friend.

Game on.

7

WILLOW

He lives here. In *my* neighborhood. What gods did I piss off to deserve this?

We'll just let everyone see who he really is after I whoop his ass.

You can tell a lot about a person by the way they play a sport like pickleball. How he handles losing, for instance.

I flip my paddle around, readjusting my grip as I stare him down. "Zeros on start!" I shout before striking the ball, aiming for Luca's feet.

He backs up a step, letting it bounce, and returns it effortlessly. The ball heads down the center line, and both Angie and I aim for it as it bounces, but at the last second, we both back off, thinking the other would take the shot. It flies past us, and I try to suppress a groan.

"Sorry, thought you had it."

"All good," she says, walking up to me. Then quieter so only I can hear, she adds, "Hey, don't let him get to you. He's just another opponent."

I grab the ball that has rolled to the fence and lob it over the net for Luca to serve. Letting out a long breath, I force my hands to unclench.

"Zeros on one," he says before serving it toward me. A solid serve with a decent amount of backspin. I anticipate the change in direction as it bounces, then strike it perfectly. The ball lands just to Luca's side, but he doesn't miss either.

We go back and forth like this for a while. Angie and Max do their part, but it's clear that Luca and I are dominating the game. He is frustratingly good, and neither side can make any real progress. Each round lasts a decent amount of time, often turning into a quick firefight at the net.

I find myself curious as to why he's just now joining this group if he can play this well. Did he just move here?

Not like I care.

After each team wins a match, I'm ready for a break. I hate to say it, but Luca is a worthy opponent. I'm impressed.

Doesn't mean I trust him though.

The four of us clink paddles at the net and say "good game" to one another before parting ways. Hopefully there are some other pairs ready to play Max and Luca, leaving me in peace.

About two hours later, when the sun is going down and the crickets come out to sing, Angie and I are finishing a match with a young married couple. We end up beating them 12-10. They played well, and I thought for sure they were going to take us right up until the end.

It's been such a beautiful night, I wanted to keep playing for as long as my body would let me. But my aching feet are telling me it's time to go home.

As Angie and I head toward the side of the court where all our stuff is, I notice Max and Luca heading that way too. Great.

I can feel Luca's stare boring a hole into me as we approach the same spot at the exact same time. Uncomfortable in the silence that falls over us, I gather my belongings and pretend to ignore him. Scuffling feet and the plinking of hard plastic balls echo softly in the background.

Max blurts, "Hey, Angie, can I talk to you about something real quick?" He points to the edge of the court.

Angie looks at me curiously for just a second before replying, "Umm, yeah, sure."

I don't miss the alarming look Luca shoots Max as they walk away from us.

It's a glimpse of the real him under that mask he wears. I'm all too familiar with the deception. I've dealt with it most of my life.

I hit my growth spurt and developed early, so I was known for being the tall girl or the "big girl" in school. My classmates got a real kick out of it and made sure I knew it too. Even all these years later, it still stings.

Luca glances back over at me with a wide, beaming smile that could not be more fake. I don't return it.

"You're really good out there," he says.

"Yeah, you too." I squat down and busy myself with putting my paddle away in my bag. I am not going to fill this silence. Instead, I take a long sip of my water bottle until he squats down beside me.

"Look, about the other night—"

"We don't have to do this, okay?" I interrupt.

"No, but if I can—"

"I really just want to forget that night ever happened."

"I know. Me, too. I—"

"Great, then we agree. If we have to be around each other on the courts, let's just stay out of each other's way." I zip my bag dramatically and rise to my feet, looking down at him and finally meeting his gaze.

I get an unexpected thrill from seeing him practically kneeling at my feet like this.

"Sound good?"

His surprise tells me he's probably used to getting his way and doesn't have a lot of people calling him out on his bullshit. He stands up slowly, dangerously close to invading my personal space, tilting his head ever so slightly. Shoving his hands in his pockets, he finally says, "Okay, if that's what you want."

"Good." I turn back toward Angie and whistle. The one we perfected back in college as our signal to get the other's attention in public. Most of the time it was me whistling to her when I was ready to leave a party or some other obnoxious social gathering.

Her head whips toward me, and she nods. I hear her say to Max, "I gotta go," before jogging back to me. Without looking back, she adds, "See you guys later!"

8

———

LUCA

"How was your date with Ginny last night?" Max asks as I drive us to Dink Shot for our regular Saturday morning games.

I turn down the music in my Jeep, shifting in my seat. "It was…good."

Max and Kayla have been trying to set me up with her friend Ginny pretty much since I moved in. After Willow made it clear she wanted nothing to do with me, I had to face the fact that I ruined my chance with her and move on like an adult.

"Kayla said she heard you two hit it off."

I suppose we did. She was sweet. Charming. Attractive. The type of woman I could imagine a future with. The date went smoothly, and we did seem to have a lot in common. As nervous as I was, I avoided alcohol to make sure I didn't have any repeats of last weekend.

At my silence, he adds, "She's already asking when we can all go on a double date."

This is what I've always wanted, right? Someone to settle down with and take on double dates? The potential for a kind and loving relationship like my parents had. I should grow up and give it a real chance.

"Yeah. That would be fun."

Max and I walk inside the building with our gym bags hanging off our shoulders, just in time for the ten o'clock ranked matches. It takes me a whole seven seconds to spot Willow stretching by the side wall with her friend Angie.

Looking the way she does, she's hard to miss.

She's wearing another one of those tiny tennis outfits that accentuates her luscious curves. The red pleated skirt barely brushes her thighs.

I nearly have a stroke when she bends forward to stretch her hamstrings, the sewn-in shorts underneath on full display, and I have to physically turn my body away from hers.

I clear my throat as I put my stuff down on one of the shelves next to Max's. If he notices that I'm suddenly unable to function like a normal human being, he doesn't mention it.

The owner, Darrell, approaches us. Max introduced us last week. "Morning fellas," he says. "You two are playing..." He runs a finger down his iPad screen, his eyes narrowing, "...Angie and Willow next. Good luck!"

I'm going to need it.

No, it's fine.

We have to learn to be around each other and play together without it being a big deal. Playing against Willow for the first time the other night went well, I thought. They were some of the most intense matches I've ever played. It was so energizing being tuned into someone else like that.

"Hey, you okay?" Max says with a jab to my arm.

"What? Oh yeah, great." I didn't even realize I was staring.

He pulls an arm over his chest to stretch out his shoulder as I set my paddle down, watching as Darrell approaches Angie and Willow. Angie's grin is wide as Willow rolls her eyes and drops her hands to her sides. My heart sinks a little.

When she meets my gaze from across the room I turn away quickly, starting my stretches and praying I don't embarrass myself any further. Today I just need to focus on playing. Let her see that I'm not a total dick and that we can exist in the same space just fine.

"Luca." Max snaps his fingers in front of my face.

I blink. "What?"

"I asked if you wanted to grill out tonight."

"Oh, sorry. Yeah, that sounds great."

"What's going on with you?"

I shake my head dismissively.

"You forget to eat breakfast again?"

"Nah, I'm good. Let's play."

The four of us take our spots at court number one to start playing our ranked match. Another one is about to start on the next court over, and a small crowd has already formed to watch.

Last week, someone explained that the team closest to the windows always serves first, so naturally, Angie and Willow take their positions behind the baseline by the window.

She likes to go first.

I would certainly let her go first if we were together.

Fuck, I need to stop. I can't be having those thoughts.

I focus my attention on adjusting the sweatbands on my arms and wiping my palms on my gym shorts. When I look back over, I notice Angie has the same watercolor tattoo as Willow, and in the exact same spot. They must really be close.

On our side, Max stays back and I stand just behind the kitchen.

Willow shouts, "Zeros on start!" before hitting it to Max's square. He returns it easily, and we get into a decent rhythm. After about twenty minutes, Max and I are up ten to nine. One more point and we win this match.

Directly in front of me, Willow is laser-focused and determined to win, barely sparing me a glance, but I know she's assessing me. She wants nothing more than to crush me after we each won one apiece on Wednesday.

I felt a little clunky at the start, but Max and I are playing well together.

Max sets up his serve, and we go back and forth a few more times until eventually I score the final point, giving us the win. Everyone around us cheers, and I look to Willow and smile. She played really well, and I thought it was a great match. But the look she levels me with makes my blood run cold.

Way to go, Pickleboy.

Max and I walk up to the net to tap paddles and congratulate them. "Good game," three of the four of us say. A muscle in Willow's jaw ticks.

If I thought playing together would get her to warm up to me, then I've obviously misread the situation.

I grab my water bottle by the side wall and take a sip, when a tall, attractive man with curly black hair tied up in a topknot wraps Willow in a crushing hug.

Who the hell is this guy? They certainly seem friendly.

How soon after our date did they get together?

Not that it's any of my business. Isn't that what I'm doing with Ginny, trying to move on?

"Who is that?" I ask Max, shaking out my clenched hands, realizing that my breathing had picked up. "Is he in our group too?"

"Why?" he asks innocently.

"He...uh...looks familiar is all."

"If you say so." He's not buying it, but I don't care. "His name is Faris. He plays with the weekend group here, but he doesn't live in West Brook."

"I see."

"Mm-hmm, I bet you do." He's enjoying this way too much. "Come on, let's keep playing."

"Yeah, I'll meet you out there in a minute."

Max walks away, and I steal one last glance at Willow and this Faris guy before digging into my bag and pulling out my phone, opening my texts with Ginny.

ME

I had fun last night. When can I see you again?

I need to be with someone I can envision a real future with.

It's time to move on from Willow.

And from my ex-wife.

9

LUCA

In the break room, the smell of stale, cheap coffee permeates the air as I fill up my water bottle. The bright halogen lights bounce off every surface with a harsh glow, burning my retinas. I head back to my desk, opening my emails and taking a sip of the coffee I brought from home. There's not enough caffeine in the world to get me through this.

It's just a job. It's not your life.

I'm thinking of skipping pickleball tonight. Maybe if I give Willow some space, eventually she could be around me without getting pissed off. I'm not even trying to date her anymore; I just want us to get along.

At every turn, I manage to do the wrong thing, and I haven't been able to get on solid footing with her. It's making me anxious. I learned at an early age how to diffuse tensions and lighten the mood with the people around me, but none of that seems to work with her.

"Morning, Luca!" Geoff says. My co-worker throws his jacket over one of the two chairs opposite my desk and drops into the other one.

"Hey, man, what's up?"

"Ready for this meeting? I hear Kevin's in one of his moods again."

I roll my eyes. "Love that for us. What's on your mind?"

He rests an ankle over his knee, rubbing his leg. "I'm just a little overwhelmed. We've been working on this project for so long, and it's gotten bigger than we anticipated."

"Whatever happens, we'll deal with it. We've designed a good program. I'm proud of the work we've done, and you should be too."

"Couldn't have done it without you. This is your baby."

"Now it's *our* baby," I say with a smile.

He stands and grabs his jacket, folding it over his arm. "You coming?"

"I'll see you in there."

As Geoff walks out of my office and through the conference room doors across the hall, I let out a long breath, squeezing my eyes shut.

I can do this.

After a solid forty-five minutes where nothing much was accomplished besides Kevin ripping into the software, we're all able to return to our desks. Chris, one of the coders on my team, follows me to my office and closes the door behind him.

"What is up with Kevin today?" he asks. "He seems more combative than usual."

I scrub a hand down my face. "I honestly don't know. Maybe he just needs to get laid."

"Right?" he says with a shaky laugh. "It's going to take forever to make all of his changes."

"I'm happy to stay late tonight if you want to work on it together."

"Seriously? That would be great, thank you. I was freaking out a bit after some of his comments."

"No problem. We can order food, my treat."

"How can I say no to that?" He smiles as he grabs the door handle. "Alright, I'll let you get back to it."

"Make it a *great* day!" I say with as much sarcasm as I can muster.

Chris laughs, a real one this time. "I'll add it to my action items, and we'll circle back with the deliverables."

"Later, man."

While I may not love this job as much as I used to, I'm grateful for my team. They believe in the work we're doing just as much as I do.

Guess I'm staying late and have a good excuse for avoiding Willow now.

I wonder if she remembers how well we got along in the days leading up to our date when we were messaging back and forth on the app, or if she's managed to block it all out.

Staring at the endless lines of code on my monitors, my gaze slowly wanders down to my phone...

ME

so about that Faris guy from pickleball

MAX

What about him?

ME

what's his deal? do you know him?

MAX

I don't know him that well

But Kayla works with his husband

I let out a breath.

He has a husband. They're just friends.

It's concerning how much relief that brings me.

ME

count me out for tonight

working late

MAX

I'll tell her you said hi

10

WILLOW

Chad and I just broke up

oh man I'm so sorry!!

you ok?

yeah I'm fine

he's a prick

I'm coming over

I'm out with my mom

I'll let you know when I'm back

Ok. Love you

love you more

I adjust the laptop on my knees as I settle deeper into my soft, cushy couch, crossing my legs and putting another tangerine pillow behind my back. My hair is up in a messy bun, no makeup, and I'm wearing fuzzy sweatpants and a T-shirt I designed that reads *I'd Hit That* with a pickleball and paddle underneath.

Luca didn't show up for our regular session the other night, and it was honestly a relief. It's been so exhausting finding new ways to avoid talking to him.

I may have acted a little immaturely last week after we lost our ranked match, but he just keeps pushing my buttons. I haven't been able to rise in the rankings in weeks, and he only dropped a tenth of a point, still the highest score in our group. Everything just feels like it's been going downhill for me ever since he came into my life two weeks ago after we both swiped right.

I see him laughing and joking around with Max, and I can't help feeling like they're talking about me. Maybe I'm just being paranoid.

Pickleball used to be an escape from all my problems, where I could get in the zone and at least *feel* like I had some control over my life. I'm a good player, but I haven't been on top of my game in a while. And being around him certainly isn't helping.

ANGIE

oh and the list is up. I got Max

ME

at least you didn't get stuck with Luca

ANGIE

honestly he seems…nice?

ME

I don't buy it

ANGIE

maybe he just had a bad night

ME

I don't care

ANGIE

I pad barefoot into the kitchen to top off my coffee, Henry close on my heels, his nails clacking on the hardwood floor. My morning is looking pretty good. I've been working on some prefab book cover designs and opened up commissions again, and I already have a request from an author for their debut novel.

I love working with authors. They're my favorite clients. They understand the creative process, and it's so much fun helping bring their worlds and characters to life.

My phone buzzes again.

FARIS

Hey partner!

ME

hi!! see you tomorrow for pb?

FARIS

Wouldn't miss it

Although Tinder Guy is pretty cute, maybe you should ask to switch partners

ME

that's the last thing I need

FARIS

Is it though?

ME

...

not you too

Whose side are they all on? Am I being too judgmental?

I'm just so tired of thinking about Luca.

These past few weeks, he has suddenly been everywhere I am, and I can't seem to get away from him. It doesn't matter how cute he is, I don't want to waste my time being friendly with people who are just assholes in disguise.

I know exactly what kind of person Luca is.

Later that afternoon, Angie and I are an hour into *10 Things I Hate About You*, cursing ourselves for eating too much ice cream, when both our phones start buzzing.

GROUP CHAT

SIMON

Luca is dating someone

I just found out

Angie looks at me with wide eyes.

FARIS

NO

ANGIE

SHUT UP

FARIS

WHO

A loud huff draws my attention.

"What?"

Angie shakes her head and types furiously on her phone.

I press play to resume the movie, cutting off Angie from saying anything. I'm glad Luca's dating someone. Maybe now he'll finally back off.

11

———

LUCA

Thank God it's Friday and I can finally start my weekend. I didn't even have enough energy to change out of my work clothes, simply flopping unceremoniously onto my old couch the moment I got home, giving my brain a chance to wind down.

After about twenty minutes, I grab my book off the side table.

I'm right at the part where the hero is facing the demon shifter who took the human queen hostage to participate in his realm's magical trials, just as my phone buzzes.

MAX

You check the list yet?

ME

not yet, lemme look

MAX

I'm with Angie

My heart rate picks up as my thumbs furiously type to

bring up the tournament website on my phone. I sit up, knocking my book to the floor as I scan the list for my name.

Carrie F. | Luca G.

Damn. A small part of me hoped it would be Willow, just to have a chance to make it right between us. As hard as I try, I can't stop thinking about her.

Who did she get partnered with?

I scan down the list.

Willow B. | Faris I.

Ah, they must have signed up together. That makes sense.

MAX

???

ME

Carrie

I don't think I've met her

MAX

Oh she's okay. You'll be fine

Can't wait for this tournament!

I pick my book up off the floor, opening it to where I left off and flatten out the crease in the pages. My eyes scan the same sentence over and over without absorbing a single word before I finally slam it shut.

I need to figure out what to do about Willow, or I'm going to drive myself crazy. I already know that she doesn't put up with any bullshit, and she hates inauthentic people. So I just need to apologize and own up to everything. Clear the air, and hope she can forgive me.

I want us to be friends.

I want her to like me.

I walk into my bedroom to change out of my work clothes but can't decide if I want to be lazy or head to the gym for a workout. I'm pretty wiped out from this week, so maybe I'll just stay longer at pickleball tomorrow to make up for it.

Wait. I have that double date with Ginny, Max, and Kayla tomorrow night.

Fuck.

Why am I thinking so much about Willow when I should be focused on Ginny and getting to know her better?

Guilt washes over me.

Do better, asshole.

It's times like these I wish I could call up Dad. He was always the voice of reason when I started spiraling like this. I grip my phone, resisting the urge to listen to his voicemail. I don't know why I torture myself with it nearly every day. It won't bring him back.

"Love you. See you soon" were his last words to me.

Most days I wish I had siblings too. With Mom and Dad both gone now, it can feel pretty lonely.

With my phone still in my hand, I pull up Max's text thread again.

ME

plans tonight?

MAX

Heading out to Kayla's parents' house in a bit with the kids

ME

gotcha, have fun!

see you tomorrow

MAX

Excited for the double date!

ME

me too

Guess it's just me, alone with my thoughts tonight. I reach into my top drawer and pull out my sweatpants.

12

———

WILLOW

With the tournament still over a month away, I convinced Faris to stay an extra hour at Dink Shot this morning. He wants to win just as much as I do, but if he's only practicing once a week, we need to get as much out of these sessions as we can.

The only problem is, to make sure we are in sync as partners, we need to be playing more doubles matches. I don't play with him nearly as much as I do with Angie, but we're still a solid pair. I will not lose to Jerry and Margaret again because he and I didn't prepare enough.

"Come on, one more match!" I yell. "Suck it up!"

Faris wipes his brow with the back of his hand. His shoulder-length hair is down but pulled away from his face with a headband. "You're insufferable, Will. You're lucky I love you."

I shoot him my sweetest smile and blow him a kiss.

"I'll tell you what," he says, lifting his chin. "I'll stay if we play doubles."

"Deal."

"And I get to pick who we play against."

My eyes narrow as he looks around the facility, turning his whole body for dramatic effect with his index finger pressed to his chin, until he lands in the direction of Luca and Carrie. *Shit.*

Honestly, I didn't even think to see who his partner was once Angie came over after work yesterday. The last thing I was thinking about was him or the tournament.

Carrie is essentially Pickleball Barbie. She's a perky, hot blonde with perfect proportions.

I wonder if she's single. Maybe I should ask her out and get my friends off my back about Luca.

I don't know her all that well, but she seems nice. The two of them have been laughing together all morning, and every time I look in their direction, she's giving him doe eyes or touching his arm.

Between Ginny and Carrie, it seems Luca has been very busy.

Not that I care.

He's obviously free to date as many women as he wants.

Faris is grinning from ear to ear, because the two of them are just standing around with no one else to play with. Except for us.

If only Angie were here to provide a buffer, but she had plans with her mom today.

"Hey!" Faris yells and waves.

They turn around.

"You guys up for doubles?"

"Absolutely!" Luca says without so much as looking at Carrie.

I pull Faris by the arm to the far side of our court so we don't get stuck making small talk with them. "Dick," I say under my breath, and he just laughs.

Luca and Carrie walk over to our court, and before they can

introduce themselves, I toss Faris the ball. "Let's go—your serve."

Carrie gives us an awkward wave and shoots Luca a glance. He just shakes his head and smiles, unfazed.

Faris smirks. "What's wrong, Will? You're acting weird all the sudden."

"Just serve it already," I say, sneering.

"Zeros on start!" Faris calls out as he serves the ball to Carrie's square.

We go back and forth several times and eventually make it to 3-3.

On the next serve, I hit it to Luca, who returns it on Faris's side. My partner reaches out for it but seems to lose his balance. The ball flies past him, and then Faris is suddenly kneeling on the floor.

"You're not giving up already, are you?" I tease. But he doesn't move. I walk over to him when he doesn't say anything. "Hey, you okay?"

He looks up at me with frightened, wide eyes. "Something's wrong. I heard a pop."

"A pop?" I sink to my knees. "What do you mean?"

He leans forward and rolls onto his side, carefully extending his left leg. "Something feels weird, and I heard a pop, but like...from inside my head."

"Can you move your foot?"

He looks down, testing his movements gently. "Yeah, I can kinda move it side to side, and I feel my toes and everything."

"What do you think happened?"

"I don't know...let me try to stand up."

I take his arm to help him, but the moment he stands, he cries out. "*Fuck*! Ow, goddammit." He sits back down on the floor. "I can't put any weight on it. Fuck, that really hurts now."

I see Darrell approaching.

"Do you think it's your Achilles?" I ask.

"That's gotta be it. I think I tore it." He lets out a groan and squeezes his eyes shut. "I can't fucking believe this." He runs a hand through his curly hair, panic flaring in his eyes.

"Okay, hey. It's gonna be okay." I put a reassuring hand on his good leg.

Darrell kneels beside us. "I saw. Want me to call an ambulance?"

"No, I'll take him. It's not far." I squeeze Faris's leg gently. "Hey, let's get you out of here, okay."

Before I can ask Darrell to help me, Luca is already lowering himself beside me, and Max is jogging toward us. Carrie stands off to the side, chewing on her fingernails.

"What happened?" Luca asks.

"Tore his Achilles. I need to get him to the ER."

"We can drive you," he says, looking up at Max for confirmation.

I narrow my eyes. What is he playing at?

"No, no, I can take him," I say to Max, avoiding Luca's stare. "But if you guys could help get him into my car that would be awesome."

"Of course," Max says, already kneeling as Darrell stands and backs up a few steps. "Luca, you take that side."

Luca hooks Faris's left arm over his shoulder. "You good? We're going to lift you up real slow, okay?"

Faris nods. He hasn't said anything for the past few minutes, and I wonder if he might be in shock.

A small crowd has gathered as Max and Luca slowly lift him, standing him up on one leg, careful not to let his limp, dangling foot touch the floor. The sight of it makes me feel ill. I don't do well with medical stuff.

They all start to move together slowly.

"I'll meet you out front." I look at Faris. "I'm calling Simon right now." I jog to the side wall and grab our bags, fishing out my keys and my phone. I hook the bags over my shoulders, dialing Simon and running through the front doors before the guys even clear the courts.

Simon answers on the second ring. "Hey."

"Hey, Simon," I start as I sprint to my car. "Here's the deal. Faris is going to be okay, but he got hurt. Pretty sure it's his Achilles."

"Oh shit," Simon says, breathless.

"He's going to be fine. I'm taking him to St. Elizabeth now. Can you meet us there?"

"Yeah, I'll head out now. Thanks, Will."

"See you soon. Love you." I hang up with Simon and open the back door to my Jeep Wrangler to throw our bags in. I hop in and zoom over to the front entrance where the guys are waiting.

When I climb out, Luca has already opened the door and is helping Faris carefully into the passenger seat.

"Thank you," I say to Max as Luca tells Faris something out of earshot and closes the door.

"Of course," Max replies.

"Let us know if you need anything," Luca says, stepping closer. Our eyes meet, and a wave of heat cascades up my neck. His irises are dark brown with flecks of red in them, a color I've never seen in someone's eyes before.

I manage to blurt out incoherently, "Yep...I'll see y...thanks for—" *Oh my God, shut up.* I jump into the driver's seat and speed away as fast as I can.

Despite suffering a catastrophic injury, Faris is grinning.

13

———

LUCA

"Thanks for your help, guys. I'm Faris, by the way."

"Luca. Good to meet you," I say as we help him through the front doors of the facility. "You already know Max, right?"

"Yeah, we met last year at our spouses' company Christmas party."

Max nods. "The two of them have become really close."

"Well, I'm sorry we're meeting under shitty circumstances," I say.

We stand at the curb, holding Faris stable as we wait for Willow. Max pulls out his phone and types something out with his free hand when Faris leans in to me.

"Will told me all about the date, you know."

I wince. "Yeah...that was not my finest moment."

"I want you to know we're still rooting for you."

I pull my head back, my eyebrows shooting up.

Before I can respond or even form words, a silver and black Jeep Wrangler speeds toward us and parks at the curb. It's...the

65

same as mine. Same exact colors and everything. I've seen it parked here before but didn't realize it belonged to *her*.

What are the odds?

Opening the door on the passenger side, I help Faris up into the seat, careful to ease him in and not aggravate his leg.

We're still rooting for you.

What does that mean? Who is "we" exactly?

If her friends are on my side, does that mean they think I have another chance to make things right with her?

Do they think she would give me a second chance?

"You good?" I ask him.

He nods in return, and I pat him on his good leg.

"Thank you," I hear Willow say to Max as I close the door and turn back to them.

"Of course," Max replies.

"Let us know if you need anything," I say.

Our eyes lock, and time slows to a crawl. For the first time, I'm seeing those stunning eyes up close so clearly—golden-brown, maybe amber.

She blinks rapidly and turns away, mumbling something I can't quite make out. It's the first time I'm seeing her flustered like this.

Then she gets in the driver's seat and peels out of the parking lot.

"Wow, that sucks," Max says.

"Yeah, that is not good. What happens with the tournament after something like this? Do you think she'll have to drop out?"

Max shoots me a glance. "Darrell will probably put her on the waitlist. Depends on how many people have signed up."

We start to walk back inside toward Carrie.

I only met her a few hours ago, and she seems cool. Pretty sure she's been flirting with me though, which is a little irritating because I didn't want Willow to get the wrong impression. I couldn't believe it when Faris saved me by calling us over to play doubles with them.

And then he got injured going for my return. Willow is going to be crushed if she misses this tournament.

I only wish there was something I could do.

Carrie and I play a few more rounds together before she has to leave, and then Max and I stay for another half hour or so. As I'm packing up my things, Darrell approaches with his iPad.

"Hey man," I say.

"Luca, I've got an update for you."

"On Willow's friend?"

He looks at me curiously. "Sort of. We're switching up the pairs now that Faris can no longer play."

"So I'm no longer with Carrie?"

Darrell smiles.

14

WILLOW

Simon arrived at the ER just a few minutes after us. The three of us have been sitting here filling out paperwork for the past twenty minutes and still haven't been called back. I hate hospitals. They're so depressing—the bright halogen lights, the scent of antiseptic hanging in the air. People in pain or waiting for news about their loved one. Stress, sickness, unease.

I pull out my phone to text Angie and keep myself distracted.

ME

Faris is injured. We're at the ER

torn achilles

ANGIE

oh shit! is he okay?

ME

he's good. Simon is here too.

Angie and her mom are very close. Seeing them together sometimes leaves an ache in my chest. I wonder if she realizes just how lucky she is to have such a loving, supportive family.

"Do either of you need anything?" I ask. "I can run out and get whatever you want."

Faris shakes his head, and Simon says, "Will, don't feel like you have to stay."

"Oh please, you know I don't have a life."

"Pickleball is her life." Faris pauses and turns to me. "Oh no. You're not going to have a partner for the tournament now! I'm so sorry."

I put a hand on his knee. "Hey, you have nothing to be sorry for. It's not your fault. All that matters is getting you fixed up and feeling better."

"You're right. Technically, it's your boyfriend's fault. He's the one who hit that shot to me."

"Oh my God, for the last time, he is not—"

"Faris..." announces a woman in scrubs from the doors by the intake station, pausing as she squints at the paper in front of her. "Is...Mal..."

He pushes himself up to stand on his good foot, raising a hand. "Ismailoglu. Yes."

She grabs a wheelchair from the side of the room and helps ease him into the seat.

Simon takes the handles and says, "I've got it, thank you so much," with an edge of protectiveness. Simon's loyalty to Faris —and me and Angie—knows no bounds. No wonder Faris is such a romantic, he's living his happily ever after.

"Come on back," the nurse says to us.

"I'm gonna head out. Good luck," I say, squeezing Faris's hand. "Keep me updated."

"Thanks, Will," they both say.

"Love you, miss you!" Faris adds as they turn toward the large double doors leading into the main facility.

"Love you more!" I shout back with a smile before the doors close.

As I walk out to the parking lot, my phone buzzes in my back pocket.

ANGIE

guess you need a new partner

I'll see what Darrell says

ME

hopefully a spot opens up

I climb back into my trusty Jeep and scrub my hands down my face. I can't believe Faris got injured. He's going to be down and out for a long time. I don't know the average timeline for recovering from this kind of injury, but I can't imagine it's quick.

I know it was just an accident, but I was the one who made him stay longer to keep playing. I pushed him. It's not Luca or Carrie's fault either; this kind of thing can happen to anyone. I just hate that Faris is going through this.

I hope I don't have to drop out though. I really want a chance to face Jerry and Margaret and reclaim my victory before heading to the US Open. I look forward to this tournament all year.

I plug in my phone and crank up my 90s alt-rock music.

As I'm driving, text alerts start popping up on my console screen. I can't see the actual texts, just who sent them. One is from Darrell. Then a bunch from Angie.

What is going on? I'm only five minutes away from my house, so I decide to wait and catch up once I'm home, but my mind is racing.

Then a text from an unknown number pops up. What the hell? Did he find me a new partner already?

After what feels like forever, I finally pull up to my townhouse and park in the driveway. Grabbing my phone, I open the text app.

DARRELL

Hey, Willow, I got you a new partner. Gave him your phone number and he'll be reaching out soon.

Oh wow, that was fast. I back out of Darrell's message to read Angie's.

ANGIE

LOLLL good luck!!!

just heard back

text me when you know

What the hell does that mean? Who is it? My thumbs fly over the keyboard as I respond to her.

ME

wait what??

Then I remember the unknown number. I pull up the new texts.

UNKNOWN

hey I got your number from Darrell

let me know if you want to get together to play sometime

Thank God. This means I don't have to drop out of the tournament. Whoever this is, is my new best friend.

ME

who is this??

UNKNOWN

it's Luca

15

LUCA

As Max drives us home, I keep staring at my phone.

Willow hasn't responded. She must really hate this. I know how competitive she is, so maybe she won't mind it if she can see me as a way to help her win this tournament.

She is welcome to use me all she wants.

Maybe I'm crazy, but it almost seemed like she didn't mind playing with me. Or maybe that's just because it's the one time I can't try to talk to her.

Max stops in front of my driveway to drop me off.

"Thanks for the ride, man."

"See you tonight!"

Tonight. The double date. I wonder if there's any way I can get out of it. Not likely.

As I'm punching in the code to my garage keypad, my phone buzzes.

WILLOW

hey sounds good

Well...the enthusiasm is not great, but it's something. At

least she's not ignoring me, or cussing me out, or threatening to drop out of the tournament because *that* would be more appealing than being stuck with me.

I can do my part to win this thing. For her.

We're both really good, so we have a decent chance at winning. My ranking has come down to about where it should be since that first day, but still just barely above hers at 3.9.

Now it's time to commence my brilliant and totally flawless plan of trying to get her to see I'm not a complete jerk.

Max and I had a good, long morning of open play after Willow took Faris to the ER, but now I've somehow found myself with even more energy than I had before.

Instead of going inside, I drive myself to the gym.

16

WILLOW

This is the fucking worst. I still can't believe Luca and I got partnered up together for the Pickle Bowl. At least he can play a decent game. I need him to stop messing around and take this seriously though.

GROUP CHAT

ME

good luck today babe 

FARIS

Thanks Will

Should be taking me back any minute now!

ANGIE

YES, thinking of you today!!

ME: you got this!

Faris is going into surgery this morning. Thankfully, the

orthopedic surgeon had a last-minute opening this week; otherwise, he would've had to wait until next Tuesday.

I had to force myself not to gag when he explained what the surgeon was going to do in there. Something about overlaying the tendons and sewing them back together so it'll be stronger than it was before the injury. But he'll be down for a long time.

It almost makes me scared to keep playing pickleball, knowing in the back of my mind it could happen to any of us at any moment. Faris didn't do anything wrong, and there's nothing he really could have done to prevent it. It's just a common injury in this sport.

"Pickleball is putting my kids through college," the ortho doc had joked. Or was he serious?

But in truth, any of us could get hit by a bus or drop dead at any moment, so why not do the things that make you happy while you still can?

Pickleball takes me back to my days playing tennis. A slice of time just for me, where I didn't have to deal with my parents or think about Holly and what she did to our family.

LUCA

You coming tonight?

Ugh. Like I need the reminder.

ME

I'll be there

LUCA

good

see you tonight, Ace

I scrunch my nose. Seriously? We are not doing nicknames. Not now, not ever.

ME

don't call me that

LUCA

it's either that or Willy, but I think Ace fits you
better

ME

neither is fine actually

LUCA

if you say so

I set my phone down on my desk, rolling my eyes. I'm not playing his mind games.

Settling into my comfy leather chair in my favorite red sweatshirt and matching sweatpants, I sip my coffee, letting it warm me up and infuse my blood with the caffeine it so desperately craves.

Henry nudges my leg with his nose. I scratch under his ear with one hand as I pull up my latest project with the other. If I finish these web ads today, I can start on some new character art for the author I've been working with this month.

Which reminds me, I need to hit up the bookstore this weekend to see my other client's latest release. One of the most satisfying things about designing book covers is seeing them on the shelves in person.

Max and Luca show up at the neighborhood courts at the same time as Angie and me. Honestly, it's kind of nice that Max and Angie are paired up too, since the four of us can quickly and easily make it down here to play without driving anywhere or meeting up at Dink Shot. We can keep working on our game and practicing together as pairs for the tournament whenever we're all available. Anything to get an advantage in this tournament.

After warming up for a few minutes, the four of us take our positions on the court to start our first match as new pairs. I'm not sure what to expect, but here we go.

"Zeros on start," I say before serving it across to Max.

Luca and I find our rhythm quickly, effortlessly. We're able to hold down our sides of the court but also anticipate where the other is going to be. Both sides get some good shots in, and there are several firefights at the net, which I love. That's when it gets really exciting. Everything moves so fast you don't have time to think, just act. It's the point at which you have to be quick and rely purely on instinct to get the upper hand.

The first match ends with Luca and me winning 11-7. We all walk over to the side of the court for water and a quick rest. It's unusually hot for early September, so we're all pretty sweaty.

I don't miss the drops of sweat falling from Luca's tan arms or how they slide down the strong column of his neck. When he lifts the bottom of his shirt to wipe his forehead, exposing the lower half of his torso, I see his abs aren't as chiseled as I would have expected. Just a bit of softness to contrast the rest of his body. I catch myself staring and turn away.

"Good game, Ace," Luca says with a grin, elbowing me while Max and Angie are engrossed in a conversation about dogs.

I roll my eyes. "Mm-hmm."

"So how long have you—"

"Stop. You know, you're not fooling me with this good guy act you have going on. So whatever it is you're trying to do here, I don't want any part of it, so just stop."

For a moment, he's silent, and I wonder if I've gone too far. I flush in embarrassment.

"What makes you think I'm putting on an act?" He crosses his arms in front of his chest, straightening up and rebalancing the weight on his feet.

I scoff. "Seriously? What are you getting out of all this anyway? Are you trying to punish me for walking out on our date? Were those tears even real? You can't handle rejection, so you've decided to get in my head and torture me, is that it?"

"So, you *have* been thinking of me."

"Oh my God. You're so full of yourself!"

The asshole just smirks. "Are you done yet?"

"Not even close. Neither of us asked to be paired up here, okay? Let's just stick to practicing, then after the tournament we can go our separate ways."

He drops his hands. "Sorry to break it to you, Ace, but I'm not going anywhere."

"Stop calling me that!" I clench my paddle tighter as I turn around and stomp back onto the court.

I'm so over this. I need Luca to drop his bullshit and stop pretending to be Mr. Nice Guy, because it's seriously pissing me off.

When he joins me to play our next match, he steps in close, leaning in so his lips brush the shell of my ear. "Feel free to keep bossing me around, though. I like it."

He pulls away, and I'm at a loss for words.

I try to focus on my steps because my knees are suddenly weak, and my traitorous heart is in my throat.

17

—————

LUCA

I made her blush.

I made Willow Blackburn blush.

I knew I was getting under her skin, but I just couldn't stop myself. She gets so mean sometimes, it kind of turns me on. So I keep pushing.

Why do I like the thought of her bossing me around so much?

When I got home last night and stepped into the shower, my hand was around my cock before the water even hit me. I tried everything I could to not think of her. I told myself it was only going to make it harder to get over her and move on.

But now that Ginny is no longer in the picture, the only thing holding me back from stroking myself to thoughts of her in that tight little outfit is my dignity. And that shit disappeared the night I met her.

I loathed myself for the entire three minutes my tongue sampled every glorious inch of that irresistible, curvy body until I came so hard I saw stars.

And now I'm stuck at work, tormented by thoughts of her.

The eleven o'clock meeting with my team ran over, and now I only have about thirty minutes to eat lunch before my next meeting with Kevin. What kind of monster schedules lunch meetings with no food? Oh, that's right. My boss.

I jog across the street to grab a sandwich from the local deli. Luckily, they know me here and start making my turkey bacon Swiss the moment I walk through the doors. I wave to the workers and slide a ten-dollar bill to the cashier before taking a seat by the window.

While I wait, I scan my email. Nothing for work luckily, but on my personal account, I notice an email from Dad's estate lawyer.

My heart ratchets up at the memories of having to deal with mountains of mindless paperwork while grieving the loss of my father. My best friend.

Because he always had to DIY *everything*, his will was declared invalid shortly after he passed, because it failed to meet Ohio's strict requirements. His retirement account and life insurance policies passed to me without issue, but the rest of his assets have been stuck in probate ever since.

Mr. Giordano,

We have some updates about the estate of Joseph Giordano. Our office has filed the paperwork to transfer his assets into your name, and we are confident that we can get this matter resolved in the next few months.

However, a lien has been filed on this estate for unpaid funds to the Springrose Care Facility of Greendale, Ohio. Please call our offices immediately to discuss arrangements to settle the dispute.

Thank you,
Martin Stanley, ESQ

The mention of Springrose has tears pricking my eyes. Greenville's best care facility, where Mom spent the final year of her life battling Alzheimer's. Even though she didn't recognize us by then, Dad and I showed up every day and subjected ourselves to endless heartbreak.

After she passed, it was just Dad and me for the next two and a half years. We helped each other through the darkest parts of our grief, coming out the other side closer and more understanding of each other than ever before.

You learn to see people differently when you go through something like that together. You come to rely on them, letting them see the ugliest and darkest parts of yourself. It's painful and awful, but also incredibly beautiful.

The fondest memories I have with him are when we first discovered pickleball together. We started out kind of slow, Dad especially, but eventually we both got pretty good. They had just put in a court in his neighborhood, so he even snuck in play time on days when I couldn't come over, always trying to get better than me.

I rub at my chest, that familiar ache settling in. God, I miss them both so much.

"Sandwich for Luca!" the guy at the counter calls out.

"Thanks, man! Take care." I sprint back over to the office. Plopping down at my desk, I roll up my sleeves and inhale my sandwich as quickly as possible without choking, before I have to go deal with Kevin. I wonder what he's pissed about today. Like it even matters.

What am I going to do about the estate? I'd rather not go back to Greendale if I can avoid it. The memories there are still raw, painful. It was where I lived my entire life up until last year, and going back will just remind me of how much has changed and how much I've lost.

There were many beautiful memories there too, but I desperately needed some distance. I'm ready to move on from that part of my life.

I can't deal with this lawyer stuff right now. It'll have to wait.

18

WILLOW

"So, how's your hot partner?" Faris asks with a sleepy grin, lying down on one side of his sectional couch with his leg propped up on several pillows. "You guys make out yet?"

I roll my eyes. "I think those pain meds are making you delirious. We hate him, remember?"

"Yeah, literally no one is buying that," Angie says as she sits down beside me, shifting two large throw pillows in between us to lean on.

She and I came over to Simon and Faris's house to check on him after his surgery earlier this week. The doctor said everything went well. This first week will be the hardest, as he is on a four-hour rotation of painkillers and blood thinners, as well as switching out ice packs and compression sleeves. I'm not sure how he's getting any sleep, especially since that compression device inflates with air and beeps on regular intervals to help prevent blood clots.

"Plus, he's dating someone," I remind them.

"Actually..." Simon yells from their enormous kitchen

before walking into the living room carrying two large platters of food. "They broke up."

"*What?*" Angie shouts.

"She finally realize what an asshole he is?"

"*He* ended it."

Now it's my turn to be surprised. "Really?"

Simon sets the plates down on the long glass coffee table in front of us. "According to my source."

"When did they break up?" Angie asks.

"Saturday night. Right after their double date with Kayla and Max."

Faris lies there silent with a wide grin, his compression sleeve filling up with a hum.

I smack his arm before leaning forward to admire the food. One platter is a charcuterie board filled with cheeses, crackers, honey, jam, grapes, and various sliced meats; the other has grilled ham and cheese paninis.

He makes the best food. He should have seriously considered becoming a chef instead of going into finance.

Though looking at their enormous house filled with expensive furniture and artwork that could be hanging in a museum, I suppose the perks aren't all that bad.

As I reach for a sandwich, Simon says, "Willow, I made ham and cheese, but if you want, I'm sure I can find a hot Italian for you." He winks at me, and my eyes go wide.

"Oh my God, you guys, stop!"

"You really should make out with him though," he continues. "Not only is he hot, but you need to get rid of all that sexual tension between you two if you want to have a chance at winning the tournament."

I narrow my eyes. "That doesn't even make sense. Plus, you've never met him, how do you know what he looks like?"

"Stalked him online and found his LinkedIn profile. Wanna see?" He pulls out his phone and starts scrolling.

"Not even a little bit." I swat away his hand, but something on the screen catches my attention. "Wait, give me that."

I snatch the phone out of his hands and bring it up to my face.

"He works at RavTech?"

"What's wrong with that?"

I scoff. "He would work for a big, evil corporation. He probably fanboys over that nut job CEO."

Preston McIntire is well known for his unhinged tirades online, but also his scandals, including rumors about his barely legal mistresses. With his wealth and connections, he's managed to keep their names out of the press over the years, but a few have come out to confirm people's suspicions.

"What is your deal with him?" Angie says. "I've never seen you so riled up by someone before."

"Why are you all on *his* side? Do you not remember me telling you about the date? This is Tinder Guy we're talking about."

Faris says, "I swear, if you mention the crying one more time..."

"Weeping. Loudly."

"You do have that effect on people."

I swat him with the pillow.

"I remember you telling us you left after only thirty minutes and barely gave him a chance," Angie says, popping a prosciutto-wrapped mozzarella in her mouth.

"He was late!"

"And before the date, you had already convinced yourself it wasn't going to work out," Faris adds. "Like you always do."

"And I was right! He clearly has some serious issues to

work out. Just like everyone else out there. I'm done dating. For good."

The three of them exchange knowing glances.

"What?" I say, throwing my hands out.

"You never give people a fighting chance," Faris says. "It's all or nothing with you."

"Because—"

"And..." he continues over me, "you always expect the worst in them. So the moment things don't go perfectly you use that as an excuse to push them away. Not everyone is an asshole."

I shake my head, crossing my arms over my chest. Sometimes I hate that they know me so well. But if people don't want me to expect the worst in them, then they need to stop showing up that way.

"Isn't there the *slightest* possibility he was just having a bad night?" Angie asks, softer this time.

"The shit he said was inexcusable."

"Then why won't you tell us?"

"I don't want to talk about him anymore. I already have to deal with him twice a week at pickleball. It's bad enough I'm stuck with him until this tournament is over."

They all give each other that look again.

"I'm getting a drink," I say, standing, not waiting for their reaction. When I sit back down with a beer, I stare at the TV screen but don't actually watch what's on, fidgeting with the label on the bottle with my thumbnail.

Of course it's possible that he had a bad night, but why waste my time? What's the point? I'm perfectly happy with the friends I have and not subjecting myself to being hurt by anyone else. People are the worst.

My relationships have never lasted more than a few months anyway, once the fun wears off and things start to get serious. It's too painful to get attached and risk getting my heart broken.

When I came out as bisexual in high school, my first girl-friend was still in the closet. She wanted to keep our relationship a secret, which I hated. Ultimately, when her parents found out about us, she threw me under the bus and told them I had pressured her into being together. That shit crushed me, and I haven't dated a girl since. But it taught me that women can be just as bad as men when it comes to being truthful.

Everyone always betrays you.

Later that night after returning home from Simon and Faris's, I'm still on edge. I can't shake the frustration of everything they said. They're all making me feel like *I'm* the one doing something wrong here by not giving him another chance. Why do I owe him that?

Get rid of that sexual tension between you two.

It's true, Luca is stressing me out. So maybe I do need a release...but not with him.

I honestly didn't mind it so much when I was playing against him because I could take that frustration out on him, but it's harder now that we're on the same team and have to work together.

In my bedroom, I walk over to the nightstand next to my bed. I slowly open the drawer and pull out my favorite toy. I can't even remember the last time I did this.

I lie down on my soft bed, pulling my pants and underwear off and throwing them on the ground. Reaching down and rubbing slow circles over myself, I let my eyes close and my mind wander, immediately picturing a tall, muscular man with tan skin, shaggy dark hair, and a devastating smile.

Fuck.

No, not Luca.

I stop the movements and let out a long breath.

Someone else, anyone else.

I begin rubbing circles again, pressing a little harder this time, easing into the ache. With my other hand, I lift the long silicone vibrator and turn it on. I press it softly at my entrance as the buzzing begins to light me up, making me wet. I slowly press it inside me, moaning at the sensation.

In my mind, Luca appears again, but now he's wearing only a pair of bright red briefs. His hard cock is tented at the front, bare chest covered with coarse, dark hair and slick with sweat, veins bulging down his forearms. Dark eyes hooded with lust aimed at me as he licks his soft lips.

I don't fight it this time.

Instead, I take control and try to imagine what he might be like.

Feel free to keep bossing me around. I like it, he said the other day. The words shoot fire straight to my core.

I kiss him punishingly, putting all the rage and anger I have for him into it, fighting for dominance. I can make him do whatever I want. I pull away and place my hands on his chest, pushing him toward my bed.

"Sit," I say to him, and he obeys like a good boy. "You're going to fuck me from behind while you rub my clit. Do you understand?"

Voice low and gruff, he says, "Yes, ma'am."

I turn my back to him, lowering down onto him slowly.

I pull out the vibrator before thrusting it back into me at the same moment I picture his hard cock impaling me, filling me all the way up. One of his hands comes around and rubs my clit just as he was told, the other slides up over top of my breasts and slowly and gently cups my jaw. I turn my head back toward him, rocking my hips back and forth as I kiss him. Fierce, passionate kisses this time. Deep and searching. My hand pressed to the back of his head, tangling in his hair, keeping him close.

The pressure inside builds and builds, my clit swollen under my fingertips. My body ready to burst wide open. "Oh God, yes," I moan. "Fuck!"

I squeeze my eyes shut as waves of pleasure course through me. Still picturing Luca's strong arms wrapped tightly around me, coaxing every last bit of this orgasm from me. It keeps coming and coming, and I wonder if it'll ever stop. Until we finally start to come down together, slowly.

With my chest still rapidly rising and falling, I click off the vibrator and pull it out. I'm sweating through the sheets.

I lie there for a moment, my mind starting to clear, and I realize what just happened. What I *let* happen.

Fuck.

19

LUCA

I park my Jeep right next to Willow's in the Dink Shot parking lot for our regular Saturday meetup and can't help but smile at the sight.

Max and I walk through the front doors, and I spot her right away with Angie, gathered around the center tables. Her long brown hair is up in two adorable space buns, and she's wearing a white crop top with long sleeves and black running shorts. *Che bella.*

My body immediately responds by kicking up my heart rate, and a flush prickles the back of my neck. I wonder if I'll ever be able to look at her without experiencing some intense physical reaction.

God, I hope not.

Ever since I broke things off with Ginny, I've stopped fighting my undeniable attraction to Willow. While I don't expect anything to happen between us—since she still reminds me a little too much of my ex-wife—I realized it wasn't fair to Ginny that my thoughts were constantly with someone else.

I wanted to believe I could make things work and start to move on, but you can't force a connection with someone, no matter how hard you try.

I just need to figure out how to get Willow out of my system.

Her words from the other day drift through my mind.

You're not fooling me with this good guy act you have going on.

She thinks the guy who showed up for our first date is the real me, and that I've been putting on some kind of act ever since to manipulate her. I hate that she thinks of me that way, and that her first impression of me was at one of my lowest moments.

When my eyes find hers, she averts her gaze a little too quickly.

"What's up, Ace? Ready to dance?"

She rolls her eyes, but I don't miss the tiny tilt to her lips. Just that infinitely small movement is enough to make me weak. How is it possible to feel such an intense pull every time we're in the same room?

I just want to get back to how it was in those days leading up to our first date, when we messaged back and forth so effortlessly. The conversations flowing like water, stretching into all hours of the night.

"Hey Angie. Good to see you again."

"You too," she says to me and Max. "You guys have any plans this weekend?"

Max says, "Kids have soccer this afternoon."

Everyone then looks to me. "Nope, no plans."

Nobody responds, the awkward silence palpable as a wave of heat washes over me.

I shrug. "Guess I don't have much of a life?"

Angie snorts. "Hey, what a coincidence, neither does Willow."

"Hey!" Willow grabs Angie by the elbow and drags her away from us, and I can't help but smile at the sudden pink tint of her cheeks.

Is it possible she could be warming up to me? Maybe we can become friends. I already know she doesn't let a lot of people in, which I can only assume is because she's been hurt before.

We have that in common too.

The four of us do some quick stretches off to the side and then walk over to one of our reserved courts to warm up, hitting balls back and forth until we are ready to play an actual match.

Max starts off with the serve, hitting it diagonally to Willow's square. She returns it easily with a decent amount of topspin. The ball heads toward Angie, who hits it high. When I slam it back over, it flies past both Angie and Max.

"Yes!" Willow shouts from behind me.

I shoot her a smile, and to my surprise, she gives me one in return.

Willow sets up the next serve with the graceful, fluid motions of a seasoned tennis player. "Zero zero on one!"

After a minute or so, I get one past Max headed for the edge. He thinks it's going wide, but when it lands on the line and it's too far for him to reach, he says, "Ah shit!"

"Nice one!" Willow says as we switch sides, getting ready for her next serve. She extends her paddle to tap mine.

Something in my chest eases just a little bit.

An opening. A glimmer of something I can't quite name yet.

We end up beating them by an astounding eight points.

Three hours later, we've won seven matches, while Max and Angie only won two, rotating out every few games to let other groups play while also playing our weekly ranked match in between.

Willow and I grab our stuff and walk over to the shared lounge space up front to wait while Angie and Max go one more round with another pair.

She sits down in the plush chair next to mine. "You know, you're really good out there."

I shift to face her. "You sound surprised."

She shrugs. "Pleasantly surprised, I guess."

"Wow, coming from you, I'll take that as a huge compliment."

She scoffs and rolls her eyes. "Could use some work on your backhand though. You need more consistency."

"Let me guess. You used to play tennis."

"High school and college." That half-smile again. "What about you? Any sports growing up?"

"Never played tennis, but I did a lot of team sports."

"Let me guess...baseball, football, and..." She pauses and looks me up and down. The intense focus of her attention has me shifting in my chair. "Hockey."

"Impressive," I say before sipping from my water bottle.

"Anyways..." She stands, tucking a loose strand of hair behind her ear. "Good games today. Play like that at the tournament and we won't have a problem. Deal?"

That *almost* sounds like a truce. "Deal," I say as I stand and stick out my hand.

She looks down and reluctantly shakes it.

I squeeze her hand, her skin warm and soft against mine, and she looks back up at me. Something in those amber eyes has me questioning everything I thought I knew about her. There's warmth and kindness there.

A small crack in that tough exterior that I now know is only there to protect herself, not to hurt others.

I had it all wrong. She's nothing like Sadie.

The revelation catches me off guard.

Behind me, Angie yells, "Will, you ready to go?"

She nods, starting to pull away. But I hold on tight.

"See you around, Ace," I say in a low voice. I drop her hand before Angie and Max appear at our side.

Willow shakes her head, trying to regain that composure she holds on to so tightly.

"Well, Max and I finally dominated," Angie says. "Just had to play with people worse than you two."

"There you go. That should get you far in the tournament," Willow says with a chuckle.

"Let's grab some food, Will. I'm starving. See you guys." Angie turns to walk past the front desk and over to the stairs to the bar.

Willow hesitates but then follows behind, not sparing us a second glance.

As Max and I reach my Jeep in the parking lot, I get an idea. I open my door and take one of the rubber ducks off my dashboard, the one with a sweat band and a tennis racket, and I place it on the hood of her matching Jeep. Ducking is a time-honored tradition among Jeep owners.

Since she doesn't have any displayed on her dash, I thought I'd give her the first one.

Ball is in your court, gorgeous.

20
———

WILLOW

The barista hands me my hot coffee with cream, and I breathe it in deeply as it lights up my insides. This bookstore has the best coffee.

I set off to find my client's new book in the Dark Romance section. It's called *After Life*, and it's about a widow who falls in love with two morticians after the death of her husband. The moment I spot it, I let out a squeal. It looks so beautiful on display. I pick up the book and admire it up close. Red and gray funeral flowers lie over a black background, with the title in white, and the letters connected by delicate swirling lines.

Hugging the book to my chest, I step around the corner of the nearest bookshelf, and I stop dead in my tracks.

It's *him*. Luca. Is he following me? Seriously, how has he been living in my neighborhood without me even knowing, and now I can't go two days without seeing him everywhere I go?

He's far enough away that he doesn't see me, so I back away. Am I seriously *hiding* from him now? I should be the bigger person here and just go talk to him.

Instead, I pretend to look at the display next to me featuring local indie authors. Soon enough, my curiosity gets the best of me, and I peek my head back around the bookshelf.

What kind of books does someone like him read?

It's the first time since our date that I'm seeing him in anything other than workout clothes. Relaxed-fit jeans and a cream colored Henley pushed up to his elbows, showing off his tan, muscular forearms.

Before I can pull my jaw up off the floor, a small boy with shaggy brown hair and a Batman T-shirt barrels into him screaming, "Pick me up! Pick me up!" as he waves a large board book around.

My stomach drops. What the hell? He has a kid? I know we only messaged for like two or three days before our date, but he never once mentioned having children. That's a pretty big thing to keep hidden. Though I guess it's not really any of my business now.

"What do you have?" Luca says in a sweet, sing-songy voice. "Did you find a book about turtles?"

"Yes! They're my favorite," the little boy says with a big smile. He must be about...five or six years old if I had to guess.

"Mine too, buddy."

I can't take my eyes off them. What an adorable sight this would be if it weren't for the fact that this man has not been honest with me since the day we matched.

I honestly wouldn't have cared much if he did have kids, but it makes me wonder what else he's not telling me.

"Willow? Is that you?" a man behind me says, scaring the living shit out of me. I whirl around, coffee dripping down my knuckles.

Max raises his hands. "Sorry! Didn't mean to startle you."

I let out a sharp breath, trying to calm my racing heart. "Hey, Max. Sorry, I'm a little out of it today."

Max offers a napkin for the coffee I spilled. Luckily, it didn't get on my new book.

"Were you...looking for someone?" he asks with a hint of mischief, looking around.

I freeze. Did he catch me watching Luca like some creep? "Oh...no...I was just—"

"There he is!"

I turn around to find Luca with the little boy in his arms, and my heart sinks. He is so adorable, but he also looks nothing like Luca. He must take after his mother.

His mother.

Wait. Is Luca married? Another fucking lie? My body flushes with heat, and my free hand involuntarily squeezes into a fist.

When he sees me, his eyes go wide. "Willow? Hey." He clearly wasn't expecting me to find out like this, because he doesn't say anything else, just adjusts his son on his hip.

"Hey," I say coolly, sipping my coffee and forcing myself to breathe.

The little boy leans into Luca and whispers, "Who is she?"

Max saves us from the impending awkwardness and says, "This...is Willow. She plays pickleball with Daddy and his friends."

I smile warily. "And what's your name?" I may still be pissed, but I'm not a monster. I would never take my anger or frustration out on an innocent boy.

He squirms in Luca's arms before looking over at Max. When he puts his arms out, Max swoops in to take him, swinging him around and ruffling his shaggy hair.

"This is my son, Gabe." He plants a kiss on his cheek. "Can you say hi?"

Oh.

Oh.

Gabe buries his face in Max's neck. "Hi."

I look over to Luca, who is smirking, as if he knows exactly what was just going on inside my head.

After a moment of uncomfortable silence, Max clears his throat and says, "We're going to go...over there and look for Gabe's sister." He looks wide-eyed at Gabe and asks, "You wanna go find Shae?"

We both watch as Max takes his son around to the kids' section of the store. At least that was only slightly embarrassing. Could've been worse. I suppose I could have vomited?

"So...You come here often?" Luca says with one raised eyebrow.

I quickly have to suppress my growing grin when he flashes that brilliant smile of his, the skin around his eyes crinkling slightly.

"Yeah. Probably too much, to be honest."

"Not possible. You can never have too many books."

Interesting.

"What did you pick out?" he asks, pointing to the book still tucked under my arm.

"Oh." I pull it out and flash him the cover, bracing myself for the usual judgment that comes with reading romance novels. Dark romance, at that. "I designed the cover. Here to support the author."

"You made that? Can I see?"

Our fingers brush slightly as I hand him the book.

"This is incredible. Do you design book covers for a living?"

"All sorts of designs. Books, logos, ads. Stuff like that."

"That's awesome." He hands it back to me. "Congratulations."

"Thanks." I take a sip of my coffee to distract myself from his stupidly gorgeous face. I want to ask him about working for

RavTech, but that would involve admitting I was looking at his LinkedIn profile.

"Gabe sure seems to like you," I say.

"Oh, yeah, he's a great kid. His twin sister, Shae, too. Max and his family have kind of taken me in as one of their own."

"Like a stray?"

"Honestly, yeah," he says with a chuckle. "When I moved here last year, I didn't know anyone. It was a stressful time for me and...I just had a lot going on." He scratches the back of his neck before shoving his hands in his pockets. "He and his wife, Kayla, invited me over for drinks and dinner right away, and now I see them almost every day."

"Wow, I love that." I'm suddenly curious as to why he moved here if he didn't know anybody. Again, not that it's any of my business.

I take another sip of my coffee and look around. I don't know what to say to him or how to act around him right now. I feel like maybe I've misjudged the situation, and I've been too hard on him.

"Look...can we call a truce?" he asks. "Or...start over? I know we got off on the wrong foot, and I take full responsibility for that." He puts a hand to his chest. "I'd like to make it up to you by helping you achieve eternal glory and win the Pickle Bowl."

"I'd like that." I smile and point a finger at him with the same hand holding my coffee cup. "But only if you stop calling me Ace."

"Absolutely not."

Stop smiling, I tell myself. *You can't trust him.*

But even as I think that, I know I don't believe it.

21

———

LUCA

I can't help grinning like a fool from Max's passenger seat as his two kids sing along to Disney songs from their booster seats in the back of the minivan. I was in such a good mood, I let the kids splurge on way too many books and toys.

Max kept insisting I didn't have to, but I was on cloud nine. They could've asked me to take them all the way to Disney World and I would have.

"You're in a good mood today," he says. "Who knew bookstores had that effect on you, huh?"

I look out the window, avoiding Max.

"So, when are you going to ask her out again?" he asks.

"What do you mean?" I say with as much innocence as I can muster.

"Come on, don't bullsh—" He stops and looks at his kids behind him, lowering his voice. "Don't BS me. You're always staring at her, you were jealous when you thought she was dating Faris, and you broke up with Ginny last week because you're still not over her. Tell me I'm wrong."

I let out a breath. Of course he noticed. Was I really that obvious?

"We're just partners now. We called a truce."

"And is that all you want? Just a pickleball partner?"

The AC blasts cold air in my face as I fiddle with the vent. "I—"

"Uncle Luca, was that your girlfriend?" Shae says sweetly.

"What?" I say, turning to study her in her booster seat.

"You should kiss her!" she says before bursting into a fit of giggles.

"Eww! You can't do that unless you're *married*," Gabe says.

I turn back around in my seat. "No one is getting married, no one is kissing."

At least not yet.

I scrub my hands down my face just before my phone buzzes.

WILLOW

I forgot to ask, was this you?

She then sends a photo of the rubber duck I left on her hood yesterday, and I grin. I don't even try to suppress it this time.

ME

his name is Herbert

and he needs more friends

WILLOW

I don't do the duck thing

ME

why not?

WILLOW

putting toys on strangers' Jeeps and then displaying them on your dash like a trophy collection?

I dunno, just seems kinda cheesy

ME

nothing wrong with cheesy

plus it's just fun

and nice

WILLOW

fun and nice

if you say so

ME

"I'm going to be honest with you," Max says. "If by some miracle she does give you a second chance, you have to tell her the truth before it goes too far."

I nod, my smile dropping. "I know, but I just want to be her friend for right now."

At least until I can get those divorce papers signed.

The thought of sharing my past with her fills me with dread. Can't all that just stay there where it belongs so we can start fresh?

I already know the answer, and I hate it.

22

LUCA

Driving home from yet another soul-sucking day at work, I blast my upbeat music to try to drown out my negative thoughts. I have to quit RavTech. It's that simple. I'm never going to be happy in that environment.

Maybe this weekend I'll finally get serious and polish up my résumé and start sending out applications so I'm ready to leave once the curriculum software launches.

As I pull into the West Brook neighborhood entrance lined with several red maple trees, I spot Willow jogging in my direction with a large black lab. I still can't get over the fact that she lives in my neighborhood.

I go for the standard two-finger-and-thumb "Jeep wave" as I pass her, but I'm too chickenshit to see if she waves back. Just absolutely killing it over here with this charisma, like always.

I need to get out of my head and stop second-guessing myself about every little thing. We've started building a rapport. I've made her laugh, and she no longer seems to explicitly, outwardly hate my guts. Progress.

I pull into my driveway, waving to Max and Kayla across

the street doing yard work out front. The twins laugh as they kick a soccer ball back and forth.

Only an hour and a half until we play pickleball.

I change out of my stifling work clothes and into my black basketball shorts and turquoise athletic shirt. In my kitchen, I pull out the chicken that's been marinating all day and get to work making myself dinner.

I think about all the possible things I could talk to Willow about tonight. I need a list of topics in case I panic and make things weird. I can't handle awkward silences, and when I become the sole focus of her attention, it feels like my brain shuts down.

She doesn't even know the power she holds over me already.

"Hey, was that you I saw driving by earlier?" she asks as we warm up on the court. Crickets chirp as the sun begins to set in the distance, painting the sky brilliant shades of pink and orange. It reminds me of fire, just like her.

"Oh...yeah," I say awkwardly.

"Funny how we have the exact same car." Her lips quirk up in a half smile.

"I know, it's crazy, right?" I rotate my shoulders around, taking my time so I can make this conversation last longer.

Max has an event for the twins' kindergarten class, and apparently, Angie isn't feeling well. So, it's just the two of us with the rest of the group tonight.

"Matching Jeeps, except for the fact you have zero ducks."

"I'm just not as *fun* and *nice* as you, I guess," she says.

"True, but so few people are."

She rolls her eyes but huffs out a small laugh as she stretches her quads.

"So, was that your dog you were running with?" I inwardly cringe. *Of course it's her dog, dumbass, who else's would it be?*

She beams. "Yeah, his name is Henry. He's my sweet boy."

"He's big. How old is he?"

"About to turn six. I was never planning to get a dog, but I went with Angie to a farm near her mom's house, and one of the lab pups just went up to her. Then another from the same litter jumped into my lap and wouldn't leave me alone."

We both lean against the fence facing each other.

"Aw, so your dog and Angie's dog are siblings? That's adorable."

"It is," she says wistfully.

A comfortable silence stretches between us as I look around the court. It feels like something has shifted again. She's so easy to talk to, and it doesn't feel awkward at all. When I look back at her, though, it seems like she wants to say more.

She lets out a soft breath. "I was going through a tough time with my parents back then. Henry came into my life at the exact moment I needed him, like the angel he is."

I stay quiet, letting her go on if she wants to.

After a beat, she says, "Then a few years ago Angie and I moved here, and that's when I first started playing pickleball."

I nod, thinking of how I first learned to play with Dad.

"I loved it right away; it reminded me so much of how I felt playing tennis growing up. The competitiveness of it, the physicality. Getting in the zone and blocking out the stresses of the world."

"I get that. Sports did the same for me. It was one of the only times I felt in control of my life. It was simple: the harder I worked, the better I got."

"Exactly. What about you? How long have you been playing pickleball?"

"Started two and a half…almost three years ago, I guess. My dad and I played together for about a year or so before he passed away." My voice cracks on the last word, and I clear my throat.

She stands up straighter, her eyebrows pulling together. "I'm so sorry."

I blink the tears back. "But I've been back at it almost…four weeks now?"

"Four weeks…" She tilts her head to the side. "Was the morning after our date your first time back?"

I nod.

"Wow, I had no idea."

I look away and shrug. "So how long have you and Angie been friends?" I ask, changing the subject.

"Since college, so like eight years."

"I like your matching tattoos."

She rubs a thumb over her wrist. "Thanks. She's like a sister. More than…" A lock of brown hair falls across her face as she shakes her head. "Well…she's my best friend."

It seems we both have moments from our past that are too painful to talk about.

"Hey, you want to go on a run sometime?" I blurt out. "Together?"

Why did I ask that? I hate running.

Stick to the list of topics, idiot.

"Okay, sure. How about tomorrow?"

A lightness expands in my chest. "Wouldn't miss it." Not for her.

"Do you prefer mornings or evenings? Not sure what your work schedule is like or anything over at RavTech."

I tilt my head to the side. "How do you know where I work?"

Her eyes go wide. "I...am just doing my due diligence. Running background on a man I'm being forced to spend time with seems like the bare minimum, honestly."

"That's fair." I tuck away the fact that she was internet-stalking me for later. "I'm flexible. I can do any time, whatever is best for you."

I'm not a morning person, but I'd run barefoot at two a.m. with her if she asked me.

"Okay...how about when you get off work. Just text me."

"Perfect."

"Okay, let's do this. Gotta make sure we're ready for this tournament." She assesses me. "I want Jerry and Margaret regretting they ever signed up."

23

WILLOW

It's four o'clock and I'm already dressed and ready for this run with Luca. I should have asked what time he gets off work, so I can stop staring at my phone and waiting for him to text me. I swore I wouldn't do this again, get myself psyched up just to spend time with someone. But there's something about him that keeps drawing me in, no matter how hard I resist.

Like when I saw him with Max's son the other day. I keep waiting for him to show me who he really is, so I can go back to basking in the knowledge that I'm right about everyone...but at every turn, he surprises me. And I'm finding that I actually enjoy being around him.

LUCA

leaving work soon. meet at 5:30?

ME

sounds good

come over whenever

address is 87 Cypress Lane

LUCA

perfect, see you then

A few minutes before five thirty, the doorbell rings. Henry starts freaking out, and I have to hold him back by the collar as I shush him and open the door to the sight of Luca in gray gym shorts and a royal blue sleeveless tank. It takes all the strength I have to look up at his face and not stare at his unfairly toned body.

"Hey!" I say, holding Henry back. "Come on in before he has a psychotic episode."

I close the door behind Luca, letting Henry go.

"Hi, buddy." Luca kneels on the floor while an overexcited Henry jumps all over him, licking his face and running in circles.

"Sorry about him, he's still a puppy at heart."

"Oh, he's fine." He turns back to Henry, scratching his ears and getting in his face. "Aren't you, buddy? Yes, you are so good!"

The sight of my sweet Henry—who is generally more reserved and hesitant around strangers—gushing over this man makes me melt just a little bit. Luca has the biggest, most gorgeous smile on his face as he riles up my baby.

I may not be able to trust my instincts about other people, but dogs never miss. The way he loves on Luca tugs at my heart.

I blink several times when I realize I'm staring. "You ready?"

He gives Henry a head bump and says, "You wanna go on a run, buddy?"

Henry goes ape shit, wagging his tail and practically jumping up and down. I wasn't sure if Luca wanted him on our run, but I'm glad he does. Plus, it's too late now; he can't take it back.

I grab Henry's no-pull harness and leash and buckle him in before the three of us head out the front door. Henry immediately lifts his leg on the bushes, and I take the opportunity to pull my foot behind me, stretching out my quad. Luca does the same.

It's warm outside, but luckily not too hot. Ready for it to start feeling like fall. The evenings are getting shorter too, and I prefer to finish running before it gets dark out.

"Beautiful weather," Luca says, looking up at the sky as he switches legs, birds chirping merrily overhead. "Perfect for a run."

He keeps saying these endearing little things. I didn't know people actually talked like this.

"Yeah...perfect."

He pulls two wireless earbuds out of his pocket and holds one out. "Music?"

I take it from him, raising an eyebrow.

"I promise I have very clean ears."

Suppressing a smile, I twist the earbud into my right ear as he puts his in his left.

Pulling up a workout playlist on his phone, he presses play and adjusts the volume halfway down before placing it back in his pocket. "Do you two have a usual route?" He points at Henry, who is ready to get going.

"We do, but if you have somewhere else you want to go—"

"Nope. Lead the way."

We get into a decent pace, following the paved trail behind the houses and through the neighborhood. The path is clear for the most part, but occasionally we have to dodge a fallen tree branch or some large jagged rocks. The leaves have been starting to turn, painting our surroundings with splotches of bright yellow and orange. Every once in a while, we come upon a brilliant red maple.

Henry keeps looking back at us with a huge smile and his long tongue hanging out the side of his mouth. I still can't get over how much he likes Luca.

We make some small talk, but mostly we just run side by side in silence, our steps and our breathing somehow falling in sync. It feels peaceful, simply existing side by side, enjoying each other's company. Listening to the same music together.

The trail leads us back out through one of the newer sections of the neighborhood. I elbow his side to get his attention and point up ahead to the right at a new modern two-story house, with a crimson-red door and colorful flower boxes below the windows.

"That right there is my favorite house in West Brook."

He pulls out his earbud. "Really? Why?"

"I don't know, it's just so beautiful," I say between breaths. "The design, the floor plan."

He gives me a curious look.

"They finished building it last year, but while it was still under construction, Angie and I would sneak in. It's got a gorgeous open layout and…" I notice him grinning. "*What?*"

He shakes his head. "Just picturing you sneaking around construction sites and all."

That dazzling smile. It nearly makes me trip over my own feet. I slow down to a brisk walk and pretend to be checking my heart rate on my watch, which I know without looking is sky high. Luca is holding Henry's leash, and they both slow to match my pace. Pulling out his phone, he pauses the music, and I'm thrown by the sudden silence in my right ear.

"Are you hungry?" he asks out of nowhere. "Do you want to grab a bite to eat?"

"Tonight? Oh...um...I'm going over to Faris and Simon's for dinner."

"Oh, that'll be fun. Hey, how is Faris doing, by the way?"

"About as good as can be expected. They were able to get him into surgery pretty quickly after the injury, so now he's just resting. We went over there last week to check on him and help with post-surgery stuff. But it'll be a long recovery."

"How long?"

"Something like six months until he's walking normally again. Could be nine months to a year before he can do sports or intense activity, depending on how seriously he takes his physical therapy."

"Wow, that is intense."

"And you can bet me, Angie, and Simon will be all over him to do his stretches and exercises."

"I don't doubt it. You all seem very close."

I nod. "They're my family."

It's true. I don't know what I would do without them.

As we round the corner and start heading back toward my house, I suddenly wish I didn't have plans tonight. I don't want this time with him to end.

Still, I can't help but think back to our date and what went wrong.

What he said to me.

I take the leash from him and unlock the front door, ushering Henry inside. "Go get some water, honey." Closing the door, I turn back to Luca, and he's standing closer to me than I expected.

"Thanks for the run," he says softly.

"Glad you could keep up."

For a moment, I'm almost sure he's going to kiss me. When he reaches a hand toward my face, my breath catches.

Oh my God, he *is* going to kiss me.

This is really happening.

My heart kicks up to a gallop as I lean in ever so slightly.

The split second before I let my eyelids fall, he plucks the earbud from my right ear, and I'm jolted back to reality.

"Oh." I laugh nervously. "Thanks for the tunes."

What the fuck? Who says that?

He backs away with a dangerous smile. "I'll see you around, Ace."

24

———

LUCA

Willow and I dominate Saturday's open play. We have gotten into a really good groove, anticipating each other's movements and covering the court efficiently. The other pairs we played against never stood a chance.

Once our last match finishes and we're done for the day, we gather our bags from the far wall and head up front to the lounge area. Her hair is up in a high ponytail again, looking impossibly silky and soft. My hands itch to reach out and touch it.

"You want to grab lunch? Or coffee?" I ask, setting my bag on the couch. "My treat."

"Right now? Sure," she says with a shrug and that half smile. Like she doesn't want the world to know she's *too* happy about something. "The food here is delicious, but the coffee isn't great. Maybe we can hit up Starbucks on the way home?"

Home.

The word vibrates throughout my entire body. As if we already share some sort of home together.

"Sounds like a plan," I say as casually as I can. Tamping down the nerves building inside me.

"Did you drive? Can Max and Angie ride back together?"

"Max drove, so I'm sure he can take her."

Angie and Max appear, duffel bags slung over their shoulders.

Angie asks, "Ready to go?"

Willow shifts on her feet and jabs a thumb in my direction. "Actually, Luca and I are going to stay and grab some food. Max, do you mind taking her home?"

Max and Angie exchange a knowing look.

"Of course, no problem."

"Are you sure?" Angie says to Max, grimacing. "Because I think we should make them suffer a little more for ditching us like this."

"Get over yourself," Willow says, before pulling her in for a hug. She whispers something I can't quite hear, and they both erupt in laughter.

Seeing her so happy and unguarded like this is rare, but she can be this way with Angie. Safe, trusting, vulnerable. It's a privilege to witness.

I hope one day she feels safe enough to be that way around me.

"Thanks, man," I say, clasping Max's hand before pulling him in for a half hug and a pat on the back.

"Good luck," he whispers.

We both watch as the two of them walk out the front door, then I turn to Willow. "Ready, Ace?"

"Let's do it."

After ordering our food at the counter, we find our way to one of the open booths, placing the order number stand on the table as we scoot in on opposite sides.

I take in the space around us. The half wall on the far side has a counter and stools, overlooking the courts below so people can watch the matches going on. Several booths line the outer edges, and a few long family-style tables fill the interior. Along the back is a wooden bar with green neon lights underneath and a brightly lit shelving unit filled with all different types of liquor, the kitchen tucked behind it. Three large TVs hang from the top of the walls, displaying different sporting events, including one of a professional pickleball match.

"This place is pretty cool," I say, my eyes finally landing back on her. Like they always do.

"Yeah, Darrell's done a great job with it."

"You ever come here at night to hang out?"

"Once in a while. It gets crowded on the weekends though. Every so often, he hosts an event called Dinks and Drinks too, which is really fun."

"Hold up...so not only did he *not* name this place Frink's Dinks, but he didn't even name the event Frink's Dinks and Drinks?"

"Right?" she practically shouts. "Thank you!"

"Missed opportunity."

"Totally."

We both laugh, the sound blending together in the most beautiful melody. God, this feels so easy. I'm not even relying on my list of discussion topics anymore.

"What's your drink of choice?" I ask.

"Here, I'd probably get beer. But I do love a good dirty martini."

"Very nice. Very classy. That would've been the perfect drink to throw in my face when we first met."

"Waste of a good drink though."

"True, true."

I don't miss her eyes darting away at the mention of that night we got off on the wrong foot so spectacularly.

"So, what type of books do you like to read? Did you buy anything last weekend?"

She places her palms flat on the table. "I meant to ask you the same thing! I didn't peg you for much of a reader, so I'm intrigued."

"Wow, I feel like I should be offended right now—"

"No, no, I didn't mean it that way, I just...sorry." She waves her hand, flustered. "What *do* you like to read?"

"Mostly sci-fi or fantasy. But I'm open to anything. Also, I asked you first."

She lets out a soft laugh. "Well, I got three books the other day, including the one I designed the cover for. All romance. But I love fantasy as well. And thrillers. Everything, really."

"So...romance, huh?"

She rolls her eyes. "Yeah, yeah, save your criticism. I've heard it all before."

A young man in a neon yellow polo places a tray full of food in front of us and takes the order number card off the table.

"Thank you," we both say.

"I wasn't criticizing. I was going to ask your favorite book."

She reels back. "Seriously?"

"What?"

"You're asking me my favorite romance book. Why?"

I shrug. "Maybe I want to read it."

A flush creeps over her cheeks. "Really?"

"Yeah, why not?"

"Okay…" She tucks a strand of hair behind her ear. "I'll make you a list."

"Or we could go back to the bookstore sometime and you can pick one out for me."

She smiles wide, and warmth blooms in my chest. "I'd like that."

After parking in my driveway, Willow turns to me, folding up her right leg and grabbing her mocha Frappuccino out of the center console.

"I still don't know how you drink that shit," she says, scrunching her nose up at my Pumpkin Spice Latte.

"I can't believe you don't. It's one of the best parts of fall. The leaves change colors and everything tastes like pumpkin."

"Exactly. So gross."

"Wow. Duck hater. Pumpkin hater. Where does it end?"

She rolls her eyes. "It's really more about the cinnamon than any actual pumpkin flavor."

I nod. "No cinnamon. Got it."

My gaze moves down to her full lips as she sips her drink. My breathing picks up. When she lowers her cup, my eyes find hers again.

Is it okay to kiss her? Or is it too soon?

Today was perfect, and I don't want to ruin it.

The silence stretches between us, but neither of us moves or tries to fill it with conversation. It feels impossible not to give in to this intense attraction between us. Like two magnets just before they collide.

But she's not leaning in either.

I know I'm overthinking it, but if I cross that line, there's no going back.

I can't risk it.

I clear my throat. "Thanks for driving," I say as I unbuckle my seatbelt and grab my cup.

"Sure," she says softly, disappointment lining her perfect face. "Don't forget your bag."

"Oh right, thanks." I climb out, closing the door behind me, loathing my very existence. She should just put me out of my misery and run over my sorry ass. I grab my bag out of the back with my free hand and close the door with my hip.

"Good games today, Ace. I think we got this tournament in the bag." I tap her door.

What are you doing? It's not too late.

"Yeah," she says solemnly. "Thanks for the coffee. I'll see you around."

Don't let her go.

Willow reverses out of my driveway and speeds away.

I really am my own worst enemy.

25

———

WILLOW

Just as I'm about to jump in the shower, my doorbell rings, sending Henry on a wild barking rampage. Who is that? Angie isn't picking me up for another few hours for dinner with Faris and Simon, and it's only been thirty minutes since I dropped off Luca at his house.

Twice now we've been face-to-face, getting lost in each other's eyes, convincing myself he's going to kiss me, but just as quickly, the moment is over. Like I imagined the whole thing.

Maybe he does just want to be friends and nothing more.

I open the door to find Luca standing there with his hands in his pockets, his shoulders hunched slightly forward. Henry barrels past, nearly knocking me over to get to him, circling his feet a few times until Luca finally bends down and scratches his ears.

"Hey," I say, suddenly very aware that I'm in a thin, silk robe and nothing else.

"Oh, sorry," he says when he realizes it too. He straightens.

"I should've texted before showing up here. I can go. I'll go." He turns to walk away.

"No!" I say, definitely louder than necessary, stopping him in his tracks. I clear my throat as I tighten the robe. "I mean, no, it's fine. What's up?"

When he doesn't say anything, doesn't move, I open my door wider and motion behind me. "Do you want to come in?"

He runs his hand through his thick black hair before dropping it. "Sure." Henry is fast on his heels as I shut the door.

"Do you want something to drink? Water—"

"I'm sorry," he says abruptly.

I freeze. I'm not sure what he's actually apologizing for, so I just stand there and let him talk.

"For weeks now, I've been trying to figure out how to properly apologize for my behavior on our date, and...there is no excuse that makes up for it. But I'd like to explain, if you'll let me. Please."

I nod. I've been dying to know, honestly. The man I've seen these past few weeks has been nothing like Weepy Asshole Tinder Date Guy. He seems more like the person I had been flirting with for days leading up to that night, right after we matched and started chatting in the app.

Feeling that long-forgotten flutter when the conversation flows so naturally, so easily. The excitement of connecting with someone, knowing it's so rare. For me, at least.

Walking over to the sofa in my living room, I gesture to the armchair next to it as we both sit down. I move the throw pillows out of the way, grateful that I cleaned up the house this morning. My scented lavender candle burns on the side table, giving the illusion that I have my life together here, when I only lit it to cover the foul dog odor.

I quickly grab the gold chunky yarn blanket folded over the back of the sofa to cover up my lower half, blushing at the thought of wearing so little while Luca Giordano sits in my living room. It's all a bit surreal.

Henry lies down on the other side of the room on his dog bed, sensing the vibes and deciding a nap would suit him better.

Luca is quiet for a moment, leaning forward with his elbows propped on his knees and his hands tightly clasped. His head hangs low for several seconds before he breaks the silence.

"I am so, so sorry, Willow."

Willow.

Not Ace.

The sound of my name on his lips is as unfamiliar as this somber side of him. When he finally looks up at me, his eyes look dull. Almost haunted.

"I've spent every day since that first night with you regretting how I acted. You didn't deserve that, and I didn't mean any of the things I said. It had absolutely nothing to do with you, and everything to do with me...and my past."

He lets out a long breath and runs a hand through his hair again, sitting up straight. "About an hour before our date, I got a call. From my ex-wife."

Ex-wife?

I force myself to keep a neutral expression.

"You were married?" I ask without accusation or judgment.

He nods. "It was the biggest mistake of my life. My relationship with her...with Sadie, was...toxic. I had trouble speaking up for myself..."

I find that hard to imagine. He always seems so confident.

"...and she took advantage of that and put me down every chance she got. She became manipulative and controlling and shut me down when I tried to talk about it. It really messed me up."

I'm not even sure what to say. I can't imagine what that would do to someone. Luca seemed reserved around me those first couple of weeks after the date, but I just assumed it was because I was being a bitch to him and trying to freeze him out.

Fuck. Was I behaving exactly as his ex-wife had toward him?

He certainly seems to have a type.

"How long were you together?"

"Long enough."

I nod. He's being evasive, which is fair. I don't need to know all the details right now. But I can't help but wonder what he saw in Sadie in the first place. Why would you marry someone who turned out to be the biggest mistake of your life? What makes me any different from her?

"What finally did it for me was when she wouldn't come to my dad's funeral."

"What? Why not?"

He shakes his head. "Who knows. I never got a real explanation, just that she had other plans she couldn't get out of." He pauses, shifting in the chair and smoothing his hands down his jeans. "Anyway, it didn't end well, obviously, and I moved out here. A fresh start, you know? Started going to therapy again to deal with my anxiety and PTSD."

"You see a therapist?" There's so much I don't know about this guy.

He meets my gaze, nodding slowly. "Yes. I have since I was in high school."

I don't look away. I won't let him think I judge him for seeking help just because I've never been. But it's rare for a man to admit it so openly.

"Eventually, my life was manageable again, and I hadn't heard from Sadie in almost a year." He scratches at the hair on his face. After a breath, he gestures to me and adds, "And then, I finally put myself out there again."

I hug my knees to my chest, resting my cheek on top.

"When you and I matched on Tinder, it was the first time in a long time I felt...excited. Hopeful. Messaging with you felt so easy and fun, and I could not wait for our first date."

I nod again, and my mouth tugs to the side. "Yeah, me too."

But then his eyes go dark and unfocused. "She called me out of the blue that night, threatening to come out here with some bullshit story. She brought up my dad."

I let my feet fall to the floor, scooting closer to him and putting my hand on his arm. His gaze following the movement.

"I'm sorry, Luca."

"No, I'm the one apologizing here. Geez, wait your turn." He gives me a small smile. "Anyway. I just...lost it. I threw my phone against the wall and grabbed a bottle of whatever was in my cabinet. Which is beyond stupid with the medication I'm taking. You know, a little is fine, but..."

I bristle as I pull my hand back. I was hopeful that his going to therapy and taking care of his mental health meant he had everything under control. But one conversation with his ex-wife triggers an outburst like that?

How can I trust that he can manage his own emotions? That something like this won't happen again?

"Look, I'm not here to blame all my problems on her, and I hate making excuses, but that's what happened right before I saw you. That's the headspace I was in. You were...perfect, and I came into that restaurant angry and hurt. And...I know the crying was a huge turnoff."

"Little bit," I say.

"Again, I'm really sorry."

I chew on my lip as I take in everything he has said. My

heart aches for him and all that he's been through, and yet I'm not sure how I'm supposed to feel about everything.

"I appreciate you telling me all this."

"It's a lot to unpack, I know." He pauses, picking at his nail. "My therapist thinks maybe I tried to sabotage the date because...I was afraid."

"Afraid of what?"

He shrugs. "Opening up to someone. Getting hurt again."

I let out a long breath. "I get that."

He tilts his head to the side, the soft light from the floor lamp casting a glow against his exceptionally beautiful face. "Get what?"

"Keeping people away so they don't hurt you?" I fiddle with a stray piece of fuzz from the blanket, avoiding his gaze. "Sometimes it's just easier to be alone than to let yourself care about someone else and allow them to have that kind of power over you."

He gets up from his chair and sits on the sofa next to me, his knee brushing against mine.

"Do you think...we can try again?"

I have to look away. "What if I can't? What if it's too hard for me?"

"What's too hard?"

"This? Everything. I'm scared too, you know."

"Then we can be scared together." He gently pulls my chin, turning my head back to face him. "But you're stronger than you know. I see you."

"What do you see?" The words come out so low they're nearly a whisper.

He says softly, "I see someone who has been hurt more times than she can count. But to a lucky few, she is fiercely loving and loyal." He brushes his thumb over my cheek. "You don't *need* anyone to take care of you, but you think it might be nice to have someone alongside you, where you both take care of each other. Not out of obligation, but just because you want them to feel loved."

My breath catches at his words. How is it possible for him to know me so well? Something between us has shifted again, and suddenly all the pieces click into place.

"We can be scared together."

I see it now. His contradicting personalities are not a deception, but protection. Protection from a world that perceives anxiety in men as a weakness. One that pushes him to bury his feelings deep down and pretend like he is okay all the time. To put on a happy face even when he's in pain.

Before I can change my mind and pull away, I lean in and press my lips to his.

My eyes close as a shiver trickles down my spine, and after what could have been one second or one minute, his mouth opens, deepening our kiss ever so slowly. My stomach flutters like crazy when he runs a hand up my arm and behind my neck, pulling me in closer.

We stay like this for a while. Allowing this perfect and magical kiss to be the only thing in existence.

I open up to him as I fist his shirt in my hands, needing to get closer. The blanket on my lap falls to the floor as I push myself up on the couch, my knee digging into the cushion. His hand hooks under my other leg, pulling me onto his lap in one fluid motion so I'm straddling him.

I pull back for a second to look at him, but just as quickly his strong arms wrap around me, and we become a chorus of loud moans and hungry breaths. His lips are commanding yet soft, a contrast to his coarse facial hair tickling my chin.

He's already hard beneath me, so I move against him, causing him to groan. The sound is so deep and gravelly that it reverberates through my entire body. I feel like I'm on fire.

I gasp when his large hand moves up my leg toward my thigh and under my robe, as I'm suddenly reminded that I am naked underneath.

He goes still with the same realization, breaking the kiss and pressing his forehead to mine. "Sorry. This isn't what I expected to happen when I came over here," he says, breathing heavily.

Pulling back to look at his face, I can't read his expression. He squeezes his eyes shut, and the ground drops out from under me.

He came here to clear his conscience. He opened up to me about his past trauma and his mental health struggles, and I pounced on him like some sex-starved maniac.

I extract myself from his grip and climb off his lap, carefully pulling my robe back over my lower half.

"I think you should go."

Standing and readjusting his pants, he says, "I'm sorry, I didn't mean—"

"No, it's fine," I say. "I'll see you Wednesday at the courts." I walk to the front door to open it for him.

He wipes his mouth and takes a deep breath before walking outside then turns to me.

"Goodnight, Luca."

I shut the door, saving myself from any further embarrassment.

26

———

WILLOW

I still feel like shit. I've been fighting off this head cold for a few days now, and I don't think I should push myself by going to pickleball tonight.

Especially with how Luca and I left things on Saturday.

Angie decided to skip tonight too and bring her dog Cally over to hang out so we could watch one of our favorite movies together. She felt bad because I likely caught this from her in the first place.

ME

how's the new cast?

FARIS

Uncomfortable

I think I liked the soft cast better

It's been two weeks since Faris's tendon surgery, and I still feel awful that he's going through all this.

ME

sorry babe :(

FARIS

Only two more weeks until I get a walking
boot though!!

ME

and nonstop physical therapy!

FARIS

Ugh

ME

love you miss you

FARIS

Love you more!

Six thirty rolls around, and I am lying down with my head on a pillow next to Angie. We are halfway through *Labyrinth* when my phone buzzes.

LUCA

you coming tonight?

ME

I'm sick

LUCA

like actually? or are you just avoiding me?

😔

ME

don't flatter yourself

I'm actually sick

LUCA

sorry Ace

I guess we're back to "Ace." Any trace of the vulnerability

from the other night has vanished.

I click off my screen and toss it over to the other side of the couch, pulling my fuzzy gold blanket closer to my chest. A memory from the other night flashes through my mind of this blanket falling to the floor as Luca grabbed the back of my leg and pulled me on top of him.

Angie is staring at me. Thankfully, she doesn't say anything, and we continue watching the movie in silence.

I don't want to waste any more of my time over-analyzing what happened the other night or wondering where any of this leaves us. It's not worth it.

About thirty minutes later, my doorbell rings, sending both Henry and Cally into an absolute barking fit.

"Shush! You two are insufferable!" Angie yells as she stands to answer the door, ruffling their black furry heads on her way.

She opens the door, but from where I'm lying, I can't see who it is. She pokes her head out of the doorframe and then reaches down to grab something.

"What is it?" I call out hoarsely.

"Looks like a special delivery."

"From who? Was anyone out there?"

"No, but I'll give you three guesses who's behind this, and the first two don't count."

I sit up, scrunching my face as she hands me a large, heavy paper sack. Placing it in my lap, I open the bag and unwrap a huge bread bowl, with the insides scooped out and wrapped separately.

I look up at Angie, hovering over me with a wide grin and bouncing on her toes.

I place the bread bowl on my small wooden coffee table and reach back in the bag to find an enormous plastic container of chicken noodle soup. It's all still warm too.

"What the hell?"

"Damn, he's good."

"Luca did this? Why?"

Her face contorts. "You're really not that bright, are you?"

I reach over with my free hand to grab the phone I tossed aside. I've missed several texts.

> **LUCA**
>
> okay well do you WANT anything?
>
> HELLO?
>
> are you allergic to anything?
>
> okay I tried
>
> on my way, last chance
>
> food is on your front step
>
> feel better soon

"That man has it bad for you, Will."

I set my phone down. "Except that he doesn't. I told you what happened the other night."

She shakes her head, walking out of the living room and into the kitchen.

Luca clearly regretted that kiss. Yet...he brings me chicken noodle soup to make me feel better? He didn't even have it delivered; he brought it over himself.

Maybe it's a good thing he stopped things from going any further, so I can take the time to decide if this is what I want. If I'm okay with everything he told me. If I can trust that this won't be a huge mistake.

Angie comes back from the kitchen with a large plate on top of a wooden tray, placing it over my lap. "Just eat your soup before it gets cold, you dumb bitch," she says. "And tell him *thank you.*"

I sit forward on the couch and put the bread bowl on the plate. When I pour in the soup, Angie hands me a spoon and tosses the paper bag on the floor.

I take a sip and let the soup warm me from the inside. Man, that is tasty.

Picking up my phone again, I type out my reply to Luca.

ME

Thank you

27

———

LUCA

I finish my last set of leg presses with a groan, wiping the sweat off my brow with the back of my hand. I reach for my water bottle and sit up, slowing my breaths and letting my heart rate come down.

Since leaving Willow's house last weekend, my anxiety has gotten the better of me, and it's been nearly impossible to calm my racing thoughts. I even took the day off work because I knew I couldn't handle being stuck in that stuffy, oppressive office today.

Why did I stop that kiss?

At this point, I wouldn't blame her if she requested to switch partners for the tournament just to get away from me. I'm a fucking mess, and she deserves so much better than me.

As I stand up from the machine and towel down, a flash of orange and red snags my attention. The door to the gym opens, and in saunters Willow...wearing the tightest pair of shiny red athletic pants I've ever seen. A bright yellow sports bra peeks out from under the neon orange crop top she wore that first day at pickleball, hugging her voluptuous curves and baring her strong abs.

Goddamn.

She looks like fire.

My cock is instantly hard, and I have to turn my body away as I adjust myself, tucking my erection under the elastic band of my gym shorts. Jesus take the wheel. This woman is going to be the death of me.

I've been coming to this gym for months and have never seen her here before. Maybe because it's a Friday afternoon and I'm usually still at work.

I remind myself to breathe.

She spots me and gives a curt nod as she approaches the front desk to talk with the receptionist. She laughs at something, smiling wide as she adjusts the bag on her shoulder.

I can't stop thinking about what went wrong that night. How I panicked. It all happened so fast I simply couldn't process it.

I want to tell her exactly how I feel and what I want, without holding back. I think maybe she's the type of person I could tell my whole life story to without judgment. I know she is. She didn't shy away when I told her about Sadie or how I've been going to therapy for nearly a decade.

But now she probably thinks I regret that kiss. My God, those perfect, plump lips. The way she grinded on my cock. Her soft skin. Running my hand all the way up her thigh before I realized she was naked under that silk robe, and then my brain short-circuited.

If there's one thing I know, it's that I want her. Every piece of her.

I don't want to move on from her.

I can't.

She approaches with her lips twisted to one side. "Hey," she says.

"What's up, Ace?" That earns me a small chuckle and her obligatory eye roll. "Feeling better?"

"Yeah, much better. Thanks again for the soup, that was... very thoughtful of you." She readjusts the bag on her shoulder, looking off to the free weights at our side.

"You want to work out together?" I ask.

Even though I just finished my workout and was about to leave?

She shrugs. "Sure, I could use a spot."

After helping her get warmed up, we move on to some weight-training exercises. We make small talk, and I refrain from touching her and lighting myself on fire, focusing more on her safety as she lifts decently heavy dumbbells.

What's my game plan here? I need to get my act together and stop second-guessing myself. It's time for bold action. It's time to flip on that confidence.

When she finishes her last set of bench presses, I play dumb and ask, "Hey, do you know where the other water fountain is? This one out here isn't working." *Lie.*

"Oh, it's back that way," she says, pointing down a hallway I've been down many times.

"Can you show me?"

She rolls her eyes again and grabs her towel as she stands up.

My insides are vibrating.

I already know about the rooms back there, the ones they use for classes, and I know there aren't any scheduled for another few hours.

I follow her into the hallway past the view of the main gym.

"It's right there," she says like I'm the dumbest person in the world, but I quickly open one of the dark, empty rooms and pull her inside, closing the door behind me as I pin her to the wall.

My face is mere inches from hers, and I can barely breathe. My heart is pounding against my ribs. My hips pressing into hers.

"I'm...sorry about Saturday," I whisper. "I shouldn't have left like that."

She scoffs. "Which time? When you left me sitting alone in my car or after we made out on my couch?"

I force myself to maintain eye contact. "Both."

"So why *did* you leave?"

"Besides the fact that you kicked me out?"

"*You* stopped the kiss."

Because I'm terrified.

She shoves at my chest with both hands, and I take a step back. "Fuck, Luca! When I try to get close, you push me away. Then you go out of your way to bring me soup when I'm sick, like you're my boyfriend or something?"

Her eyebrows scrunch together, and she shakes her head.

"What do you want from me? Just *tell me* what it is you want."

Her words unleash something in me.

I step in closer, slowly raising my arms to rest on the wall, my forearms framing her head. "You have no idea what you do to me...do you?" My voice a whole octave lower than it was moments ago.

Her throat bobs, and I feel her squirm under my gaze.

"What do I *want?*" I repeat her question, tilting my head. A wave of confidence washes over me. "Let me make this crystal fucking clear. I want *you*, gorgeous."

My hands drop to her face as I claim her lips, leaving no question as to how I feel about her. Our tongues clash and fight for dominance, but I'm the one setting the pace this time. I'm taking control.

I break our kiss and tug gently on her lower lip with my thumb.

"I fantasize about these perfect lips…" Releasing her mouth, I graze a knuckle slowly down her chest, over the roundness of her ample tits and her hard, pebbled nipples. "This perfect body…" As my hand moves lower and lower, I whisper in her ear, "Do you want to know what else I want?" I pull away just enough to look at her face.

She nods quickly, her chest rising and falling with her ragged breaths, her hands flat against the wall behind her as my fingers graze the inside of her thighs.

I grin. "I want you on your back, spreading your legs for me so I can tongue-fuck this perfect pussy."

28

———

WILLOW

My eyes go wide as I let Luca's filthy words sink in.

Fuck.

I have never heard him talk like this before. I didn't even know he was capable of being so...forthright. So commanding. So...nasty.

"Who *are* you?" My eyes search his.

He smirks. "This is me. This is what you do to me."

Before I can say anything else, he kisses me again. Deep, demanding. It's like he's not even the same man I knew twenty minutes ago. I always believed there was another side to him, but I never expected anything like this.

Goose bumps erupt along my skin as his hands glide back up my neck and into my hair. Grabbing my ponytail and wrapping it around his wrist, he tugs my head backwards just enough to make me gasp, breaking the kiss. When he pulls away, his eyes are hooded. Lust-filled. Just like the night I accidentally fantasized about him. Except this time, the roles are reversed, and he wants to be the one in charge.

God, I want that too. I need it like I need air.

"Well?" he says in a low, gravely tone. It's a voice I don't even recognize. "I need to hear you say it."

I try to speak, but all I can muster is one single word. "Yes."

He bites his bottom lip. "Good girl."

My body has no choice but to comply as I step around him and lock the door. I lower myself to the floor, the rubber mats cushioning my knees. Lying back, I let my legs fall open, never breaking our eye contact. All I can hear is the pounding of my own heart, beating so hard and fast I think it might leap out of my chest.

This is so fucking hot, him taking control like this.

The room is dim, but I can see just enough of him from a small wall light in the corner. His eyes are feral. He palms his cock over his gym shorts with one hand as he runs the other through his hair, sinking to his knees.

I can barely breathe as he leans down on all fours and crawls over me, closing the distance between us until he is hovering just inches above my body. Lowering his hips until his hard length is pressed on top of my sensitive center, he begins moving slowly back and forth. The torturously slow thrusting of his hips creates such intense pressure and friction, I moan.

His dark eyes flare. The movement of his hips is unhurried, like we have all the time in the world. I hold my breath as he lowers his head and claims my mouth again.

The kiss is fierce. He is taking what he wants, and I want him to have everything. I run my hands up his neck and through his hair, tugging at it as his mouth moves to my neck. Propped over me on one elbow, his other hand slides up my ribs, stopping just below my breasts.

I sense his hesitation.

Before he can pull away, I take the hand at my ribs and

place it over my aching breast, squeezing tight. Reassuring him I want this just as much as he does.

A low groan rumbles in his throat. I pull him close, angling his head until my mouth finds his neck. His skin is salty, the rich, earthy scent of him somehow invading all my senses.

When he pulls away, a whimper falls from my lips. He grins as he sits back on his heels, kneeling between my thighs. With both hands, he pulls up my shirt and slowly unzips my sports bra, letting it fall open, exposing my chest.

Luca studies my body hungrily as he caresses my stomach. I'm about to tell him I need more when suddenly he's taking my breast into his mouth. Sucking and biting my nipple as I arch into him. I want him to take all of me.

He moves to my other side, sucking so hard he draws out an obscenely guttural moan from me.

He pulls back and says, "Make that sound for me again, gorgeous."

"Make me," I say breathlessly.

He wipes his mouth as he assesses me, letting out a long breath.

He slowly hooks both index fingers into the top of my red pants and pulls them, along with my underwear, down past my knees and the rest of the way down to my ankles. My shoes are stopping them from coming all the way off, so he stops to unlace and remove them first. The way he undresses me is so... unhurried. Methodical. It's driving me crazy.

When my pants are off, he stares down at me, open and bare for him.

"Fuck," he says on a groan, sliding his fingers up and down my slit. "You're already so goddamn wet."

I'm not sure I've ever heard this man utter a single swear word before, even when I was beating him in pickleball. But I really, really like this side of him.

"Keep working those nipples, gorgeous." Letting out another breath, he hooks his hands under my hips and then dives between my thighs.

That same sound escapes me again as he devours me, licking and sucking my clit to perfection. I instantly become a screaming, melting mess, and I just know this won't take long. But God, I want it to last.

I still can't believe this is really happening.

I grab my breasts and squeeze my hard nipples like he told me to, my body begging to comply with his commands.

His moans spur me on as he licks me, his tongue alternating between soft, flat pressure and hard, pointed flicking on my clit. He pushes me so close to the edge my head is spinning.

Luca pulls away and looks me in the eye as he takes two fingers into his mouth, wetting them before teasing my opening and plunging them inside me. We both gasp at the same time.

He leans back down and laps at my clit as he glides his fingers along the inside of my sensitive walls, back and forth. Working them in tandem until I can no longer form coherent thoughts. Until there's only this pleasure. Until there's only the two of us.

"Fuck, I knew you would taste this good," he says, breathing heavily.

I feel my insides begin to coil tight, the pressure and the fire building. "Oh God, don't stop," I manage to mumble, grabbing his hair with one hand, keeping him pressed against me. The thought of him stopping is unbearable. "Don't stop, please."

"Never. I've got you."

I'm practically panting. I'm no longer in control of myself. I don't even recognize the sounds coming out of my mouth, but I don't even care. I don't care if anyone outside this room can hear me. I don't care about anything right now except for this.

"Look at you falling apart for me. You are so fucking perfect."

Tension builds and builds until I can't hold it together anymore.

I'm going to die if I don't get this release.

"Say my name, gorgeous. I want my name on your lips when I make you come."

Oh fuck. I explode. "Oh my God! Luca! *Fuck!*"

My orgasm rips through me, and I scream as I ride out the pleasure on his face and his hand. He keeps the same pace, coaxing every last drop from me as I say his name over and over. I lose all sense of time, space, reality. Like I'm outside my own body.

As I start to come down, he slows his pace but waits until I'm finished to stop the movements completely.

I look up at him as he pulls his dripping fingers out of me and raises them to his lips, keeping eye contact as he cleans all traces of me off his hand. I pull him down to kiss me and moan when I taste myself on him. Fuck, why does that turn me on so much?

"You've made a mess of yourself," he whispers.

Gaining control of my breath, I reach out to pull down his shorts, my need for him again already all-consuming, when I hear the door handle jiggle. We look at each other with wide eyes. Then comes a knock.

"Hey, who's in there?" a man shouts.

"Shit!" Luca pulls himself off me. I sit up as he grabs hold of my pants and underwear, sliding them over my feet and back up my calves. I stifle a laugh as I stand on shaky legs to get a better angle to pull them up, placing my hands on his shoulders for balance.

When he pulls my pants the rest of the way up to my waist, he runs his hands around my ass and squeezes. I help him up to standing, just as we hear keys jingle from the other side. Luca bends to grab my socks and shoes as I zip up my sports bra and pull my shirt back down just in time to see the door open and a janitor's stricken face.

"Oh, hey, man! We were just heading out," Luca says, the opposite of casual.

We could pass for having just stretched or worked out together—in the dark?—but he eyes us with suspicion as Luca grabs my hand, pulling me out of the room and down the hallway.

"Let's get out of here," I say to Luca as we grab the rest of our stuff and walk out the front doors. I realize I'm still barefoot the moment I step onto the warm concrete.

Luca turns around, kneeling in front of me. "Hop on."

"Seriously? A piggyback ride?"

"A piggyback ride hater too, Willow? Really?"

I scoff and climb onto his back, wrapping my arms over his shoulders and pulling my knees into his sides.

He jogs the short distance over to our twin Jeeps.

"Did you know I was here?" he asks.

"Only as I was parking. It's not like I followed you here."

"If you say so," he croons before setting me down on the ground.

Before I can say anything back, he pins me against my car and kisses me again, this time so much slower than our previous kisses. He takes his time, claiming every inch of my mouth. Pulling my gym bag out of my hand, he lets it drop to the ground as he interlaces our fingers together, running his other hand up my arm and shoulder, resting it on the nape of my neck. I can't get enough. I need more, I need all of him.

I pull back, breathless. "Do you want to come back to my place?"

He squeezes his eyes shut, the same way he did the other night. "I can't," he says, and my stomach drops. "I need to take you out on a proper date first. I'm not sure what came over me in there. You deserve...a real date."

I let out a sharp breath and can't help but smile. "When?"

"Tomorrow night?"

"We're playing pickleball in the morning. Are you going to be able to keep your hands off me until the evening?"

"Oh, it's not even a question. My motivation to win that tournament far outweighs any desire I may have for you."

I smack him on the chest and then wrap my arms around his neck. "Then it's a date." I kiss him hard as he presses me back against my car. I feel his erection against my thigh before he pulls away again.

"Okay, I have to go before I take you right here in this parking lot." He gives me a soft kiss on the temple, breathing me in deeply.

I refrain from telling him that I would let him do anything he wanted to me right now. Right there in his Jeep, in full view of his collection of rubber ducks on the dashboard too.

Because I want this man more than I've ever wanted anyone before, and I want to hear all the dirty, nasty commands he can give me.

I climb up into the driver's seat and smile down at him as he hands me my shoes and gym bag, pulling himself up for one more heart-pounding kiss. When he steps back down, something bounces to the ground with a soft squeak. He reaches down and picks up the rubber duck he left on the hood of my car a few weeks ago.

"Oh, and here I was thinking you got rid of poor Herbert." He holds it up.

"I could never."

He places it in the palm of my hand and plants one last tender kiss on the inside of my wrist over my tattoo.

"Do you have names for all your ducks?" I ask.

"I'll be sure to do proper introductions next time."

I roll my eyes as he shuts my door.

I watch him through my rear-view mirror as I pull out of the gym parking lot until I can no longer see him. But his scent still lingers on my skin.

29

LUCA

This woman has uncovered a part of me I thought was long gone.

Early on, I learned I enjoyed being dominant and commanding during sex. Just like in social situations when I project more confidence than I feel, it was something I could easily switch on. Like an actor stepping into a role. My partners were so receptive to it, and for that slice of time, I was in control.

It was something I didn't quite understand: how my confidence in the bedroom couldn't just be my default setting in real life. My anxiety always sitting in the back of my mind, eager to return when I drop the mask.

Then Sadie came along, and I relinquished control. She abused that trust. My confidence plummeted, and I lost my ability to speak up.

"You have no idea what you do to me...do you?"

I hadn't planned on going that far yesterday. The filthy words I said to her just flowed from my mouth before I could stop them.

But it changed everything, and I can't go back.

She is my awakening.

"Hey, snap out of it," Willow says, tapping my leg with her paddle. "We're down by two, let's go!"

I lean in to whisper, "If you wanted me to focus today, then maybe you should have picked a different outfit. You knew exactly what you were doing when you put this on."

She's torturing me with another tiny tennis skirt. My fingers constantly ache to slip underneath the fabric and feel how wet she is for me.

We've only been here an hour, and I'm not sure how much longer I'm going to last before I pin her to the ground. I can't stop picturing her beneath me. Tasting and kissing her, licking the sweat off her hot skin as she comes undone from my touch. From my words.

"If we lose this ranked match and you tank my DUPR score because you can't control your dick, then I'm canceling our date tonight."

My eyes go wide. "What?"

Gary shouts from the other end, "Y'all ready over there?"

"We're good, sorry," I respond. Turning to Willow, I add, "You know all too well that bossing me around only turns me on even more."

"Eight six on one," Gary calls before sending the ball to my square. I return it, summoning the will to focus on winning this match. I may not care about my ranking, but she does.

She wouldn't really cancel our date tonight, would she?

I can't risk it. I have our whole night together planned out. She gives me the confidence I always feel like I have to fake, and I don't want to second-guess my decisions with her.

She liked it when I told her what I wanted.

When it's time to leave a few hours later, Max, Angie, Willow, and I walk through the front doors and out into the parking lot. Max offered to drive since we can all fit easily in his minivan.

I aim for the back door to sit next to Willow, since I sat up front with Max on the way here. Angie intercepts me and says, "Nice try, lover boy." She slides into the back seat and shuts the door in my face.

When I climb into the passenger seat, I glare at her.

"Spare me," Angie says. "I saw you two in there. I almost asked Darrell for a spray bottle." She twirls her fingers in a *turn around* motion.

"Jesus, Angie," Willow whispers.

Ignoring her comment, Angie asks, "Max, have you ever brought Kayla out to play?"

He starts up the van and drives out of the parking lot. "Yeah, she's come to the neighborhood courts a few times, but it's not really her thing."

"Aw, that's too bad."

"It's fine. Her parents live nearby, so on Saturday mornings they take the kids while I play pickleball, and she can get some quiet time."

"That's awesome," Willow says. "Sounds like an amazing family."

"You have no idea. It's been a game-changer having them so close."

I look back at Willow, and she's staring out the window with her chin in her palm.

For the rest of the ride home, we all make small talk, but Willow remains quiet.

30

———

LUCA

The people-pleaser in me wants to reply with something like, *Wear whatever you want* or *How fancy would you like?* But instead, I type out:

My hands shake a little at the boldness, my heart pounding against my ribs. I haven't been this way with anyone in a long time.

She doesn't respond right away, and I hold my breath until I see the little bubbles pop up as she types.

She then follows up with a picture of two dresses on hangers side by side. One is a cute, flowy sundress, a faded sort of red with white polka dots. Almost like a vintage style that she would look great in.

The other? Lord have mercy. The other is a small scarlet red dress with tiny straps. The fabric looks stretchy, ready to hug every single curve on that spectacular body until I peel it off her inch by inch. I already know *this* is the one I will see lying in a heap on the floor tonight.

ME

you know exactly which one

just for that, do not wear panties

WILLOW

I wasn't planning to

My cock twitches.

Marone, this woman.

I grab my keys and make my way out the door. I had debated whether or not to buy her flowers, because I'm not sure if she's the flower type, but I decide to go for it. I don't know what kind she likes, but I do know that plain roses just won't do. Not for her.

With an hour left to go, I'm standing frozen in my bedroom. I've come to the startling realization that there's no possible way I can bring her back to my house tonight. This place is a wreck, and I haven't even finished going through all my moving boxes from last year. I barely have any furniture. It just screams sad bachelor pad.

I swallow down one of my pills as my body thrums with

nervous energy, pacing aimlessly around my living room. My thoughts are racing, and I can't seem to focus on one productive task. All I can think about is her.

I really need to get my shit sorted out.

One thing at a time.

Can I just invite myself over to stay at her place?

I'm overthinking it.

Yesterday she invited me over. It'll be fine.

I'll pack an overnight bag and keep it in the car, stashing my extra bottle of anxiety meds in there as well, just to be safe.

Oh shit...I need to buy condoms.

Breathe. You're spiraling.

Forcing myself to start getting dressed, I finally settle on a gray button-up shirt and black dress pants. I take my time, consciously slowing my movements to allow myself to regain control. My breathing returns to normal, and my thoughts begin to sharpen.

My first real date in so long. This has to go well.

With steady hands, I type out one last text:

ME

See you soon Ace

31

WILLOW

Sliding into my favorite red dress, I take a moment to admire how it accentuates my curves. It took me a long time to love and appreciate my own body. Growing up, I was bigger than most of the girls in my school. I was strong and athletic but also tall and curvy. It was impossible to just blend in with the crowd.

I have about twenty minutes until Luca picks me up for this date, and true to my word, I leave my underwear in the drawer. This dress does not do well with panty lines anyway.

I take a sip of water to tamp down the faint nausea floating in my stomach.

Am I ready for this? After everything I've been through? That voice in my head screams at me to run away and protect myself, but I ignore it.

ME

I'm actually…nervous?

ANGIE

awwwwww

ME

ok fuck you

ANGIE

🤍🤍🤍🤍🤍

I sit at my vanity and finish putting on the last of my makeup at the same moment my doorbell rings.

Okay, so…he's early.

Henry is barking and going nuts. It's pure chaos.

I sprint to the front door to let him in, still needing to get my shoes on. A memory flashes through my mind of running out of the gym barefoot after we nearly got caught fooling around in the Zumba classroom.

When I open the door, Luca is standing there, stunning as ever in a fitted gray button-up shirt that accentuates his toned shoulders. His black hair is carefully styled at the top, and he's holding a stunning red and orange bouquet of exotic flowers.

Henry flies past us to relieve himself on the front lawn, but we just stand there, unable to take our eyes off each other.

"Hey," I say, still taking in the sight of him.

"Hey gorgeous."

I love how it's "Ace" when he's being playful and trying to

get me to laugh, but "gorgeous" is something else entirely. He says it reverently, like it means more than he's letting on.

He steps up to me and pulls me in with his free hand for a hug, and I tense. I'm not entirely comfortable with physical affection, and somehow this feels even more intimate than what we did at the gym yesterday. But soon I find myself wrapping my arms around his torso and relaxing into him, the shape of his body molding perfectly to mine.

When he angles his head back, his mouth brushes against mine, and I push on his chest. "Lipstick!"

"I don't care," he says, tightening his grip on me and walking me backwards into my house. Henry runs back in, just before Luca kicks the door closed behind him. He kisses me for a good minute before pulling back and studying me. His reddish-brown eyes go wide when he finally notices the tight red dress and my long hair cascading in waves down my shoulder.

I smile as he remains frozen in place. "You okay there?"

"*Bellissima.* You look...incredible." He pulls on his jaw.

Burning heat rushes over my cheeks as I twirl the ends of my hair around my finger.

He wipes his chin on the back of his hand and offers me the flowers. "These are for you," he says softly, tracing my mouth with his thumb. I can only imagine what my face looks like after that make-out session.

"They're perfect. Thank you, Luca." I lean back in for another kiss, unable to resist those lips. I may never grow tired of kissing him.

"Let's get these in some water." Taking my hand, he leads me to my kitchen, stopping to look around like he's lost. "Okay, so I've never actually been in here. Do you have a vase?"

I laugh as I extract my hand from his. "I'll get it."

Handing him back the bouquet, I open one of the cabinets

containing a simple glass vase. Luca has already found a pair of scissors on the counter and gets to work trimming the stems. We work in sync, anticipating and complementing each other's moves, like we do on the court.

His arms come to my hips, pulling me close. "One last kiss." He claims my mouth, and everything else fades away. It's never just one kiss. Neither of us can get enough.

It's never been like this for me before, this insatiable need for someone else. I've been careful not to let people get too close, but somehow Luca has pushed past all my barriers. Even more surprising is that it doesn't scare me as much as I thought it would.

I gasp for breath. "Okay, shoes and lipstick."

"Bring it with you," he says. "To reapply after dinner."

His eyes dance with mischief before adding, "I'm just going to recover over here with Henry."

I yelp when he smacks my ass playfully and turns around to go sit on the couch. He pulls my sweet boy in for playful scratches and nose nuzzles while whispering praises in his ear.

I am in so much trouble.

32

LUCA

We get seated at Thai Essane, the best Thai restaurant in town, at a small, dimly lit corner table. Votive candles cast a soft glow on Willow's beautiful face and her plump red lips.

"What?" she says, continuing to read the menu. "You're staring."

"I can't help it."

I haven't opened mine yet. I keep smiling at her until she folds her menu and puts it down in front of her then stares back at me.

Moving my chair closer to hers, I brush her long, wavy hair behind her shoulder and rub along the back of her neck. She answers with a hum as her eyelids flutter closed.

How could I have missed out on this date the first time? If only I had shown up sober and dealt with everything like an adult. For a month now, we could've been together like this.

I have to make up for lost time.

"What are you getting?" she asks, picking up her menu again.

I guess I should figure out what I'm ordering soon. The heady aroma of sauces and the savory mix of herbs and spices make my mouth water.

Reluctantly, I withdraw my hand from her warm, soft skin and take a look. "Umm...I don't know yet. I'm having trouble concentrating for some reason."

She peeks out from behind her menu and bats her long eyelashes at me. "Well, what do you *want?*" Echoing her words from yesterday, knowing it's exactly what unleashed that commanding side of me the first time.

That's it.

I set down my menu and reach under the table, pulling her chair all the way over to mine with my right hand, and run my left hand up her thigh. Higher and higher until it settles just beneath the hem of her tight red dress. Similar to the way it did during our first kiss on her couch when my hand drifted up underneath that thin silk robe. And just like that night, I'm met with no underwear.

But this time I don't second-guess myself.

I lean in, my lips brushing the shell of her ear as I feel her shudder beneath me. "I behaved this morning when you teased me with that god-forsaken skirt, and I'm trying very hard to be a gentleman tonight, but you and that red dress are making it very...difficult."

Her head tilts, those matching red lips a mere inch from mine. "What if I don't want you to be a gentleman? What if I want you to say every nasty thought swimming around in that pretty head of yours and command me until I'm a whimpering mess for you?" She pouts, and my hand squeezes her thigh, causing her to yelp softly.

So she wants to be a brat, huh? Two can play at this game.

With my other hand coming to rest on her chin, I turn her head to look out toward the other patrons in the restaurant.

Some just a few feet away. I whisper, "Only if you can be a good girl in front of all these people."

Her thighs clench under my grasp, and I smile with satisfaction, dropping my hand from her chin and resting it on the back of her chair. "Oh, you do want to be my good girl, don't you?"

"Yes," she replies, her breath picking up speed.

"Are you wet for me right now, gorgeous?" My confidence unwavering, I let one finger slip around to the top of her inner thigh, finding it slick and warm as I press in ever so slightly. *Fuck.*

I have never been this bold with someone in public before. I can't help it. The way her body responds to my touch just spurs me on even more.

She leans in closer, her eyes glazed, when the waitress comes back over and says cheerfully, oblivious, "Sorry about the wait, folks, what can I get you to drink?"

I casually pull my hand away from Willow's drenched thighs as I calmly say to the waitress, "I'll have an Old Fashioned. Please."

"Perfect, and for you, ma'am?"

We both look to Willow, who appears to be flustered. I suppress a smile. Knocking her off her game has become one of my favorite pastimes.

"I'll...uh..."

"You like dirty martinis, don't you, gorgeous?" I offer evenly with a tilt of my head as I lick the finger that was just caressing her under the table.

"Oh...yes. Right. A dirty martini, please."

Once the waitress leaves, I stop torturing her. Looking into her lovely, round amber eyes, I can't help but smile. Genuinely this time. My heart rate picking up at the sight of her.

I take her hand in mine. "So, I promised you a proper date.

And I may be out of practice here, but I do believe that entails getting to know each other a little better."

She clears her throat. "Yeah, I'd like that."

"Should we start small with work stuff or go straight to our childhoods and tragic backstories?" I ask with an elbow on the table and my chin resting in my palm.

She huffs a laugh and says, "Do you have a tragic back-story? Is that why you're pretending to be so happy and positive all the time?"

"Oh, that?" I wave my hand around. "That's just my trusty defense mechanism built off decades of people-pleasing and compartmentalizing big emotions, fueled by a mild-to-moderate anxiety disorder."

We talked about it before, but I'm curious how much she does want to know about my baggage, and what she's willing to put up with.

"Cool, sounds super healthy," she says with a laugh. "At least you're self-aware. That's half the battle."

"Okay fine, we can do tragic backstories later. Honestly, I'd love to hear more about your design work."

"Oh...well...I was always creating as a kid, like drawing and building stuff, but I never felt like I could portray what I was picturing in my mind. Until I discovered photography and graphic design. Then it was all I wanted to do."

"So, you turned your passion into a career. That's amazing. I wish I had the courage to do that."

"What stopped you?"

I shrug. "My parents pushed me to pursue a more stable career path. I was always drawing as a kid too, but they would tell me I couldn't make a living that way, so I had better study something more practical."

Her lips twist to the side. "I'm sorry they told you that. My parents were never really a factor in my decisions. My coach was actually the one who helped me secure a tennis scholarship and pushed me to pursue the things I loved."

I smile and take her hand in mine. "I'm so glad you had that kind of support."

"And then the night of my graduation party, he put his hand up my shirt."

Holy fuck.

"Are you serious? That's so messed up."

She flattens her lips into a straight line and looks away, but I squeeze her hand.

"I am so sorry that happened to you."

Before either of us can say more, the waitress arrives, setting down our drinks. We give her our food orders and then clink our glasses together.

After taking a sip, I'm about to ask more about this tennis coach I suddenly need to pay a visit to, when she says, "I remember you telling me that your dad passed away recently. I'm sorry."

I nod, blindsided by the change in topic.

"Do you have any other family around here? Siblings?"

I set my drink down, turning the glass in my fingers. "I'm an only child, and my mom passed four years ago too."

She places her soft hand over mine. "That must've been so hard for you."

"I was really close with them. Mom was diagnosed with early-onset Alzheimer's at the age of fifty-one, shortly after I started college. Watching her slip away for the next three years while she forgot who we were was almost as agonizing as losing Dad in a split second to a heart attack a few years later."

"Oh my God. I had no idea. To lose both your parents so young is…"

Tears sting the back of my eyes, so I clear my throat and say, "What about you? What's your family situation?"

"Ha! How much time do you have?" she says, but just like the other day, her voice is laced with pain.

I intertwine our fingers, pulling them to my lips to kiss her knuckles. "I have all the time in the world for you."

Her cheeks take on a pinkish tint. I notice one tiny freckle under her left eye on the apple of her cheek, and I have the sudden urge to kiss it.

"I'm not super close with my parents," she says.

I think back to our talk the other day when she said something about getting Henry during a particularly tough time with her parents.

"My older sister, Holly, ran away from home when I was fifteen. It put a lot of strain on our family, and I ended up having to grow up way too fast that year. They just shut down and stopped taking care of me and themselves. So it became my responsibility. But eventually, I hit a point where I just couldn't do it anymore." She looks down at our hands like they hold the answer to why this happened to her. "I don't even know if Holly is still alive."

"That's awful. I'm so sorry." I pull her hand to my chest and hold it there. Wishing I could take away every ounce of her pain.

We stare at each other solemnly.

How many times can two people say "I'm sorry?"

But there's another shift.

We just told each other things we don't normally share, and neither of us turned away.

33

LUCA

After finishing our dinner, I take her to get ice cream at a small local shop down the road. We eat side by side while walking through a nearby park, admiring the colors of the trees and the cool, crisp air as fallen leaves crunch under each step. With her high heels on, she is the same height as me, maybe half an inch taller.

When she had emerged from her bedroom earlier, her face was a mix of apprehension and challenge, as if testing me to see how I would react to being shorter than her.

Like any of that matters to me.

But in that moment, I realized it must have mattered to *someone* in her past. Someone had made her feel insecure over something so insignificant, and how I reacted would determine if we could even be together. So, I simply pulled her forehead to mine and whispered against her lips, "You...are perfect."

I wasn't lying. She really is.

"Okay, so I have to know about RavTech," she says before taking a bite of her pistachio ice cream. "I'm sorry, but how can you of all people work for someone like Preston McIntire? He's a comic book supervillain."

I groan. "I know. Honestly, I've never met the guy. His dirtbag son is my boss though."

"Yikes." She shivers and pulls her shawl tighter with her free hand. "So why work there? What do you do anyway?"

"I'm a software developer. I'm currently heading up a big project that is launching soon. Once it's done, I plan to look for another job. The corporate life is not for me."

"What kind of project?" She finishes her ice cream before looking around. I take the cup and spoon from her and throw our trash away in a nearby garbage can.

Interlacing our fingers, I continue, "It's meant to help teachers build a curriculum that works for all students, especially those who need extra attention."

"Is that something you wish you had growing up?"

She doesn't miss anything.

The side of my mouth turns up. "Am I that easy to read?"

"Not in the slightest. But I am starting to figure you out a little bit more, Luca Giordano."

"And?"

"And you're nothing like I thought you'd be. Yet everything I hoped for."

I pull into our neighborhood, our hands intertwined and resting on her leg as she rubs her thumb over mine. The sensation shoots sparks up my forearm as I park my Jeep in her driveway.

She reaches for the door handle, but I lean over and pull her back toward me.

"I can open my own door," she says with a small shake of her head.

"I know, but let me. Just this once. Maybe you'll like how I do it."

I climb out and walk to her door, opening it for her and extending a hand to help her step down. My eyes roaming from her high heels all the way up those long tan legs, to that tight red dress hiked up nearly past her thighs.

"Thank you," she says.

"Nice, right?"

She rolls her eyes, fishing out the keys from her purse as we walk to her townhouse. When she stops in front of me to unlock the door, I brush her long hair over her shoulder, kissing her neck as one of those tiny red straps slips down her arm. I feel her shiver beneath me, goose bumps erupting over her skin.

I rub my hands up her shoulders, gently putting the strap back in place before pulling up her shawl. "Hmm, so cold out here. Let's get you inside and warmed up, shall we?"

The click of the lock instantly has me nudging her inside, nearly tripping over her feet. The door isn't even all the way closed before I spin her around to face me, wrapping her in my arms and kissing the warm column of her neck. It's been killing me all night not kissing those perfect red lips and smearing her makeup. But I have plans for those lips.

I suddenly notice the lack of dog breath and black mountain of fur circling my legs. "Wait, where's Henry?"

"Angie took him for the night," she says with a smile.

I press my forehead to hers. "Look at you planning ahead." I gaze down at her mouth and run my hands over her arms again. "Did you have a good night?"

"Mm-hmm."

I rub my thumb over her chin. "You ready to have some fun, gorgeous?"

Her breath hitches, and she nods quickly.

"Good. Because I've been picturing those beautiful red lips on my cock all night. You want to be a good girl? Then get on your knees and paint my dick red."

Willow doesn't hesitate, a slow feline grin forming as she lowers herself to the ground and unbuckles my belt, pulling it free from the loops with a snap. I unbutton my shirt part of the way, and by the time I pull it over my head, she already has my pants down at my ankles. She looks up at me hungrily as I softly caress her cheek with my thumb.

When she slowly peels off my briefs, my cock springs free a hair's breadth distance from those lips, and my balls tighten. God, I want this to last, but I'm barely holding it together already. And she hasn't even touched me yet.

I really hope I don't embarrass myself here.

Her hand wraps around my shaft, slowly pumping back and forth as she flicks the head with the tip of her tongue. The sensation nearly sends me over the edge before she licks me from base to tip.

Fuck me.

I'll be lucky if I last another minute like this.

When she takes me into her mouth, I have to shut my eyes to hold on a little longer.

Quick, name all the Founding Fathers.

Umm, George Washington?

I gather her hair behind her head and away from her face.

Those scarlet red lips devour my cock, making an absolute mess of us both, and just when I think she's taken me in as far as she can, she pushes forward until I can feel the back of her throat.

Ahh ahh, Jefferson?

"Goddamn," I say on a moan.

I finally look down at her, my breathing ragged, still holding her hair back with one hand and stroking her cheek with the other. "Look at you taking me so well." I swipe at the smeared lipstick around her mouth, and she hums at the praise. "You are so fucking perfect. This mouth was made to suck my cock."

Her moan vibrates through me as she picks up her pace and gently takes my balls with her other hand. I definitely won't make it much longer.

I don't know, John something?

She is sucking and licking me to perfection, that tongue working wonders. Gagging on my cock over and over and over.

Fuck it.

I take the hair in my hand and wrap it once around my fist. "I'm close," I warn, giving her enough time to decide what happens next. When she pulls me even closer, squeezing my ass as she whimpers, I know it's all over for me. "Oh, God yes, here it comes."

And then I explode.

The force of my orgasm is so intense it doubles me over, and I worry I might actually lose consciousness. I continue to come down her throat for what feels like eternity, my knees shaking, but she takes all of it. She doesn't stop until she's milked me of every last drop, and I'm pretty sure I've died and gone to heaven.

When I finally come to my senses, she's looking up at me, and her throat bobs as she swallows it all down. With red lipstick smeared everywhere and a tiny drop of my cum on her swollen lips, I go to wipe it away with my thumb, but she licks it up before I can.

I'm still trying to catch my breath when I realize in this moment that I would do absolutely anything for this woman.

34

WILLOW

My first orgasm came quickly.

I had been ready for him the moment I saw him standing on my front porch tonight, looking so damn fine. Then everything that followed has been like a fever dream.

This man is sweet, sexy, commanding, and gentle, all at the same time.

"Your turn," he had whispered to me before lifting my red dress and eating me out on my living room couch, much like he did at the gym yesterday. He had me screaming his name in no time.

And now, for the past forty-five minutes, my red dress long ago thrown into a heap on the floor, Luca has been edging me as I beg for release. Torturing me on my bed by taking me nearly all the way up to the peaks of pleasure, before pulling me back down and starting all over again.

"Please, Luca, I can't take it anymore!"

"This is for being a little brat at dinner, you know that?" His voice is pure dominance, but it's all part of his game. Now that I have him figured out, I'm just trying to enjoy the ride. But I'm coming undone.

I'm usually the more dominant one in bed. Handing control over to someone else in such a vulnerable state requires a level of trust I've never quite reached with anyone. Until now. And I've been missing out. I had no idea it could be like this.

"Please, baby. I'll be so good for you. I'll do whatever you tell me. Please!"

He looks up at me with hooded eyes before standing. I take in the sight of him. Tan, olive-brown skin, messy black hair falling over his forehead, trimmed facial hair...and that body. He is both muscular and soft. Like the other parts of him that seem contradictory, but it's just him. He is both and everything all at once.

"Hmm...please what?" he asks.

"Please fuck me. I need you." I don't care that I'm begging.

He fists his cock as he stares down at me and hums. "Just because you asked so nicely."

After grabbing a condom off my nightstand, he rips the foil open with his teeth. The anticipation is killing me. I haven't done this in a while, but I have no doubts, no regrets.

I'm on the pill, but I'm relieved he brought condoms. I'm so out of practice I wasn't even thinking about it.

I need him closer. I need him with me. Inside me. Everywhere.

After rolling the condom down his hard length, he slowly climbs onto the bed, hovering over me. Resting his forehead on mine, he takes a deep breath, the mood shifting. "Tell me you're sure," he says softly, gazing into my eyes.

He needs the reassurance that I'm okay. That I still want this. That I still want *him*.

I frame his face with my hands, the coarse hair tickling my

palm as I kiss him deeply. "Yes, I'm sure. I've never wanted anything more."

He notches himself at my entrance, stroking his cock up and down to spread around my wetness. In one slow, fluid motion, he eases himself inside me, inch by glorious inch, filling me all the way up.

Oh my God.

I shift my hips, and he tenses.

"Ooh. Hold still. I need a minute."

The full sensation of him inside me is so intense I can barely breathe. But I need more. "You feel so good," I whimper in his ear, tugging his hair.

Never breaking eye contact, he lowers himself down to his elbows, pressing our hot, sweaty bodies together. His weight on top of me is comforting and grounding. He slowly pulls out of me just to the tip, before thrusting back in while claiming my lips with another passionate kiss.

I moan into his mouth, my eyes fluttering shut.

After a few more slow thrusts, he pulls all the way out, the warmth and fullness in me suddenly gone.

My eyes fly open as he rolls us both over, making me squeal. Our combined laughter is my new favorite sound.

Luca's hands are still on my hips as he guides and lowers me back down on top of him, seated to the hilt as he fills me up once again. He pulls then pushes my hips, setting the pace for how I ride him.

He runs his hands up my back and to my neck, sending shivers down my spine, before pulling me closer for another heart-stopping kiss. I continue grinding on him as we both start to fall apart.

When I push myself back up with my hands on his chest, his eyes drink me in as I take control and work myself closer to climax. He grabs my breasts and squeezes. Pinching and twisting my nipples, pulling every explicit sound from me.

"Play with yourself," he commands, grabbing one of my hands off his chest.

I lean back and take my fingers into my mouth, wetting them before rubbing circles over my clit, right where our bodies meet. His hands roam back and forth over my ass, finally settling back on my hips. Pushing and pulling as my own motions get sloppy. Digging his fingers into my skin.

I can barely think straight. There's no more thinking, only feeling. Only this moment where we are united and my every nerve is on fire with need. For him.

"I'm close, baby," I moan. God, I don't want this feeling to end. I never want it to end.

"Not until I say so," he orders. When my eyes roll back, he squeezes my thighs. "Eyes on me."

Oh fuck. I can't hold on much longer. I take my hand off myself, trying not to topple over the edge too soon. Our eye contact is so intense I'm about to combust. It's too much.

"You ready to come all over my cock, gorgeous?" he asks, panting, running a hand up my neck and grabbing a fistful of hair as he thrusts up into me.

I can only nod and whimper.

"Good girl. Keep moving for me." I move my hips again. Before I know it, his other hand is at my clit, his thumb pressing hard and circling back and forth. "Now."

And that's all it takes.

"*Oh fuck!*" I scream. Like fireworks set off inside a building, my orgasm is too intense to be contained. I can barely breathe as my body convulses. The waves of pleasure are so fierce I have to anchor my hands on his chest, slick with sweat. He grabs my wrists, holding me in place.

A moment later, he's crying out too as I feel his cock pulse inside me, still hitting that sweet spot so perfectly. His hands return to my hips, moving me back and forth on him, until we both come down together, gasping for air.

I lean down and claim his mouth, running my hands along the side of his head and into his hair. He caresses my sweaty back, making his way down my ass and over my leg. Neither of us able to talk or even think.

Still blissfully falling and falling together.

35

———

WILLOW

After making me drink an entire glass of water, Luca holds me in his arms. My back pressed into his front, his coarse beard hair tickling my neck. Our legs intertwined.

This is the point at which I would normally kick someone out of my bed so I could fall asleep. But I don't dare move an inch out of Luca's strong arms. He traces tiny shapes over my skin, sending shivers throughout my body, and I lean into his warmth.

"What are you doing tomorrow?" he asks quietly, nuzzling the nape of my neck. "Please tell me we can lie in bed all day like this."

"Mmm, that sounds lovely, but I have to work. I have a deadline coming up."

"Working on a Sunday? Bummer." He peppers my shoulder with slow, soft kisses.

"It's actually a pretty cool project. I get to create the graphics for a music festival in Colorado."

"Really? What kind of graphics?"

"Like the names of the bands and artists on stage. All the

graphics that get put up on the screens during a set. Animations too. The festival already has a set color scheme and set of fonts, so I create a package from that to keep the look cohesive."

"I'm not sure I understood all that, but it sounds insanely fun."

"It is. I love taking on different projects. Keeps me from getting bored."

He huffs out a breath. "That must be nice. Can't say I relate."

I turn in his arms to face him. "Is it really that bad?"

"Unfortunately, yes. I dread going in every day. It's sucking the life out of me."

"I had no idea," I say softly, running my hands through his hair, my fingernails gently scratching his scalp as his eyes flutter shut. "Why don't you quit if it's so bad?"

"That's my plan once this project is done. I need to see it through to the end. I want to get it in those classrooms and see it with my own eyes." He shrugs. "Besides, the job pays well, and I already used a lot of what my dad left me as a down payment on my townhouse. Wait...shit."

He scrubs a hand down his face.

"What is it?"

"I forgot to reply to the lawyers about my dad's estate a few weeks ago. It's a whole mess involving his will and the rest of his assets, but they said it could be resolved in the next few months. It might be enough money for me to live off of while I figure out what to do."

"You should find something that makes you happy."

"*You* make me happy." He squeezes my hip and plants a soft kiss on my temple, breathing me in.

I groan through a smile and smack his chest.

"What, too cheesy?"

"Pretty cheesy. Come on, if you could do *anything*, what would it be?"

He rolls onto his back and places his arm over his eyes. "I don't know. Something that matters."

"Like what?" I slide my fingers over his chest.

Lifting his arm, he squints over at me with one eye still closed. "Can I tell you a story?"

"You can tell me anything."

I want him to. I want to know everything about this man and every side of him. All the different pieces that make up who he is.

"Well...when I was a kid, I was shy. Like, really shy. I didn't have any brothers or sisters or a whole lot of friends. I did have lots of cousins though, but we didn't see them outside of holidays. Plus, I was the youngest of all of them, so we weren't close."

"Your parents were older when they had you, right?"

"Yeah. They had trouble conceiving for the longest time. I was their 'miracle baby.' Anyway, I was the kid who brought a notebook everywhere and would just draw for hours by myself."

I rub soothing circles over his skin, my fingers tangling in his chest hair.

"I got to middle school and felt as if nothing was going right for me. I was not a carefree kid, always worrying about something. No one understood why I was so on edge all the time, myself included. And I was...lonely."

He meets my gaze.

"My mom and dad encouraged me to join some of the team sports at school. I was pretty athletic and a fast learner, so I got really good and ended up making some amazing friends. Joining these teams and having friends brought out a totally different side of me, building up my confidence and self-esteem. It turned everything around for me."

"That's so great."

"So, I don't know…maybe there's something I can do with kids and sports and…mental health? There's still such a stigma around it, especially for men and boys."

"Then you should do it."

He shrugs. "I wouldn't even know where to start though. I'm not trained in any of that."

"You told me before that you wished you had the courage to turn your passion into a career," I say, propping myself up a little higher. "You should absolutely do it. The world needs more people like you, Luca."

"Oh yeah? And what kind of person am I?"

I brush away a strand of hair from his forehead as he angles back toward me, placing a hand on my hip.

"Someone who is passionate and feels deeply…someone with a good heart…someone who wants what they do to mean something in this world."

He presses a kiss to my lips and wraps his arms around me, rolling me on top of him as I squeal.

"What about someone who can't keep his hands off you," he says with a small thrust of his hips, his erection growing, rubbing against my stomach.

"Mmm, yes, I was just getting to that," I murmur, running my hand down between us to stroke his hard shaft.

He gasps.

"Someone…" I pause to lean down and brush my lips against his. "…who has a devastating cock. One that I need to *feel deeply* inside me."

"If you say so." He reaches up to my neck, pulling me close for a kiss that I feel all the way down to my toes.

I drink in every sensation, savoring every second with him until daylight peeks through the curtains.

36

WILLOW

The coo of a mourning dove gently pulls me from sleep. I stretch out my hand for Luca as I slowly roll over, only to find his side of the bed cold and empty. I jolt upright, trying to get my bearings, squinting as I look around my painfully bright room. The bedside clock says it's ten a.m. when I hear something clatter from outside my bedroom door.

What the hell was that?

I quickly throw on one of my favorite oversized pickleball T-shirts that reads *Banger? I Don't Even Know Her!* and open the door to find Luca in my kitchen making breakfast. The aroma of bacon, eggs, and coffee hits me, and my mouth instantly waters.

At the stove, Luca's hair is messy, and he's wearing nothing but a pair of black boxer briefs. The toned muscles in his shoulders ripple as he reaches for a spatula off the counter and stirs one of the pans.

Jesus Christ. The sight of him like this has me biting my lip and wondering how many hours I have until I absolutely have to start working. Or if I can blow it off.

His head whips in my direction, and he winces. "Sorry, did I wake you?"

"It's okay." I yawn as I come up behind him and wrap my arms around his bare torso.

It feels so natural to hold him like this.

I kiss the back of his neck. "Did you sleep okay?"

"Like a rock. What about you?"

"Can't complain. Probably could've slept another five hours though." I squeeze him tighter. "Is this all for me?"

"Oh...did you want some too?"

I pinch his side, making his hips jolt back into me.

He spins around, wrapping his arms over my shoulders and pulling me close. Our bodies pressed together as my head buries into the crook of his neck.

"Hope you don't mind, I went rummaging through your fridge."

"Of course I don't mind. Especially when you make me coffee too."

"Made a whole pot," he says into my hair.

"You're too good to me." I pull back and kiss him.

The taste of mint on his tongue reminds me I haven't brushed my teeth yet, but he doesn't seem to care.

"Sit," he says with a twinkle in his eyes before swatting me on the butt and turning back around to tend to the eggs. A hint of that commanding voice I heard so much of last night has me squeezing my thighs.

I take a seat at the counter and watch as he turns off the stove and fills two plates with eggs. The timer for the oven goes off, and he pulls out the sizzling bacon, soaking up the grease with a paper towel before adding two pieces to each of our plates.

He hands me mine and then pours steaming hot coffee into

my favorite cup. A large red mug that reads *Tears of My Pickle-ball Opponents.*

Lucky guess.

"How do you take it? Cream, sugar?" he points to the counter where he's already set everything out. He certainly has found his way around my kitchen.

"Cream, please."

He stirs in the creamer and then walks around the counter to hand me my mug, planting another soft kiss on my temple.

I could get used to this.

"Thank you," I say as he walks back into the kitchen to pour his own mug. "This is all so incredible, but you didn't have to do all this. You're going to spoil me."

"Don't tell me what I can and can't do," he says with a wink. "Besides, this isn't even close to me spoiling you."

I feel my cheeks flush with warmth as I look down at my plate. I don't let people take care of me often. I'm not used to anyone doing things for me that I'm fully capable of doing myself, let alone enjoying it. Is this what it's supposed to be like?

It's been two whole weeks since we talked at the bookstore. The day I began to realize maybe I had judged him too quickly and perhaps he deserved a second chance.

I never imagined things would turn out like this.

He takes the seat next to me, setting down his food and coffee, before casually placing his hand on my thigh. His fingertips rub the sensitive spot on the inside of my knee, sending a shiver down my leg.

I feel his eyes on me. "You're staring again."

"Sorry," he says without a hint of remorse. "I can't help it. You just look so beautiful like this."

"Like what? Bed head and smeared eyeliner?"

"Just…you. Sleepy, content…eating something I made. Letting me take care of you."

I take a bite of eggs and moan. "Where did you learn to cook?"

"My mom and my Nani. They had me help them in the kitchen most weekends growing up. I have a lot of fond memories cooking with them."

I put my hand over his. "Well, they taught you well. This is delicious."

"Thank you, but this is nothing. Just wait until our next date when I make you dinner."

"Yeah? You're already thinking about our next date?"

"Gorgeous, I'm thinking about our third, fourth, and fifth dates."

My stomach flips when he looks at me and smiles. How does he do that? How can he be so sweet and romantic when just a few hours ago he was saying the filthiest, raunchiest things I've ever heard?

I turn away to take a sip of coffee—his eye contact too intense for me right now—and a small orange bottle on the counter catches my attention.

"Can I ask you…about the medication?"

"Anything."

"How often do you have to take it?"

"That one I take twice a day. But I also have another one I can take as-needed if it gets bad."

"What happens if you don't take it?"

"Basically, the worrying thoughts get louder. Right now, the meds keep them from overwhelming me."

"What kind of thoughts?" I ask wearily.

"Like…questioning everything. Wondering if I'm going to say the wrong thing or make the wrong decision. Every little task becomes stressful because my brain is trying to prepare for all the worst-case scenarios all the time."

I nod. That makes sense, it's just a lot to wrap my head around.

"I've been managing it since high school. It's not something I want you to worry about."

"You know, you didn't seem anxious or question the... things you said last night." I feel my face flush with heat again as his lips form into a sly grin.

"Because I feel safe with you." He says it like it's the most obvious thing in the world.

I feel safe with him, too. He makes me want to throw out all my fears and doubts. Yet, something is still holding me back.

"Besides," he continues. "Making you blush is one of my greatest achievements. Second only to making you smile."

After eating the rest of our breakfast and enjoying a quiet, relaxing morning together, Luca eventually gets dressed in a black fitted T-shirt and jeans he brought from home. I help him gather his things and walk him to the front door.

Circling my arms around his neck, I kiss him hard.

"I had a fun night with you," he says, putting his hands on the sides of my face, rubbing a thumb across the top of my cheek. "Easily in my top five for dates."

I swat him in the chest.

"Okay, okay. Top three."

"I should've thrown that drink in your face."

"Can I call you tonight?"

"Yes, please."

He kisses me again, slowly. Tenderly.

When he pulls back, I already feel that longing for him.

"Don't let my flowers die, Ace," he says before driving away as I try to contain my growing smile. It's never been like this with anyone before, and I'm not sure what to do. I'm trying not to get too into my head about everything and just enjoy this feeling for once.

Maybe it's not so bad, letting someone in. Letting them care for you.

Is it crazy to believe things could actually work out for me?

37

———

LUCA

Mondays. The bane of my existence.

Trudging into the office, I steel myself to face another day of soulless corporate bullshit. Another day of this sheer and utter madness after the most unbelievably romantic weekend with Willow. Life-changing, really.

I've always had trouble sleeping, ever since I was a kid. But just that short time with Willow in my arms was the soundest I've slept in my entire life. It all felt like a wonderful dream.

At ten o'clock, I get a message from Kevin through our in-office messaging app.

KEVIN MCINTIRE: Can you come up to my office?

My heart starts pounding. I hate these vague messages. Did I do something wrong? Is everyone getting laid off? Just tell me now so I don't spiral and imagine the worst.

ME: Sure, I'll be right up.

My head is swimming as I take the two flights of stairs up to his office. We've been on top of our deadlines, so I can't figure out what he wants to see me about. Maybe it's just more office chit-chat. It's probably fine.

I knock twice on his open door before noticing Kelly, our HR rep, standing next to Kevin's desk as he leans back in his leather chair. I almost don't notice him glancing at her ass, because my heart is practically leaping out of my throat. There's only one reason Kelly would be here for this meeting too.

Oh fuck.

But then Kelly starts walking past me. "I'll see you for our meeting this afternoon, Kevin."

"Bye, Kelly."

My shoulders sag. She's not here for this. I'm probably not getting fired. Today, anyway.

I clear my throat. "You wanted to see me, boss?"

His gaze finally leaves Kelly's backside. "Yes, Luca. Come in. Shut the door, will you?"

Okay, shutting the door doesn't mean anything. It's fine.

I take the seat facing him as he clasps his hands together, placing them on the desk. "I wanted you to hear it from me first, but we are putting a hold on your curriculum project."

I freeze.

"A hold? For how long?"

"Indefinitely."

I open my mouth, but no words come out. Blood is rushing in my ears as my hands come up to massage my temples. "I'm —" I take a breath. "I'm sorry. Indefinitely? Why?"

"Financials are in, and we're readjusting Q4 numbers. Board would like to see more significant growth going into next year."

"But...we're scheduled to launch in a few months. It's almost ready. Can't we just finish it out?"

"Sorry, man. You know how it is. Launching now will require a lot of manpower, and frankly, more money than we'd like to spend. It's just not happening."

My breathing picks up as I wipe my sweaty hands on my slacks. "I honestly don't know what to say right now."

"Would you mind breaking the news to your team? It should come from you."

Oh really, it should? You feckless corporate fuckboy.

God, how I want to strangle his fucking neck right now.

"Luca?" he says when I don't respond. "Did you hear—"

"Yeah, I fucking heard you," I say before thinking.

Shit.

He tilts his head, pinching his eyebrows together. "What did you just say to me?"

What am I doing? Every instinct is screaming at me to shrink down and apologize profusely. Maybe there's still time to take it back, and we can pretend it never happened.

But the simpering words die on my tongue.

I can't do this anymore.

"Fuck you, Kevin," I say steadily, standing up to tower over him. "I quit."

I take off my badge and place it on the table before turning on my heel and walking out of his office and down the stairs to my desk. Once my door is shut, I let out a harsh breath and run my shaking hands through my hair.

Holy shit.

I just did that.

That might have been very, very stupid.

But it felt so goddamn good.

I look around my office for any of my things I need to take with me. I figure I have only a few minutes before Kevin tries to barge in here and deliver some grand, fuck-off speech. Luckily —and also a little sadly—there's only a handful of personal items here in this cold, sterile office. A picture frame with a photo of my parents, some drawings from Max's kids of turtles and princesses, as well as my meds and my favorite ballpoint pen.

I stuff it all in my laptop bag, which *I* bought, but leave the company-owned computer on my desk. Good riddance.

I move at a brisk pace to the elevators, out of sight from Kevin and the rest of the team. A pang of guilt runs through me for abandoning my coworkers. Quitting like this and just leaving them before explaining what is happening with the project is such an asshole move.

I shoot off a quick text in our group chat while I ride the elevator down to the lobby.

RAVTECH GROUP CHAT

ME

I'm so sorry to do this guys, but I'm out. I can't stay there any longer. Kevin is shelving the project and I just blew up at him. I know I let you all down.

Meet up tonight? Beers on me.

Marching through the front doors toward the parking lot, I undo my tie. The noose around my neck is finally gone, and I can breathe again.

The air smells sweeter, fresher.

I take the extra time to lower the hard top off my Jeep. I'm practically vibrating. I haven't felt this way in a long, long time.

Of course, a part of me wonders how I'll pay the bills in a few months, which would normally send my anxiety skyrocketing, but in this moment, I know I made the right decision.

That place was killing me.

I finish securing everything in place when my phone buzzes several times.

RAVTECH GROUP CHAT

TIM

Don't apologize. You're my hero!

EMMETT

We'll be fine

GEOFF

I'm in for drinks tonight

CHRIS

I kinda want to walk out too???

EMMETT

Fuck you Chris, you're staying

I smile as I climb into the driver's seat. I'm so relieved the guys are supportive.

Because there's only one person in the entire world I want to be with right now.

38

WILLOW

A pause.
Furniture shopping on a Monday? During the day? What is he up to?

ME
wait, did you quit?
like for real??

LUCA

for real

you in?

ME
I'm in 😌

Luca shows up with the top off his Jeep. When I hop into the passenger seat, he immediately runs his hand up the back of my neck and pulls me in for a crushing kiss. He seems lighter. Pure joy is radiating off him.

"I can't believe you quit your job," I say as we pull apart, and he hands me a Mocha Frappuccino. I assume his is a Pumpkin Spice Latte.

"I know, me neither," he says with a wide grin, his eyes crinkling in the corners. "But I don't even care. I should've done this a long time ago. I feel so *free* right now!" He pounds the steering wheel as he reverses out of my driveway.

When we leave the neighborhood and start driving down the main roads, the wind blows my hair around, and it becomes too noisy to talk, so we just hold hands and enjoy the ride, sipping on our drinks as his upbeat music blares through the speakers.

I'm curious as to what finally pushed him to quit. But if it was really as bad as he says, I'm glad he's finally out of there. Luca does not belong in a place like that.

As we stop at a red light, I look at the ridiculous rubber duck collection on his dashboard and pick one up. "This a new one?"

"Oh yeah, I just got him the other day! What should we name him?"

I chuckle, twisting my lips to the side in contemplation. "Hmm…" It's a firefighter wearing a black hat and red shirt, with a hose in one hand and an axe in the other. "What makes you think it's a *him*? Women can be firefighters too, you know."

"I stand corrected." He puts a hand over his heart. "What should we name this brave and fearless *signora*?"

"What about…Ember."

"Ooh, that's perfect. I love it."

"Me too," I say as I put Ember back on the dashboard next to all her new friends.

Inside the enormous warehouse-style furniture store, Luca interlaces our fingers and kisses the back of my hand, pulling me toward the section of the store with rows and rows of couches.

"What do you think of this one?" he asks, pointing to a cute cream sofa and matching loveseat.

I raise my eyebrows. "Well…I like it okay…but do *you* like it? Does it even matter what I think?"

"Of course it matters," he says simply. "You'll be sitting on it too." The way he says it, as if it's the most obvious thing in the world.

I flinch inwardly at the idea of planning a future with someone. He said it so casually, like of course I would be involved in this decision, completely unfazed by thoughts of me being in his life for the foreseeable future.

Letting this strange new warmth settle in me, I smile over at him. "Yes, sitting…among other things," I say before taking a sip of my Frappuccino.

He narrows his eyes and pulls me close. "Among many, many other things," he says, planting a kiss on my temple and smacking my ass playfully.

I pull him down another row to a light tan sectional that looks extremely soft and comfortable, and also about the right size for what I imagine he would need in his living room. I haven't been inside his place yet, but I'm familiar with all the floor plans of his section of townhouses. It's very similar to mine.

Plopping down on the plush cushions, I rub the spot next to me for him to join. "This one could work. What do you think?"

He sits down and runs his hand back and forth over the cushion. "Yeah, I like it." He looks over at me. "Looks good. Really, really good."

Running my fingers through his shaggy hair, his eyes flutter closed at my touch. "Alright, spill it. What happened this morning? I'm dying to know."

"I told Kevin to go fuck himself."

I put a hand to my chest. "You didn't!"

"I did." He grins, taking a sip of his disgusting pumpkin drink. He's so damn happy right now.

"How did it feel? I bet it felt amazing."

"It really did. It all just came out. But I honestly don't regret it. I had to get out of there."

"I agree, babe. I'm so proud of you." I interlace our fingers together, rubbing my thumb over his. "So, what did he say that made you so mad?"

He turns his head, resting his cheek on the cushion between us. His tone turning more somber. "They killed my project."

"Oh shit. I'm so sorry."

"Guess it wasn't profitable enough for them."

"The things that help people the most usually aren't. Corporations aren't in business to help anyone but their stockholders. Fuck 'em."

He nods. "I feel bad for leaving my team high and dry like that though."

"They'll be fine. You did what was right for you. I know you're probably all up here right now..." she taps on my forehead. "But everything is going to work out. I believe in you." I crush my mouth to his. A hint of cinnamon on his full lips, but I don't mind.

His free hand instantly slips around my waist, ready to pull me into his lap when I start to laugh and pull away.

"Not here!"

"But we agree it's got to be this couch, right?" he says, reaching back out and squeezing my ass. "It just *feels*...right. Don't you think?"

"Hmm...yes...I think this is the one."

"Good. Because I have plans for you on this goddamn couch."

39

———

WILLOW

"What time is it?" Luca asks sleepily from my bed as I climb back under the covers.

"Ten thirty." I pepper his bare chest with kisses.

"Wait. Ten thirty? In the morning?"

I laugh against his warm skin. "I've been waiting so we could make brunch together."

His hand glides up my back under my shirt in slow, languid strokes. "You could've woken me up."

"But you looked so peaceful. When was the last time you slept in on a Tuesday?"

"Not since college, for sure," he says, pulling me in for a kiss. "But even then, I never slept this well."

"Really? Why not?"

He shrugs. "I've always had trouble sleeping. I don't know why."

"I didn't know that. You've always fallen asleep so quickly with me."

"Exactly."

194

My stomach flips as his words sink in. I don't know how this man always manages to make me feel so...wanted. Needed.

I lean down to kiss him again as I straddle his hips, his morning wood rubbing against my center through my shorts as he squeezes my thighs. I cannot get enough of him. He's like a drug. And I'm a hopeless addict.

After finishing up work that afternoon, I head over to Luca's house, where he has been busy in the kitchen prepping to make chicken rigatoni for dinner, while brownies bake in the oven for dessert. I certainly wasn't going to stop him. At the rich smell of chocolate, I'm drooling.

"Babe, how much longer on those brownies?" I shout from the living room.

"About to take them out, but we've gotta let 'em cool."

"Ugh! They smell so good. I'm not going to be able to wait until after dinner."

"Patience is a virtue, Ace."

I hear the oven door open and the scraping of metal as he pulls out the tray, setting it on the counter.

"Okay, fifteen minutes and we're in the clear."

"Come here then." I put my arms out for him to join me on his ratty old couch.

All the new furniture should be here tomorrow, luckily. I offered to come over today to help clean up and prepare for the delivery, even though he seemed a little embarrassed about letting me see his place. It definitely gives off college frat boy vibes, but it isn't terrible. I've seen worse.

He climbs on top of me as we snuggle on his couch. With his warmth and his weight pressed into me, I immediately feel at peace. Especially when Henry comes to rest at the base of the couch next to us.

At some point, I jolt awake, not realizing we had even fallen asleep. But Luca is so comfortable I just sink back into his embrace. Until a clanking noise from the kitchen gives me pause. What is that?

Leaning on my elbows, I peek over into the kitchen to see what's making that sound, when a sense of dread washes over me. Oh shit.

"No! No, no, no. Henry, no!" I yell, clamoring off the couch. But it's too late. The brownie pan is on the kitchen floor, licked clean.

"What happened?" Luca calls from the couch, still waking up.

"Henry ate all the brownies! Shit!" *Chocolate.* I'm spiraling. "We have to get him to the emergency vet's office right now, but I don't know where it is. And my regular vet is all the way downtown."

Luca is already at our side, his calm and reassuring hand comes to rest on my leg. "Hey. It'll be okay, we'll just take him over to Max's. He's off on Tuesdays. Come on." He pulls me up to standing.

Max. Of course. Thank God he's just down the street.

Luca grabs Henry's harness and starts buckling him up as I put my shoes on. He stands at the front door with Henry on a leash, his hand extended. "Come on. It's going to be okay."

I let his calming words flow through me as I take his hand.

We cross the street to Max's house and Luca raps on the front door, hurried but not frantic. When the door opens, Max looks at us in surprise and bewilderment.

"He got into a pan of brownies," Luca blurts out. "What do we do?"

Max quickly squats down to assess Henry. "The whole pan?"

"Yes," Luca and I say together.

"Come in, come in," Max says as he stands and takes Henry's leash. "We'll take care of him, okay?" He says that last part to me, and all I can do is nod.

I'm still so shaken. I've never had to deal with an emergency for Henry before, in all the years I've had him. I'm so glad Luca and Max are here, because I'm already a complete wreck.

Max leads Henry through the hallway and into a bright open kitchen, where he looks in one of the upper cabinets, pulling out a bottle of something.

"Who do we have here today?" Max croons, kneeling back down to Henry's level.

"This is Henry," I say shakily as Luca's strong hands come to my shoulders.

"Hello, Henry!" He looks up at me and asks, "And how much does he weigh?"

"Umm...ninety-five pounds at his last check-up?"

"Oh, big boy! Okay, so we need about...five teaspoons."

"What is that?" Luca points to the bottle.

"Hydrogen peroxide. It'll make him vomit. It's not going to be pretty, but we need to empty his stomach."

"But he's going to be okay?" I ask.

Max strokes Henry's fur. "He'll be fine. He's not showing any symptoms of toxicity yet, so we're good."

"Thank God."

He measures out the liquid with a syringe as a timer goes off on Luca's phone.

"Oh shit, I forgot. I'm supposed to start the chicken for dinner."

"Go, I'm fine," I say, even though his presence calms me in a way no one else can.

"We can just pick something up instead."

Max waves his hand. "Nah, go ahead, we're good here. We're just going to give him this..." He pauses to squirt the liquid into Henry's mouth, holding his muzzle until he swallows it all down. "...and take him out back until he throws everything up."

Luca looks to me. "Are you sure? I can stay."

"Go ahead and start dinner. I'm good. Promise."

He wraps me in a tight embrace, and I instinctively hug him back.

"I'll be back over as soon as I can." He kisses my temple and adds, "Text me any updates."

"You want barfing updates?"

"Yes, please," he says, squeezing my hand once before walking out the front door.

Max removes Henry's leash and walks to a set of sliding glass doors. "Come on, boy! Let's go!"

Henry bolts out the back doors and into a large grassy backyard, happy as can be. My heart soars at the sight of him frolicking in the yard, checking out all the new and exciting smells like it's the best day ever.

I follow Max out back, unsure of what to say to Luca's friend without him here as a buffer.

"Thank you so much for helping out with Henry," I say awkwardly, hugging my elbows into my sides.

"Are you kidding? Of course. Happy to help."

"I'm glad you were home. Where are those cute kids anyway?" I look around at the giant swing set and toys strewn about, but it's awfully quiet.

"Their grandparents picked them up from school and took

them to the park. Kayla works until six most nights, and they love to see them."

I remember him telling us about how they take the kids every Saturday morning so they can have a break. Must be nice having parents nearby who are so involved in your life.

"Oh, right, Kayla works with my friend Simon, right?" I suddenly remember.

"Yep."

I realize I don't know much at all about Max, even though we've been playing pickleball in the same group since I moved here. Guilt washes over me.

"I'm...sorry if I've ever been rude to you on the court. I'm not very good with people."

"I don't think you've been rude. Intimidating, maybe, but not rude."

I laugh, and just then Henry goes still, angling his head down.

"Here we go," he says, jogging over to Henry and kneeling next to him as I follow behind.

Right on cue, Henry starts puking his brains out on the lawn. It's the most disgusting yet comforting thing I've ever seen. I still can't believe he ate an entire pan of brownies, that little shit. I'm so grateful Max was here, since my vet's office is over thirty minutes away.

I shoot off a quick text to Luca as promised, letting him know the puking has commenced.

"You ready for the tournament?" he asks.

"I think so. I've got him playing four days a week now, so I'm not sure there's much else we can do to prepare. But I'm excited."

"Things seem to be going well with you two."

"Yeah, he's great."

Henry continues spilling his insides all over the grass, and I try not to look at the dark brown mess or risk getting sick myself.

Max is unfazed as he keeps his eye on Henry and says in a more somber tone, "He's been through a lot, you know."

"I know," I say softly.

"I like you, Willow. I think you're really good for him."

"He's good for me, too."

More heaving. God, it just keeps coming.

"Luca is my best friend, you know? And we may not have known each other as long as you and Angie have, but that's who he is to me. He's *my* Angie."

"*So don't break his heart*" is left unsaid, but I hear it all the same.

It has me seeing Max in a whole new light. "Thank you for being there for him when he moved here. I'm glad he has you as a friend."

I have to stand and turn away. I was not expecting to get emotional in front of Max Goldberg today.

When it seems like Henry is finally done, Max stands and says, "We'll let him hang around for a bit, make sure he doesn't re-ingest the...mess. But he should be good to go."

"Really, that's it?"

"That's it. I recommend getting some hydrogen peroxide to have on hand for this kind of thing. Hopefully you never need it though."

I let out a long breath. "Thank you so much." This is the point at which most people would probably hug, but I don't do that. "If you're taking new patients, I'd love for you to be our vet."

"Who are you seeing now? If you don't mind me asking."

"Dr. Ambrose downtown. Do you know him?"

"Yeah, of course. Great guy. But I would be honored if you

chose to come over to us. Good to have someone a little closer if something like this happens."

Max scratches Henry's head one last time as I say goodbye before I leash him up and walk back to Luca's house for a delicious home-cooked dinner.

40

———

LUCA

Our morning was spent reading our books together in comfortable silence while waiting for the new furniture to be delivered. Her head heavy in my lap as I played with her hair. Not getting a whole lot of pages read because I kept looking down at her gorgeous face. Silently thanking whoever is out there for placing this woman on my path. Begging my own worried mind not to mess this up.

Henry stayed next to us on the floor the entire time, recovering from his incident with the tray of brownies yesterday. I still feel so guilty for leaving it out on the counter, not realizing he could reach it if he got on his hind legs. Willow was pretty shaken up, but luckily Max was there to help.

The furniture truck arrived about an hour ago, just as Willow was leaving to drop off some food we made for Faris and Simon.

And now, I finally have a new bed, sectional, loveseat, coffee table, and a small dining set. I've still got a mountain of other things to get done, since after leaving the furniture store on Monday, we practically cleared out the entire home section of Target buying me new curtains, dishware, sheets, pillows, and blankets.

But as I look around my living room of coordinated blues and various neutral shades—and even a tall Areca palm for the corner—I can't help but smile.

After an entire year, I'm finally getting settled into this townhouse. Leaving Greendale was necessary, but I haven't had a place that felt like home in a long time.

I'm still not quite sure what I'm going to do about work yet, but I'm giving myself a few weeks to rest and figure out what I want to do. I have enough money to get by for a while, and I just feel like I need time to slow down and gain some perspective.

I cannot go back to some soulless corporate job. I just can't.

Looking at my watch I can't help but wonder when Willow will return. I imagine soon, since we only have about an hour until our regular Wednesday night pickleball session.

Right on cue, my phone buzzes in my pocket.

WILLOW

heading home now to get ready

ME

pack your overnight bag too

you're coming home with me tonight

WILLOW

bed all set up??

ME

all ready gorgeous

WILLOW

our first sleepover at your place!

ME

see you soon

I close out of my messages to see a new email from my divorce lawyer. When I open it, my stomach drops.

Sadie still hasn't signed the papers. Even though both our lawyers assured me it would be done by now.

What is she doing? What fucking mind game is she playing?

I shoot off a quick reply, asking him to do whatever it takes to get them signed. I can't have this hanging over my head any longer. Not when things are moving so fast with Willow. I don't want to do anything to jeopardize what we have.

We arrive at the courts a few minutes early.

It had taken every ounce of strength in me not to take Willow straight to my bed the moment she showed up on my doorstep wearing that tight black tank top and short white tennis skirt. Her hair was up in a high ponytail, but already I was picturing it wrapped around my fist.

She insisted we wait until after pickleball to break in the new bed, and that I should focus all my pent-up energy on playing tonight. I told her I'd do my best, but I have no self-control when it comes to her.

Willow and I stretch together along the edge of the court, always taking a little extra time these days to warm up after what happened with Faris.

The tournament is coming up in just ten days, but we already play so well together. I've never been so in tune with someone else before, even when I was playing team sports growing up. It's like we can anticipate each other's moves without even saying a word.

Everything with her is just so...easy. Uncomplicated. I can't believe how lucky I am.

After beating Max and Angie 11-7, we all gather at the side of the courts to take a break.

Willow jabs a thumb toward the clubhouse. "I'm going to go use the restroom. Be right back." She plants a kiss on my cheek, and I tap her ass lightly with my paddle.

"Hurry up, Ace."

She shakes her head, sauntering away.

I watch every step she takes until Angie elbows me.

"Oh, hey," I say. My eyes go back to Willow as she walks into the building.

Angie follows my eyeline. "You know you guys are like... disgustingly cute, right? Like we all talk about you behind your back."

"Jealous, are we?"

"Yes, actually! But that's not what I came to talk to you about. I'm going to venture a guess that she hasn't mentioned her birthday to you, right?"

I tilt my head to the side. "Umm...no. Why?"

"That tracks. It's on Sunday, and I didn't want you to be caught off guard."

I shake my head. "Wait, are you serious? *This* Sunday?"

"I thought you might want to know."

I don't even know what to say. "Well, yeah of course. But... why wouldn't she tell me?"

Angie shrugs. "She doesn't like to make a big deal about birthdays."

Apparently. But why keep it a secret?

"She'll be..." I think back to her Tinder profile. "...twenty-seven?" I'm almost sure we were the same age when we started talking.

"Yep."

I cross my arms. "Okay. Thank you for telling me. Do you guys have something planned already? Can I tag along?"

"I've been wanting to do something for her, but she kept shooting down all my ideas. So I kind of gave up."

"Well...I could plan something." I scratch my chin, trying to process all this.

"But when? The tournament is next weekend," she says.

I think for a moment, squeezing my eyes shut, and an idea strikes.

It's crazy but...maybe I could pull it off.

"Are you free Saturday night?"

She blinks. "Are you sure?"

"Of course, are you kidding? I'll take care of everything." I pull my phone out of my bag. "Can I get your number?"

She sticks out her bottom lip in a pout.

"What?"

"You really like her."

"I do. She's...incredible."

Angie takes my phone to input her contact info. "That's good to hear," she says, handing it back to me.

We both look toward the clubhouse where Willow has just come out, heading back to us.

Angie's head whips back to me, her tone suddenly serious. "Because I'm sure it goes without saying that if you hurt her in any way—"

"Let me guess. You'll kill me?" I laugh, but she just stares up at me as I shift uncomfortably on my feet.

She doesn't even crack a smile.

41

WILLOW

"What do you want to watch?" I ask Luca as I sit down on his new sectional couch with a large bowl of popcorn. Tucking my feet under my legs, I pull a soft navy blue blanket over my lap as Henry plops down on the floor in front of me. As I scratch his fuzzy head, I glance over at Luca, who is standing between the kitchen and living room, quietly typing away on his phone and not listening.

He has been acting weird since last night. I remember him talking with Angie when I came back from the bathroom, and I didn't think anything of it at the time, but ever since then, he's been on his phone more than usual, and it's just not sitting right with me. What were they talking about?

Angie is my person, my rock. With anyone else I might be suspicious of something going on between them, but not her. Never her.

But now I'm sitting in Luca's newly styled house, trying to talk to him, and he's not paying attention. I wring my hands in my lap as a similar moment from our Tinder date flashes through my mind.

"Babe?" I say sweetly, causing his head to pop up, his eyes wide.

"What? Sorry," he says, pocketing his phone. "I've been trying to figure something out. Did you say something?"

"I just asked what you wanted to watch." I offer a small smile, pushing down that inkling of dread trying to climb up my spine.

"Whatever you want. I'm up for anything as long as it's with you." He sinks down next to me, kissing my temple.

"What are you trying to figure out?" I ask. "Maybe it's something I can help with."

He waves a hand. "It's not important. I'm sorry I was distracted."

Why is he being so weird about it? Why won't he just tell me? It almost feels like he'd rather be somewhere else.

Grabbing the remote from the coffee table, I put on a new show that I've been wanting to watch for months, called *Golden Daggers*, about two elderly women who are secretly trained assassins, working for some of the richest and most powerful people in the world.

I snuggle in closer to him as he puts one of his arms around me, interlacing our fingers together, and with the other, pulls the blanket over us.

All of his new furniture was delivered and set up yesterday before pickleball, and last night was my first time sleeping over, and I haven't left. We made great use of the new bed, breaking it in...over and over again. I thought maybe we would be doing the same on this couch tonight, but he's been so distracted it's turned me off.

It has been a whirlwind couple of weeks together, so maybe it'll be nice to slow down and just be still with each other for once.

"You feel so good," he whispers in my ear, holding me tighter.

I lean deeper into the crook of his arm. "You too," I say, turning my head slightly. He kisses my temple again.

Maybe I'm overthinking this. This is such new territory for me, my brain is probably trying to create problems that aren't even there. I need to stop trying to ruin a good thing.

Ever since he quit his job, we've been spending all our time together at my place. But with his new furniture and his home all set up, we can finally spend equal time over here now too. He even insisted on buying food and water bowls for Henry, along with another dog bed, so he can come over here with me.

This man keeps surprising me.

Holding him closer, I try to commit these moments to memory...because a part of me is sure they'll be taken from me one day.

42

WILLOW

Tomorrow is my birthday, and I still haven't told Luca yet. I know I should have by now, but he's going to want to make a big deal out of it, and I also haven't told him the whole story about why I hate celebrating my birthday in the first place.

Things have been going so fast with him, I can hardly believe it's only been a week since our perfect do-over date, and two weeks since our first kiss on my couch. These days, we spend all our time together making love and playing pickleball, and now I feel like I've missed my window to casually bring up my birthday without making it weird.

At least he's taking me out on another date tonight. I think I'll tell him then and get it over with. Explain everything and let him know that our night alone together is all the celebration I need. He might be disappointed that I didn't tell him earlier, but I think he'll understand. I know he will.

In my bedroom, I finish getting ready in front of my full-length mirror while listening to the latest episode of *The*

Kitchen Sink podcast on my phone. I prefer watching the videos to just listening to them, but either way is good. Their banter as siblings is just so much fun, it makes you wish you were part of their family.

I hear Luca arrive to pick me up just as the hosts are telling a story about body bagging.

"You are the worst when it comes to that!" Larissa says.

"Only with you," Bradley replies with a laugh. "But it's just so funny!"

"I think it's bad sportsmanship. You know how easily I bruise. That shit hurts so bad."

"You're just mad because I'm better than you, and you've been a sore loser ever since we were kids."

"Yeah, and you would beat me up then too. Trying to be the big tough guy to compensate for the fact that you have no real skills."

"Bitch. Love you though."

"Love you too."

"What in the world are you listening to?" Luca asks from the doorway.

I whip my head in his direction. "Have you never listened to *The Kitchen Sink*? The pickleball podcast?"

He puts his hands up and laughs. "I've never heard of it. I'm not online all that much."

"Me neither, but this show is awesome." I pause the episode. "The hosts are brother and sister, and they talk about all kinds of things related to pickleball. Tournaments, equipment, players, techniques, telling stories, all that stuff."

I continue getting ready in front of the mirror as he wraps his arms around me. He swipes my long hair over one shoulder, exposing my neck, grazing his lips softly against my skin and sending shivers down my spine.

"Well, I'll definitely start listening now," he says in between kisses. "You're getting me into all sorts of new things. *Kitchen Sink*...romance books...*Golden Daggers*."

"I still can't believe we binged the whole show already." I spin around in his arms and drape mine over his shoulders. "I think the new season drops in a few weeks though, so we shouldn't have to wait too long."

"Thank God. I'm dying to know what happens with Pearl and her missing husband."

"Same."

He kisses me softly on the lips before pulling away and taking out his phone. Once again glancing over at me before typing something as he walks out of my bedroom. I barely even saw him yesterday after we finished all the *Golden Daggers* episodes because he said he had "stuff he needed to do" but wouldn't tell me what it was.

I need to find out what he's hiding from me.

Luca parks his Jeep in the half-full parking lot of Dink Shot as I glare at him.

"What are we doing back here?" I finally ask. "I thought we were going out."

"Just grabbing something real quick," he says with a quirk of his lips. What the hell is going on with him?

He takes my hand as we walk up to the entrance. When Luca opens the door for me, I step inside, and he puts a hand on the small of my back, guiding me to the left toward the stairs leading up to the bar.

"What is going on?"

He doesn't answer, just continues nudging me up the stairs. My patience is wearing thin as we reach the landing. Before I can demand that he tell me what we're doing, Angie jumps out from around the corner and screams, "Surprise!"

I startle as she hugs me. "Wait, what? What the fuck is going on?" Once I'm over my initial shock, I squeeze her back tightly.

Only when we separate do I even notice the long table in the center of the dimly lit room where several familiar people are gathered. Simon, Faris, Max, Kayla, Gary, and a few other people from our neighborhood group.

I'm frozen in place and don't know what to say or do.

Luca is grinning from ear to ear. Is *this* why he's been acting so strange the past few days? He was planning a birthday party for me?

"Surprise," he says in a sing-songy voice before planting a kiss on my temple. When I don't react, he leans back in and whispers, "Don't worry. Later, we're going to talk all about why you didn't want to tell me it was your birthday."

My stomach drops. Is he pissed? I didn't consider the fact that he might be upset with me over this. Disappointed sure, but mad?

Worry claws at me as I try to come up with an excuse, fumbling until he nips at my earlobe and adds, "I'll let you pick your punishment."

Heat floods my face, and I have to work hard to keep my expression neutral in front of all our friends. He interlaces our fingers with a devious grin as we walk toward the party table to take our seats, and I remind myself to breathe.

Simon appears from the side of the bar and wraps me in a hug. "Happy birthday, Will!"

"Aw, thank you. I'm so glad you're here. Sorry if I'm still a little shocked."

"Well, you have this one to thank for all that." He angles his head at Luca. "Who, by the way, you haven't introduced me to yet."

I roll my eyes. "Simon, this is Luca. Luca, Simon."

"Pleasure to finally meet you, Simon."

"Pleasure is all mine." They shake hands, and Simon practically has stars in his eyes.

"Alright, that's enough." I push Luca toward the table, winking at Simon.

Faris's face lights up as Luca approaches him with his hand outstretched. "Luca! Good to see you again!"

They shake hands like they're already best friends, and Luca leans down for a half hug, whispering something. They both laugh as they separate, and I narrow my eyes.

"Hey, we don't keep secrets around here." I wince the moment I hear my own words. They both level me with the same condescending expression.

"Will, we're here for your surprise party even though you failed to tell my boy here it was even your birthday," Faris says. "So...you know...maybe just come take a seat." He pats the chair to his left as he moves his crutches out of the way.

"*Your boy*? What, are you like besties now?" I come around the table and hug him tightly, then sit down with a fake pout, Luca taking the seat on my other side.

"I can't believe you're all here!" I say to everyone at the table over the loud thumping music, putting on my most convincing smile as I try to quell my rising nerves.

It'll be fine. They're here because they want to be. They're your friends, and they love you.

The evening continues as everyone orders food and drinks and engages in lively conversation. But I find myself unable to eat anything, my stomach still twisted in knots.

"So, you guys ready for the big tournament next weekend?" Simon asks.

"It should've been *us*, Will!" Faris raises his fists in the air.

"I know. But once you're all healed, we'll get you trained back up, hopefully in time for next year's tourney."

"Eh, don't count on it," he says, pushing around the food on his plate. "I think my pickleball days might be over."

I gasp. "Don't say that! We'll help get you back out there."

"I don't know. We'll see," he says, shrugging.

"Are you worried about getting injured again?" Luca asks. The concern in his voice makes my heart skip a beat.

"Maybe a little. It's hard to say for now, cause I'm still dealing with it. Not gonna lie, it's been pretty rough."

I take Faris's hand, resting my head on his shoulder. "I'm so sorry."

I've been spending so much time with Luca these past few weeks, and not nearly as much with one of my closest friends, when he's clearly been struggling. "And I'm sorry I haven't been around more."

"Get out of here with that. I'm just glad you finally got over yourself and gave this guy another chance." He lifts his chin toward Luca. "I'm happy for you two."

"Love you," I say softly.

"Love you more," Faris replies, planting a kiss on the top of my head.

After another hour of conversation, my nerves have eased a little, but I still can't wait to go home. Luca rubs the top of my thigh as if he can sense my discomfort.

I force a smile and stand up. "I'll be right back."

"Okay," he says, his eyebrows drawn together.

I walk around the corner to the bathrooms, and before I can close the door, Luca is behind me, nudging me inside, locking the door behind us.

"Okay, what's going on?" he asks. "What's wrong?"

"Nothing," I say unconvincingly, looking down at my feet. "I'm fine."

He rubs his hands over my arms. "Did I do something wrong?"

"No, really. This is great...it's so thoughtful of you."

"Then what is it? Tell me." He gently cups my face, bringing my gaze back to his. The worried look in his eyes nearly breaks me.

"I just..." I close my eyes, forcing out a breath. "Birthdays are hard for me. I don't like celebrating them...because I just...it brings back a lot of painful memories."

"Oh." He pulls me in closer, wrapping his arms around me. "I didn't know. I thought you just didn't want anyone going out of their way for you. God, I'm so, so sorry."

I pull away to look into his eyes. "No, you don't have to be sorry. You didn't do anything wrong. I should've told you sooner. This was all so incredibly thoughtful of you," I say again. And I mean it.

"Then...why would Angie let me plan this?"

I look away.

"She doesn't know?"

I shake my head, still unable to meet his gaze.

"Why? What happened? Please help me understand." His hand is warm as he takes mine and kisses my knuckles.

"Not here, okay? I'll be fine, I promise. Let's finish the party and then go home, it's not a big deal."

He looks around the bathroom. "No, that won't do. Let's see. We can find a window around here to sneak you out of...or wait! I'll pretend to be blackout drunk, then you get annoyed and take me home. That way *I'm* the asshole, and no one has to know the truth. Sound good?" He takes my hand before I can say anything and unlocks the bathroom door.

I laugh as I pull his arm back. "Wait, stop! You don't have to do that."

"Why not? Let's get you out of here."

I tilt my head. "You'd do that for me? Just like that?"

He frames my face with his large, strong hands and looks deeply into my eyes. Pressing his forehead to mine, he says, "I would do *anything* for you."

43

———

LUCA

"**O**kay. Ready to go back out there?" I ask, brushing her hair over her shoulder.

She quirks an eyebrow as she looks around. "What's the rush?" Her hand finds the front of my pants, my dick twitching at the sudden and unexpected contact.

A ragged breath escapes me. "Wait, here?" My heart starts pounding.

Her palm slides up and down my cock, which is quickly getting hard. "Why not? You were the one who wanted to celebrate my birthday so badly." She licks the sensitive spot under my ear.

"That's not fair. Ah fuck."

"Since when have you known me to play fair?"

"I...uh..." I clear my throat, grabbing her hand. "I can't. I'm sorry. I have a thing about public restrooms."

She cocks her head, a smile playing on her lips. "Really?"

"I know I literally just said that I would do anything for you, but not here. Anywhere but here." Just the thought of it makes my skin crawl. The germs, the wet floor, the faint smell of piss. It's enough to make me go soft again.

She extracts her hand as I curse myself for ruining the moment.

I skim the pout of her lip with my thumb. "Let's get back out there so we can finish up and leave. Then I'll give you your birthday present at home."

We make it a whole thirty minutes before she gives me the look. It's go time.

I clutch my stomach with a loud groan.

Max's head whips in my direction. "Hey, man. You okay?"

I shake my head, putting on my best dramatic performance. "I don't know. My stomach is just really hurting all of a sudden."

"Aw, babe, do you think it's something you ate?" Willow asks, fighting back a smile.

"I'm sure it's nothing, don't worry about me."

I let another minute go by before groaning again, this time louder, more pathetic. Really doing my best to sell it. Looking at Willow, I say, "I'm so sorry, but I'm really not feeling well. Do you think you can take me home?"

Max leans in. "We can take you back if Willow wants to stay."

"No!" we both say at the same time. Probably blowing our cover.

Willow adds, "No, no, you guys stay. I can take him. Thank you for the offer, and thank you all for this party. This was so amazing."

Angie jumps to her feet and wraps Willow in a hug, shooting me a look. Yeah, she knows we're full of shit. They all probably do, but I don't care. I promised I'd get my girl out of here, and no one is going to stop me.

"Bye, everyone. Sorry for ruining the fun!" I shout to our friends, bending over slightly, still clutching my stomach.

We say our goodbyes before Willow and I disappear into the stairwell and walk out the front doors. Each step to my car getting quicker and quicker until we are safely out of view of the others, collapsing in a fit of laughter.

The aroma of lavender washes over me as we step through Willow's front door, followed immediately by putrid dog breath. Closing the door behind us, I take a moment to steady myself. The silence is deafening, both of us knowing we have to talk about what happened tonight, but suddenly my stomach is churning for real, my chest constricting.

I don't do well with confrontation.

I imagine all the worst-case scenarios for how this could go, but I reach for her hand anyway. Using her touch as an anchor to hold me in place as I try to find the courage to say what I need.

Because I have to try, for her.

"So…I know you said that birthdays are hard for you, and I understand…but…it kind of hurts that you didn't tell me."

"I know, I know. I just…" She sighs. "I was going to tell you tonight on our date and explain everything, but…we've only known each other for a few weeks, and I didn't want you to feel obligated to—"

"What?" I interrupt. "To celebrate you? Spoil you? Have you not caught on yet that I'm crazy about you? That I *want* to do all those things?"

She shrugs, and that small movement lights something

within me. I take her by the chin and make her look at me. "You know that, right? I told you tonight that I would do anything for you, and I meant it."

She shakes her head. "I just..."

"What? Talk to me."

"I'm sorry I didn't tell you. I didn't mean to keep it from you," she says. "I'm not good at this whole dating thing, you know? I forget sometimes how to be open with another person. How to let them in."

I pull her in for a crushing hug and exhale into her hair. "I know, I get it. I'm still learning too. I just want you to feel safe opening up to me, okay? I want you to trust me."

"I do too. But..."

"But what?" I pull away, and she meets my gaze, her eyebrows drawn together as I take her hand in mine.

"I'm scared."

"What are you scared of?"

"I don't know. You and me. All of this. How fast things are going?" She looks away when she adds, "How I feel about you."

I pull her hand to my chest and squeeze.

"I've never felt this way about anyone, Luca. It terrifies me. I...I don't want to mess this up."

"You can't mess it up," I say, running my thumb over her soft cheek, right over that lone freckle. "Plus, I already screwed things up enough for the both of us on our first date, remember? And we survived that just fine."

She huffs a laugh, and warmth radiates throughout my body.

"So...why don't you like birthdays?" I ask gently. "What happened?"

Willow unlaces our hands and turns to take a seat on her couch. I follow closely and sink in next to her, wrapping my arm around her.

She lets out a breath. "I told you about my older sister who ran away from home and left me and my parents."

I nod, pulling her close.

"Well, she ran away the night before I turned fifteen. I woke up on my birthday and found out Holly was gone, and my entire life was turned upside down. My parents were both completely preoccupied trying to get a hold of her and find her, understandably...but they forgot my birthday."

"I'm so sorry. That must've been hard for you."

"I know it sounds childish, but that day is inextricably linked with Holly abandoning us."

"It's not childish at all."

"I've only heard from her once since that day. She moved in with some older rich guy, changed her name, and just left it all behind. Left *me* behind. Not that we were super close to begin with. She was kind of chaotic and wasn't all that nice to me, but she was still my big sister. I still looked up to her."

She maintains a blank expression, and I want nothing more than to take away her pain.

"I figured when we were all grown up, we would become best friends and would have each other. But not only did I *not* have her in my life anymore, my parents completely checked out after that. And I was more alone than ever." She pauses. "I haven't cried again since that day."

"I had no idea," I say, holding her tighter.

"Of course you didn't. Not even Angie knows the whole story. I mean, she knows my sister left, but I never told her it happened on my birthday."

My heart aches for her. No wonder she has such a hard time letting people in. If her own sister could leave her—on her birthday, no less—then why bother trusting anyone or getting close to them?

I turn her face toward me. "Hey. She doesn't deserve you.

You are the most...amazing person I've ever met. And anyone who doesn't know just how special and incredible you are doesn't deserve to know you. I'm sorry you had to deal with all of that growing up. It wasn't fair to you. You should have been allowed to be a kid, and the adults in your life failed you."

She nods, holding her wrist, the one with the watercolor heart tattoo, and rubs it softly with her thumb. "I learned a long time ago that your real family is the one you choose. I drew this heart for Angie, and she insisted we get it tattooed together our first year as roommates. It's a reminder that we always have a choice in who we give our heart to."

I tuck a strand of hair behind her ear before kissing her. Just a soft, reassuring press of our lips. Leaning my forehead on hers, I steel myself for what I want to say. For the words trying to burst forth.

I shouldn't say it. It's too soon.

But it's the truth. It's my truth.

I'm choosing to give my heart to her.

And I have to tell her.

"I love you," I say softly.

Her eyes fly open as she leans back, searching my face. Her eyebrows knit together.

"You don't have to say it back. Maybe it's too soon, but...I couldn't go one more second without letting you know just how much you mean to me, Willow. You're incredible. You are brave, you're talented, beautiful. And I love you."

Her expression softens as she frames my face with her hands and leans back in, crushing her lips to mine. Harder this time.

I said the words, and she didn't run away. She didn't freak out. I hold on to that and pour all of my love into this woman.

When she climbs up on my lap, I rub a hand over her soft thigh and up to her ass before giving it a light smack. She smiles against my mouth, and I open for her as she grinds herself on my cock. A soft gasp escapes her lips when I press her hips down harder, creating that sweet friction.

"Mmm, you like that?" I whisper in her ear. "What else do you like?"

"I like it when you tell me what *you* want," she says breathlessly. "I want that side of you only I get to see."

I was hoping she'd say that.

She yelps when I suddenly brace one arm under her and one behind her back, throwing her over my shoulder as I stand to carry her to the bedroom. The words flow so easily for her as I run my hand up her thigh and yank down her underwear before smacking her bare ass. "Take this off, gorgeous."

I set her down on her feet and lie back on her bed, eyeing that short, tight dress pulled all the way up her thighs as she shimmies out of her bright red thong. "Then get over here and sit on my face until you come all over my mouth and drown me in your pussy."

44

WILLOW

For the first time in twelve years, I wake up on my birthday with a smile.

Luca is standing in my bedroom doorway, shirtless, with a tray of my favorite breakfast foods and a fresh, steaming cup of coffee. The smell hits me, and I sigh with contentment, wondering what I did to deserve a man like this.

Henry barrels into the room panting and wagging his tail, knocking things over like a bull in a china shop.

"Good morning, gorgeous," Luca says as he sets down the mug on my nightstand, careful not to get tripped up by my large, obnoxious dog. "Nothing special about today, but breakfast in bed is what my mom used to do for me on...this kind of ordinary, unremarkable day."

The mention of his mother makes my heart squeeze. He doesn't talk a lot about her or his dad, and I know it's still painful for him. So the fact that this is something she did for him means the world to me.

He places the tray over my lap and lies down on one elbow

at the foot of my bed. From under the tray, he produces a large manila envelope and holds it out for me.

"And what's this?" I ask, taking it from his grasp.

"Definitely not a present," he says.

"That's the only part about birthdays I still accept, actually."

"You'd be a fool not to."

"Hey, while we're on the subject, when is *your* birthday anyway?"

"July seventh."

"Ooh, seven seven. Are you lucky?"

"I think maybe I am," he says, rubbing my feet over the comforter.

I open the envelope and pull out what's inside. On heavy cardstock is a beautiful, full-color illustration of me and Luca, back-to-back on the pickleball court. I'm holding a ball and paddle, giving him a smirk over my shoulder as he grins at me. The cartoon style is distinctive, characterized by sharp edges and exaggerated shapes. And the detail...

At the bottom is a curvy signature. His signature.

"You *made* this?"

"Do you like it?" he asks quietly.

"Luca...this is..." I'm at a loss for words. "You said you liked to draw, but I had no idea you could do something like this. It's remarkable. You are really talented."

He smiles brightly.

"When did you even do this? Didn't you find out it was my birthday like four days ago?"

"On Friday, while you were working."

The day he was suspiciously busy with secret plans he wouldn't tell me about, while I was foolishly questioning his feelings for me. Worried he was distancing himself from me and this relationship. I'm such an idiot.

"You did this in one day? For me?" My head is swimming, like I don't even believe this is all real. Am I still dreaming? Have I not woken up yet?

He tilts his head and gives me a curious look. "Okay, my new mission in life is to make it so you're not so surprised when I do these kinds of things for you. I don't know what *cretinos* you've been with in the past, but this is bare minimum."

I chew on my bottom lip, staring back down at the drawing. "I suppose I could get used to it."

"You better," he says, leaning in and kissing me, then nudging the tray of food. "Hurry up and eat. Any longer and I'm going to have to heat all this back up." He sinks down onto the floor to rough-house with Henry.

Luca really is spoiling me.

Setting the new standard and ruining me for all other men.

After finishing our breakfast and coffee together, Luca heads back to his house, since Angie and I made plans. She insisted on taking me out for my birthday, just the two of us.

I know she is the one who told Luca about my birthday, and I'm honestly glad she did. I don't know why I was so scared to tell him, as if it would change anything between us. I just know that no one else has ever cared for me this much, and revealing a piece of myself to him that I've kept hidden away for so long finally feels like a weight has been lifted.

As I wait for Angie to arrive, I put the finishing touches on the custom T-shirts I secretly made for me and Luca. One thing I love about being a graphic designer is making ridiculous shirts for me and my friends, usually just inside jokes that no one else would understand, but that we find hysterical.

I put together the design for these pickleball shirts pretty quickly, thinking it would be fun to be matching for the tournament. Only now I'm second-guessing myself. It's the kind of thing I would have judged someone else for. It feels...cheesy.

Except he loves cheesy.

My lucky Italian boy with the heart of gold who collects rubber ducks on his Jeep because it's fun, and makes me breakfast in bed, and tells me that I make him happy.

He'll fucking love it.

Love.

Last night he told me he loved me. I knew it was coming before he even said it, but I couldn't bring myself to say it back. Not yet.

I've never said it before.

I have to be sure.

45

WILLOW

"I have to come clean about something," I say to Angie as I set down my glass of merlot on the outdoor picnic table at our favorite winery.

"You're dying," she deadpans.

"No."

"You're pregnant."

I snort. "God, I hope not."

"Luca faked being sick last night so you two could leave the party early and bone?" She casually takes a sip of her Chardonnay.

My eyes go wide.

"Knew it. You have no poker face."

"Just resting bitch face."

"You do have the best RBF, I'll give you that."

"Thanks, but that's not what I'm confessing to."

"Oh? There's more?" she says with a laugh.

I take a breath. "Angie. I'm invoking Ernest."

She goes still at the mention of our safe word. Named after

a tiny stuffed teddy bear I had in college, "Ernest" is only to be used in dire situations when we need the other person—usually Angie—to stop joking around and be, well…*earnest.*

Her eyebrows knit together as she sets down her glass. "Okay. I'm listening." She reaches her hand out, and I take it.

I proceed to tell her everything I said to Luca last night about Holly and my birthday. When I finish, a single tear falls down her cheek, and I swipe it away.

"I feel like such an asshole," she says. "I'm always pushing you to do all this stuff on your birthday. Every year. And all this time you've been hurting. Why wouldn't you tell me, instead of letting me drag you all over the place?"

"I'm sorry. I'm telling you now."

"I've only ever wanted to celebrate you, so you know how important you are to me." She rubs her thumb over my wrist.

"I know, it's why I love you. It's why I let you do it."

I take a sip of my wine as we sit in silence.

"Do you remember the first time you took me out for my birthday?" I ask, taking a bite of cheese from the plate Simon made us.

She thinks about it. "Was that the year we did karaoke at that dive bar on campus and had the entire place singing Happy Birthday to you?"

I nod. "I didn't tell you then because our friendship was still so new. We had been roommates for two months, and we were already inseparable. I never had a friend like you before, and I was afraid of revealing such a painful part of my past so soon and scaring you away with my trauma. I never told anyone about this until last night."

"Wait…" She holds up her hand. "You told Luca before *me?*"

"Ernest."

"Sorry."

We look off in the distance, the sun beginning to set over

the vineyard, casting a warm glow over the neighboring hills. The air is turning chilly, so I pull out a flannel blanket from my bag and drape it over both our laps.

"So it's getting serious?" she asks gently.

"Yeah. It is."

"You're scared shitless, aren't you."

"Terrified."

She laughs and puts her arm around me. "He's head over heels for you, babe. He cares about you."

"He loves me," I whisper, still looking out at the scenery, unblinking.

She whips her head in my direction. "Are you serious? He said that?"

I nod slowly.

"And what did you say?"

When I wince, she lets out a groan.

"You didn't say it back?"

"I couldn't," I say, shaking my head. "Not yet. He's been so open about his past and who he is, but I could barely tell him about my family. This major part of my life. I'm not good at this, Ang."

It feels impossible to let someone else see the darkest parts of me. Even Angie. How could someone possibly love me if I can't let them in?

"Look at me." She squares my shoulders so I'm facing her. "You are one hundred percent correct. You suck at relationships."

I huff out a laugh. "Thanks?"

"But none of that matters with the right person. Anyone deserving of you will be patient while you figure out your shit. They're not going to run at the first sign of you doubting what you have. No matter how hard you try to push them away."

"Wow, when did you get so wise?"

She shoves my shoulders playfully. "Fuck you, bitch, I'm always wise!"

"I beg to differ."

She tsks. "This isn't about me. Look, I know this kind of thing is hard for you, but if this man says he loves you, I believe him. I've seen you two together. He's all in. He's just waiting for you to join him."

I take a bite of pepper jack, letting the creamy and spicy flavors distract me while I mull over her words. Could it really be that simple? You just...open yourself up to someone and trust that it'll all magically work out? How can you put so much trust in another person?

I suppose I've already done it with the woman in front of me. How hard could it be to do it again?

"Babe, this is the kind of love you read about. It doesn't even sound real unless you've experienced it for yourself. Do you realize how special that is? I've always wanted that."

"With John?"

She purses her lips to the side.

I cock my head. "Not with John? I thought he was your first and only love."

She shrugs. "It's complicated. There was someone else I wanted to be with before John, but he never knew I existed. It ended up being all in my head."

"You never told me this before."

"Because it was just a crush. It didn't mean anything. I was young and stupid. I look back on that time and cringe at how childish it was."

"Then he's a dick. He doesn't know what he missed out on."

She laughs, and I pull her to my side, her head coming to rest on my shoulder as we watch the sunset. My heart feeling lighter.

"Thank you," I say softly. "This has been the best birthday ever."

46

LUCA

This is not at all how this week was supposed to start.

I park my Jeep in Willow's driveway, the back filled with my hastily packed luggage. After taking a few deep breaths of the cool morning air to calm myself, I summon the courage to knock on her door. Immediately, Henry starts barking on the other side, and I realize I probably should've given her a heads up that I was coming over, but this entire day is already not going the way I had expected it.

I only wish there was another way.

Willow opens the door, and I smile at the sight of her.

"Hey you," she says.

I hold her face and pull her in for a kiss. A deep kiss. My entire body lights up, and I have to pull back, breathless, before I change my mind.

"Hey you," I say back, committing her gentle lavender and coconut scent to memory to get me through this day.

"What are you up to?" she asks, running her palms up my chest.

"I have to head out of town...actually." I take her hands in mine as her head tilts to the side, her messy bun dropping slightly.

"Oh really? Where are you going?"

"I have to go settle my dad's estate. It's a whole thing. His property has been tied up in the courts since he passed, and I have to meet with the lawyers in person. I can't put it off any longer."

While planning Willow's surprise party with Angie, I also had the pleasure of fielding urgent calls and emails from his estate lawyers telling me this couldn't wait, and if I failed to show up this week to settle the dispute, then I risk putting my finances and everything my parents left me in jeopardy.

"You're going back to Greendale?" Her face lights up. "Do you want company? My week is pretty light, and I can bring my laptop in case I have to work."

My chest constricts. God, I don't deserve her. I want so badly to tell her to come, but... "I can't risk you running into Sadie," I say slowly. "I don't want her to meet you."

She can't. I refuse to let her touch what we have.

"Besides, it'll be totally boring." I wave my hand around, trying to sound casual. "I should be back tomorrow anyway."

I don't miss the disappointment in her face, but she absolutely cannot come with me to Greendale. Especially since I might have to pay a visit to Sadie to get these fucking divorce papers signed.

"Oh. Okay, if that's what you want," she says softly, and it feels like a dagger plunging into my heart.

"It's not what I want at all," I say, stepping closer and wrapping my arms around her waist before she can pull away. "What I want is to stay here...buried in you all day." I kiss her neck, but she's stiff beneath me.

"Will you let me know when you get there?" she asks evenly.

"Of course. It's about a six-and-a-half-hour drive. I'll be back before you know it." I kiss her one last time. "I love you."

I turn around and walk to my Jeep before she can say—or not say—anything. I'm trying not to worry too much about the fact that she hasn't said it back. I didn't expect her to just yet, not with her fear of commitment. Lord knows I probably sprung it on her way too early.

Still, I wonder how many more times I'll be able to say those words without her saying them in return before it breaks me.

I wave at her as I back out of her driveway, her arms cradling her elbows as she leans against the doorframe. Her smile wavers, and everything in me is screaming to go back. To tell her of course she should come with me. That I never want to go anywhere in the world without her.

I should have told her the divorce wasn't final yet. She deserves to know the whole truth, and I don't want to keep anything from her. I don't want any secrets between us. It scares the ever-loving shit out of me though.

Some things never change, I guess. Deluding myself into thinking that if I ignore all my problems then they will go away on their own. Classic.

Voicing the truth out loud to Willow may be the thing that dooms us, but we can't build a future together without being completely honest.

I'll tell her as soon as I get back with the signed papers.

I just hope it's not too late.

47

LUCA

I arrived in Greendale last night—much later than I planned, thanks to traffic—so the lawyers' office ended up being closed. I texted Willow to let her know I arrived and that I missed her. Grabbed some shitty food from the twenty-four-hour diner down the street, then proceeded to toss and turn all night in a shitty hotel bed. I only sleep well when I'm next to her.

Now I'm sitting in a scratchy burgundy chair, ready to sign a mountain of paperwork and be done with all this, so I can drive home and be with the woman I love.

A tall man appears in the doorway, dressed in a black suit that must be two sizes too big. His handlebar mustache giving off serious Burt Reynolds vibes.

Martin Stanley. I remember him from when Dad died.

"Mr. Giordano? Right this way."

I follow him down a narrow hallway of cream walls and brown carpet until we reach a small office. The far wall is covered by a floor-to-ceiling bookshelf, filled with old, dusty law books.

He motions to one of the chairs facing his mahogany desk, setting down a stack of papers. "I have the paperwork ready for you to sign to release payment to the Springrose Care Facility," he says.

"Great."

Let's get this over with.

"But we also just received word that the judge has a last-minute opening to hear our case about resolving your father's estate first thing tomorrow morning."

My stomach bottoms out.

"Tomorrow? No, I have to get home today."

"Mr. Giordano, I highly recommend we take this opening, or it could be another year before this case is heard."

Fuck. I want to go home. But I need to get this done so I can move on from this place.

The man riffles through another stack of papers. "I see here your father's property is currently valued at five hundred fifty thousand dollars, and his other accounts exceed one point five million."

I freeze. That can't be right.

"No, I think you're mistaken. I already got the 401K when he passed. Your office explained that the retirement and life insurance went to me without issue because I was the named beneficiary."

"Correct, you did receive those funds. This is the total amount from his bank accounts, which include the remainder of your mother's assets as well."

None of this sounds familiar. "Wait, why am I just now hearing about this?"

"It's all right here." He hands me a piece of paper with a bunch of legal jargon and numbers on it. "It's possible that when your father passed, not all of the money was accounted for. I know for a fact that Springrose drained a lot of their savings. I'm sorry for any miscommunication."

Memories from that time are hazy, so it's entirely possible they did tell me, and I just didn't retain any of it. I was so wracked with grief that I just signed whatever they put in front of me so I could get the hell out of there.

But we're talking one point five million dollars. Two million if you count the property. I could do so much with that money. I wouldn't have to work again for a long time and could put it toward something that matters.

I run my hand through my hair and let out a breath. "Okay. Fine. Let's do it."

"Excellent."

After discussing the details with Mr. Stanley, I drive back to my hotel to extend my stay another night. I find a place to grab some lunch, calling Willow on the way, but she doesn't answer. When I get to the restaurant, I shoot off a quick text to have her call me back. I want to explain over the phone why I can't come home tonight. I need her to hear me when I say how much I miss her.

I don't want to stay here another day, but if it means closing out this chapter of my life, then it'll be worth it.

But that also means I need to deal with Sadie.

Thirty minutes later, I'm sitting in Sadie's driveway. I thumb through the papers in my lap, praying she doesn't pull some bullshit about why she won't sign. This has gone on long enough.

I take a moment to breathe, just like my therapist taught me. In for four, hold for four, out for four, hold for four.

I can do this.

I knock on the door to the house we once shared. It still looks the same as when I left.

Sadie opens the door, and my stomach tightens.

"Well, look who it is," she says with an oily grin.

"You know why I'm here. Let's just get this over with so we can both move on. Okay?"

"Aw, not even a hello? Or a please? Where have your manners gone, Boo? Let's be adults about this."

"I am not playing this game, Sadie. Sign the papers. *Please.*"

"Come on in, let's have a chat."

"There's nothing to talk about." I hold up the stack of papers. "Here's a new copy, in case you lost yours. I've already signed, and the yellow flags are for your signature."

She scoffs. "Come inside, or I'm not signing shit."

I rub my jaw. "Fine."

Her growing smile has me on edge. She's always scheming, and I know she's up to something. I need to hurry up and get the fuck out of here.

Just as I step into the house, my phone vibrates. It's Willow.

Goddammit. I can't answer with Sadie here. I reluctantly decline the call, cursing my impeccable timing, and set my phone on the coffee table face down along with the papers.

"Okay, I'm inside. Sign it."

"Do you want something to drink?" she asks as she walks into the kitchen. "Water, tea? I could make you an Old Fashioned, like the good old days."

"What are you doing? What is this?"

She comes back into the living room with two glasses of water and sets them down. "You're the one who showed up on my doorstep. *Our* doorstep. Don't pretend you didn't want to see me."

I shake my head. She's delusional as ever.

I don't even have time to respond before her lips are on mine.

48

WILLOW

I think I might throw up.

I've spent the last two days feeling every possible emotion, trying to understand why Luca didn't want me to go with him to Greendale, and then, why he didn't come home last night.

I haven't heard from him in nearly twenty-four hours.

I was at the gym when I missed his call yesterday. His text asked me to call him back, but when I did, he sent me to voice-mail. Nothing since.

I told myself there had to be a logical explanation and not to panic. Maybe he decided to stay another night in his home-town and forgot to call. Maybe he was on his way and got stuck in traffic, and his phone died.

But when I woke up to zero calls or texts from him this morning, I knew something was wrong.

Was he hiding something from me this whole time?

Did he go there to see Sadie?

Or did something happen to him?

As I mindlessly scroll on my phone, a text from Angie pops up.

ANGIE

still no update?

do I need to get Wesley on the case?

ME

what's your brother going to do?

ANGIE

he knows people

just say the word

ME

I appreciate it, I'll let you know ;)

I need a distraction, or I'm going to go crazy here. I spent some time with Faris yesterday after he got his cast off and they had fitted him for a walking boot. He still has to use crutches and is only allowed to put twenty-five percent of his body weight on his bad leg for now. Plus, all the physical therapy he is scheduled to do.

Along with helping Faris put together a schedule and routine, I've been doing my best to stay busy with work, trying not to let the intrusive thoughts win out, but in truth, I've barely slept, barely eaten.

I figure there are only two possible scenarios for his silence at this point: something catastrophic happened or he's leaving me. And both options are too excruciating to think about.

Yesterday, I was angry. Last night, I cried. But this morning, I'm just numb.

I hate that this is what I've been reduced to. Waiting around for some guy to call, letting *his* life and *his* actions dictate how I feel. Craving his attention and validation.

I promised myself I would never be this person.

Why would I expect him to be different?

Luca has given me no logical reason to believe that he would do this to me, and yet...everyone does in the end. Everyone is always hiding something. Everybody always leaves.

And to think I almost said "I love you" back to him. I wanted to so badly.

I look over at the red pickleball shirts I made for us, slung over the back of the couch, as I sit there curled up with a blanket. We only have a few more days until the tournament, and I was hoping to get some extra play time in with him this week. Now I don't even know when or if he'll be back.

Those stupid fucking shirts.

I debate whether to even bother going to our regular Wednesday session tonight. I'm way too distracted to be of any use to anyone right now.

And *that* is what finally sets me off.

I pull up my thread of unanswered texts with Luca and start typing.

ME

> I hope you are okay, and that there's a perfectly good explanation for your silence, but I have the sinking suspicion that this is the end for us. I thought you were different. But you really are the same guy who showed up that first night we met. You showed me who you were, and I was right about you from the start. But I never wanted to be more wrong in my life. Don't bother answering this text either. Please delete my number if you haven't already done so. Have a nice life asshole.

Maybe it's a bit dramatic, but he's the one who left town and ghosted me. After telling me that he loved me. And I almost said it back, like some lovesick, needy chick.

I refuse to be that person.

I refuse to let him have that much power over me.

I should never have let it get this far.

I decide to go play. Fuck him. I don't need him to play the sport I love. I was playing long before he stumbled into my life, and I'll keep playing long after he's gone.

I arrive at the courts determined to prove I don't need him, that I'm still the same person I was before. Until I have a sinking realization that turns my stomach: with Luca gone, I no longer have a partner for the Pickle Bowl. I'll have to drop out.

That asshole knew how much I wanted this.

It's like he found one of the few things that mattered to me, the one thing I was excited for, and decided to ruin that for me too.

Just like my high school coach tainted my love of tennis, I guess it's only fitting I let another man I trusted ruin the sport I love.

Angie and Max are warming up on the court, talking and laughing. The moment they spot me at the fence, I freeze. I don't know what to say to them, or how to explain what happened with Luca.

But Max is his best friend. If something bad happened to Luca, he would know, right? And clearly, Max is unbothered about the well-being of his buddy right now, like it's any other night.

Which leaves only one scenario left.

I turn on my heel. The burning rage and pain erupting from within.

"Willow, wait!" Angie calls after me, running until she

catches up on the sidewalk. With a hand on my elbow, she spins me around to face her. "What is it?"

My eyes burn, and I swipe at the tears beginning to fall down my cheeks.

She rears her head back. "That fucking asshole." She runs over to her bag and yells something back to the group. I can't hear anything over the sound of blood roaring in my ears.

Without another word, Angie links her arm in mine to walk me home.

49

LUCA

I pull into Willow's driveway at 9:22 Wednesday night. More than sixty hours since I made the monumental mistake of leaving for that god-forsaken town without the woman I love.

When Sadie tried to kiss me yesterday, I ran out of that house so fast I left my phone and the divorce papers on her coffee table, setting off a series of unfortunate and problematic events.

Since I haven't memorized a phone number since I was a child, I had no way of calling or texting Willow. The thought of not getting a hold of her had me spiraling. I managed to find an Apple store downtown, where I proceeded to sign up for Instagram on one of their MacBooks and send several messages to her professional account. But they were getting ready to close, so I couldn't stick around to see if she replied.

I slept like shit, showed up this morning for my hearing with the judge looking like I got hit by a train, and then got the fuck out of there.

Without a phone, I had to rely on memory to get me back

here. Except my memory is shit, and I took a wrong turn some-where in Indiana. After stopping at some run-down travel stop to buy a *paper map*, I sped the rest of the way here, miracu-lously avoiding any more traffic or getting pulled over.

I know I've missed our usual Wednesday night matches together, and that she wanted as much time on the courts this week as we could get before the tournament Saturday. I've let her down. In so many ways.

But that ends now.

I don't even bother closing the door to my Jeep before I'm sprinting to her porch, knocking on her front door.

"Willow? It's me!"

Nothing. Just the sound of Henry barking up a storm.

"Please, I need to talk t—"

The door flies open, but instead of Willow, it's Angie. She crosses her arms and levels me with a glare that would have most men weeping. This woman, who is a head shorter than me, is somehow looking *down* at me, and it's unnerving as hell.

After what feels like an eternity, she finally says, "Glad to see you're not dead."

"Please let me in, I need to talk to her."

She cocks her head, sizing me up. "For your sake, I hope you have a fucking great explanation."

"I do," I rush out. "My phone was—"

She cuts me off with a raised hand. "Save it. I don't need to know."

Angie looks over her shoulder toward Willow's bedroom and then back to me.

"Look. I like you, Luca. In all the years I've known her, I had never seen her as happy as she's been these past few weeks with you. But whatever just happened while you were gone? This kind of thing *cannot* happen."

I just stand there and nod.

"I think you two are really good for each other…" She opens the front door wider, letting me take a step inside. "But I do hope you remember our little talk the other day."

My head pulls back.

What talk?

She grabs her purse off the side table as she steps past me. Turning back, she rakes her thumb across her throat before walking backward out the door and out of sight.

Christ, that woman is scary.

I shake off the lingering fear of her petite, blonde friend as I close the door and make my way to Willow's bedroom. The sight of her perched on the edge of her bed in her tennis outfit, tears streaking down her face, stops me in my tracks.

"I haven't cried again since that day."

Oh no. No, no, no.

I kneel between her legs, wrapping my hands around her soft calves. "I'm here, I'm right here. I'm so sorry. I didn't have my phone, I was hoping you got my messages."

She stares at me. "What messages?"

"Instagram. Your work account. I couldn't call you, so it was the only way I could think to contact you. I got stuck dealing with lawyers and a court hearing, and I just couldn't get out of there. I'm so, so sorry." I wipe a tear from her cheek. Tears that shouldn't be there. "Why are you crying? Talk to me."

She wipes her nose on the back of her hand and looks off to the side, shaking her head. "I didn't see any messages. I thought you left."

"I'm so sorry I had to go, and that I didn't take you with me—"

"No," she says, stopping me. "I thought you left…me."

My jaw drops. "You thought I wouldn't come home to you?"

I'm such an asshole. I should have realized what leaving would do to her.

"I don't know what to think. You said you loved me—"

"I *do* love you."

"—and then you didn't want me to come with you. And when I tried to get a hold of you, you ghosted me."

"My phone—"

"I know, I know. And I get it now, I just...that's what it *felt* like. And...I need time to think." She pushes my hands off her legs as I feel the ground underneath me open up.

"Time to think about what?" My breathing picks up, my heart pounding against my ribs.

"This isn't easy for me, you know. I...I'm not sure I like who I was while you were gone. Constantly checking my phone, obsessing over where you were or whether you were even okay."

I ease up off my knees and sit next to her on her bed. "I *wasn't* okay. All I could think about was getting home to you."

Home.

It's the second time I've said it tonight. But I know it's true.

"I thought maybe you wouldn't come back, and..." She looks away. "Part of me was almost a little...relieved. Like I was right all along, and I could just go back to how I've been living my life. Not relying on anyone else or waiting for them to leave."

Suddenly, I can't breathe.

What have I done?

"Willow, that's not what's happening. That's not me. Look, I know it's hard for you to trust people," I press. "And it kills me that you thought I left you. But I'm here. You know me. You know what we have is special." I take her hand in mine and kiss her knuckles.

She sniffles. "But what if I don't want to feel this way?"

"What way?" I squeeze her hand, desperately holding on to her.

"Like...at any moment you could just...destroy me."

I lean my forehead against hers, my hands moving to the sides of her face, silently begging her to stay. "You have had the power to destroy me since the moment we met. You own every part of me, Willow. I will do whatever it takes to earn your trust, however long it takes, because I am already wholeheartedly yours."

She sobs.

"I missed you," she whimpers.

I press a soft kiss to her lips, running my hand behind her head. "God, I missed you too. I love you, Willow. I do. I love you so much it hurts."

She leans back, extracting my hands, and my heart rate picks up again. *No.* Please don't pull away, please don't run from this.

Before she can say anything, I lie down on her bed and open my arms wide. "Come here."

She hesitates, but then lies down facing me. I pull her closer, fitting her head into the crook of my neck, wrapping my arms around her warm body, her leg settling between mine. Her inhale is sharp, an aftershock from crying so hard.

I never want her to shed another tear for me. Ever.

Her hair is soft as I run my fingers through it. I breathe in her sweet scent, needing to memorize every detail of this moment, just in case this is the last time she ever lets me hold her. I pray this isn't the end.

Please, God, don't let this be the end.

We lie there in silence for maybe half an hour. When her breathing slows way down, I wonder if she's fallen asleep, until I feel her hand glide slowly up my back. Pulling back to look at her face, I swipe a stray hair away and place a soft kiss on her temple. "What are you thinking?"

"I'm thinking...that I've been trying so hard not to fall for you..." She pauses, and I hold my breath. "That I didn't realize it had already happened."

"Yeah?" I hold on to this glimmer of hope with everything I have.

She looks up at me with wide, glassy eyes and places a hand on my jaw. Her touch sends a wave of warmth down my neck as I lean into her palm. "It sounds like we already have the power to destroy each other, so it's too late to go back."

"What are you saying?" I ask desperately, unable to tell if her words are about to heal me or annihilate me.

"I'm saying...you better not fucking break my heart, because neither of us will survive it."

I let out a sharp breath and kiss her softly, deliberately. Pouring as much of my love into her as I possibly can. When she deepens the kiss, I moan into her mouth, wanting her to know just how much she affects me. How much I need her.

We lie there kissing, exploring each other's bodies. I let her set the pace, because I still don't know exactly where this all leaves us. She's upset and vulnerable, so I will follow her lead. I would stay like this forever if she wanted.

She then hooks a leg over me, rolling me onto my back. I begin to lose my composure as I pull her weight down, needing to feel the friction between us. I'm already about to explode when she pushes herself back, straddling my hips. She peels off her top, exposing her gray sports bra, which I zip down slowly. Her full breasts drop slightly as they're freed, and I ease myself up into a sitting position, greedily squeezing one as I take the other into my mouth.

Sucking and biting her hard, pebbled nipples, I try to pull

every sound from her full, beautiful lips. "You mean so much to me, you know that?"

Framing my face with her hands, she explores my mouth with her tongue, and I whimper.

Fucking *whimper*.

I'm so far gone for her.

Her hips grind over my cock, driving me absolutely wild. Her intensity and passion ready to unleash that side of me only she gets to see. But tonight she is taking charge, I can feel it. She needs to feel in control again.

"Tell me what you need," I say between gasps, cupping her jaw.

"I need you, baby. All of you."

"You have me. Whatever I have, it's yours."

She pulls away and takes off her skirt and her underwear.

I undress quickly, reaching for a condom before sitting back on the bed, propped against the headboard. She takes my hand and shakes her head.

"What is it?" Does she want to stop?

"I don't..." She looks down at the condom still in my hand. "I don't want anything between us."

I think I'm having a stroke. Did she just say what I think she said?

"I...I've never done that," I say, slightly panicking.

She tucks a loose strand of hair behind her ear. "Me neither. But you know I'm on the pill...and...there's no one else."

"Are you sure about this?"

She nods.

"Willow, I need to hear you say it."

"Yes. I'm sure. I need you," she says again.

I let out a shaky breath as I set the condom back down on the nightstand.

My hands settle on her hips as she lifts her leg over top of me, lining us up perfectly. The head of my cock just barely presses into her as she slowly moves her hips to start letting me in.

Her entrance is so wet as I slide inside of her with one single movement, enveloped in her warmth, and I've never felt so safe and loved. Our bodies join like two halves finally reunited. Nothing between us. We move in sync, slow and languid. Making love like we're the only two people left in the universe.

50

WILLOW

Luca's new bed is so comfortable I don't want to get up, but the tournament is today, and I need to get moving. Luca has already gone downstairs to make us breakfast, and the aroma of coffee is beckoning me.

Ever since he came back from Greendale, we've been inseparable.

I went with him to buy a new phone after he explained everything that happened, and I found his Instagram messages. They were buried in a different section of my DMs because I wasn't following him back.

@LUCA.GIO.77

hey gorgeous it's me

lost my phone so I hope you get this

I have to stay ANOTHER night here 😭 But the lawyers got us a hearing tomorrow with the judge for my dad's estate. Cross your fingers it all goes well. I'll tell you everything when I get home!!

I love you and miss you so much

After I read them, I felt silly for reacting the way I did. But what are the odds that he would lose his phone out there? It's actually pretty sweet the lengths he went through to contact me.

He's been strangely vague on the details of *how* he lost it, but I guess it doesn't matter.

I just wish I could've been there for him, since it sounds like being there and dealing with everything for his parents triggered his anxiety. Which again begs the question of why he insisted on going alone in the first place, when he knew it would be hard on him.

I could've handled myself just fine if we had run into Sadie. I know he doesn't want us to meet, but I would like to be a source of support for him, no matter how hard it gets.

Isn't that what we do for the people we love?

Of course, I haven't said the words "I love you" back to him yet. I just need more time, and I think he understands that. It's taken everything I have just to be open and vulnerable with him again, and I didn't want to say it before I was ready.

But I think after we win this tournament today, I want to take that next step. To hold nothing back and trust him fully.

Even if it terrifies me.

"We can be scared together."

I finally peel myself out of bed, the cool air chilling my naked body. Riffling through my duffel bag for something warm to wear, I spot the matching shirts I made for us, tucked away at the bottom. I almost forgot I grabbed these at the last minute when I packed to come over here.

I smile as I change into a sports bra and my new shirt, adding a zip-up hoodie over top and pulling on a white tennis skirt. I grab his matching shirt and fling it over my shoulder, walking downstairs to the kitchen.

Behind the counter, Luca is dressed in glorious gray sweatpants riding low on his hips. His bare torso on full display, begging for my touch. Messy morning hair half covers his forehead as he looks up at me. "Morning, gorgeous."

"Good morning," I say, mirroring his smile. I inhale deeply and sigh as I walk toward him. "Mmm, smells delicious, what is that?"

"Our usual. Bacon, eggs, coffee. Plus, some blueberry pancakes to carb up."

I point to the tall pot sitting on the back burner. "And what about that?"

"Ah, yes. That is the sauce for dinner."

"You made spaghetti sauce at seven in the morning?"

"Technically, I made it at six, but yes, it needs to simmer all day." When I raise an eyebrow, he pulls all five fingers in his left hand together and gestures at me. "This is my Nani's recipe from *Venezia*, going back over six generations. I think I know what I'm doing."

I shake my head as he goes back to making breakfast. God, he looks so good like this. Relaxed, half naked, cooking my favorite foods. This is what every morning with him could be like.

On the dining room table next to me are two large cardboard boxes I don't recognize.

"What's in these boxes?"

"Oh, just some stuff I brought back from our old storage unit. Some photo albums, stuff like that."

"Aw, are there pictures of baby Luca in here?" I say hopefully.

"Definitely. You can take a look if you want," he says with a hint of *my life is open to you.*

I open the flaps to peek inside. Resting at the top is an old wedding photo in an elegant gold frame. This must be his parents. I hold it up for him.

I hear him turn off the stove before coming around the kitchen counter to my side, wrapping an arm around me and resting his chin on my shoulder as we stare at the photo. I gently wipe away the dust that has settled on the glass.

His mother is wearing a gorgeous white lace dress with long sleeves, and on her slender finger is the most stunning silver princess-cut diamond ring I think I've ever seen.

"Wow, she is so beautiful."

I can see so much of Luca in both of their faces. The striking dark brown eyes and high cheekbones from his mother. The strong nose and jet black hair from his father.

His smile is a wonderful blend of both of theirs.

The two of them look so young and happy. So in love.

He turns his head to face me, squeezing me tighter. "They would've really liked you."

"Yeah?" I hate that I'll never get a chance to meet them. They would be so proud of the man he's become.

"Oh yeah." His face lights up. "My mom especially would appreciate how you keep me in line. You two would've gotten along so well."

I squeeze his arm. "Did you hear from the lawyers yet about the hearing?"

"No, not yet. Hopefully the judge makes his ruling this week." He finally notices the shirt hanging over my other shoulder. "Hey, whatcha got there?"

"Oh!" I set down the photo before holding up the shirt with two white pickleball paddles crossed behind a ball, and text underneath that reads *DILL WITH IT*.

His eyes go wide. "Did you make that?"

Without a word, I unzip my hoodie with my other hand, exposing my matching shirt underneath.

"*Yes!*" he says as he swoops me up in his arms, spinning me around. "That is awesome!"

He sets me down and kisses my temple.

"Matching shirts, huh? Who knew Willow Blackburn had it in her to do something so...*cheesy*."

"You don't have to wear it if you don't—"

"Are you kidding? I love it. We are so going to dominate today and win that trophy." He snatches the shirt out of my hand and pulls it over his head, then looks down at himself. "I love you so much."

I almost say it back without thinking.

He walks back into the kitchen and says, "Now...eat up, we've got a big day ahead."

A full plate is placed on the counter in front of me. Followed by a steaming mug of coffee, creamer already mixed in.

It's Pickle Bowl time.

51

LUCA

From the driver's seat, I steal a glance over at Willow. I still can't believe everything that has brought us here to this moment. We had a rough start, but now I feel like the luckiest man in the world. I have the woman of my dreams by my side, and we're about to go kick some ass in the pickleball tournament that brought us together.

I'm still so pissed about everything that happened in Greendale though. The only good part of the trip home was getting to visit the cemetery where my parents are buried. I hadn't been back since Dad's funeral. I miss them both so much it hurts, and I wish more than anything they were still here to meet Willow. I wasn't lying when I said she and Mom would get along. My chest aches for the moments we'll never be able to share.

I did leave feeling like I had a little closure, but it doesn't take away the pain of knowing I'll never see them or hug them ever again. That grief never goes away.

I park at Dink Shot for the Pickle Bowl. It's finally here. What we've been working toward all these weeks. Bringing our intertwined hands to my mouth, I kiss her knuckles. "You ready, Ace?"

"Let's do this."

She leans in for a kiss, and I take my time with her. Savoring this moment, reminding myself that she's still here. That this is real.

Walking through the front doors, I notice it's not too crowded yet, but I imagine in about an hour, this place is going to be loud and crazy. Benches have been set up along the interior space between the courts for people to watch, as well as additional seating upstairs in the bar.

There's a buzz in the air that has me bouncing on my toes. I haven't participated in a sports tournament in ages, not since college hockey. But I suddenly feel energized and excited as the adrenaline pumps through my veins. I want to win this so badly for her.

Willow elbows me. "There they are."

"Who?" I follow her line of sight to an elderly couple, both with short white hair, wearing matching track suits. "Is that...?"

"Jerry and Margaret," she says with a glare.

A laugh bubbles out of me. "*That's* Jerry and Margaret? My love, they've got to be like seventy years old."

"Seventy-two. And don't let them fool you. They are quick and they are merciless."

"I think you've been watching too much *Golden Daggers*, Ace." I shake my head as I take her hand and pull her away from her geriatric rivals. Angie and Max wave us over from the other side of the courts.

"Oh, wow. Matching shirts?" Angie says with a quirk of her eyebrow. "Who are you and what have you done with my best friend?"

"Jealous? I'll make you one later," Willow says before setting her stuff on the ground by the wall and hugging Angie.

Max extends his hand to me. "What's up, buddy?"

"What's going on?" I shake his hand and clap him on the back. "Where's the family?"

"They'll be here soon. Grabbing food so they don't turn into little terrors."

"Adorable little terrors," I say. "You guys all ready?"

"We're ready. Best of luck."

"Good luck to you. See you on the other side."

A few hours later, Willow and I have managed to win both of our matches to advance to the semifinal round, but honestly, it's a miracle we're still in it. Our rhythm has been off, and we've had to fight for every point. In both rounds, we've only won by two.

And I think it's my fault.

I've been distracted by thoughts of Dad ever since I got back from Greendale. Dealing with his will and the hearing, visiting their graves...it's just brought up so many emotions, and I'm struggling to focus.

He should be here for this.

We played pickleball all the time together after Mom passed. It's impossible not to think of him. Both of them.

But while my mind is elsewhere, I'm dangerously close to losing us this tournament and failing Willow. I need to get my head in the game, because I promised I would do anything for her. And I meant it.

WILLOW

I don't understand what the hell is going on with us. We've never been so out of sync before. Usually, we can anticipate each other's movements and timing like we can read the other's thoughts, but today it's just not there.

Whatever is happening, we just need to work through it. I have to trust that we're prepared and that we know each other well enough to win this next match and advance to the finals, where we potentially face off against my arch-nemeses from last year's tournament.

Angie and Max were eliminated in the last round, so it's up to us to keep this thing going.

We have to win this.

The sound of balls colliding with paddles echoes all around us as Luca and I rest on the benches. These tournaments take a lot out of you, especially since the matches end at fifteen points instead of eleven. Maybe we should have spent more time conditioning and training up our endurance.

With all the people gathered here and multiple games going on at once, the air has turned warm and stuffy, making me feel claustrophobic. Fanning myself with my shirt, I close my eyes and lean my head on Luca's shoulder, neither of us saying a word until the next round starts.

"Twelve twelve on two!" Luca shouts before slamming the ball over the net. The frustration is rolling off him, and it's really unsettling. He's usually so calm and steady when we play, but I know he feels this disconnect too. I don't know how we're even still in this, let alone tied at twelve points apiece.

Our opponents this round are solid. Their returns are tight, and the guy has a wicked topspin on his serves. If it does end here, I can walk away knowing we lost to a great pair and gave it our all.

But holy hell, I want to win.

After some intense back and forth, I finally get the ball past them to secure our thirteenth point. Luca and I tap paddles as we switch sides, but neither of us is smiling. Our usual laughter and banter replaced with quiet focus and determination.

The match ends with Luca and me somehow managing to win fifteen to twelve. Completely exhausted and drained, we meet our opponents at the net to tap paddles. "Good game," we all say to each other.

The woman shouts, "Congratulations!" and I force a smile in return.

I guess we should be celebrating. We should be elated that we're going to the finals. Just one match away from winning the entire tournament. One more win and I can claim the victory I've been chasing since I first started playing pickleball three years ago.

But there's no joy, no revelry. Not from us. Not yet.

Luca pulls me in for a tight, sweaty hug and whispers in my ear, "We've got this, Ace. We're right there. One more win, okay?"

I nod as he kisses my temple, but I can't shake the sinking feeling that something is just...wrong. We're barely winning these games. It's like we're strangers playing together for the first time.

Maybe I'm not as good as I thought I was.

Maybe I don't deserve to win this.

"I'm going to go walk around, clear my head," I say.

"Okay. I'm gonna use the restroom. Meet you back here so we can end this thing?" His smile is small but reassuring.

"Absolutely." I kiss him quickly. Even our kiss feels off. What the hell is wrong with us today?

As I walk around the courts trying to get my thoughts together, I spot Faris and Simon in the distance. I jog up to them, needing their grounding presence right now.

"Hey!" Faris says as Simon waves.

I wrap them both in a hug at the same time, careful not to pull Faris off balance while he's on his crutches.

"I'm so glad you're both here."

When they pull back, Faris asks, "What's wrong? What's going on with you?"

"Ugh, I don't know. We're off out there. You saw us, we shouldn't even be in this!"

Faris puts a hand on my shoulder. His steadying touch immediately calms me. "Hey. Just breathe. You're doing fine. It's probably just nerves."

Simon adds, "I don't know what you're talking about. I thought you guys looked great out there. And you're just one win away!"

"You've got this, Will. We're rooting for you."

I let out a long breath. "What would I do without you two?"

Faris snorts. "Can you imagine? You'd be so miserable."

That pulls a laugh from me. "Okay, I'm going to go walk around a bit. I'll see you after?"

"You bet," Faris says. "We'll go somewhere and celebrate."

"Love you, miss you."

"Love you more!" they say in unison.

Something catches my attention from up in the restaurant area. A small boy waving his hands wildly at me. Gabe. He's sitting on Kayla's lap while his sister is busy talking to an older woman with white hair. Must be Kayla's mom.

I return the wave as something warms in my chest. A gentle reminder that there are more important things waiting for me after this tournament.

As I aim for the front lobby, I start to feel a little better. All I can control is myself and my attitude, and playing the best I possibly can. Everything else will play out as it's meant to.

A voice comes over the loudspeaker, giving everyone an update on the match that just ended. "...And stay tuned for the Pickle Bowl Final, where Willow Blackburn and Luca Giordano will face off against Jerry and Margaret Feldman!"

There it is. It's official. It's go time.

When there are fifteen minutes left until the match, I walk back to the benches and take a long sip of water. Luca isn't back yet, so I look around for that strong, familiar face to reassure me that everything is going to be okay. I catch sight of a beautiful, striking woman with the same brown hair as me, walking through the front doors of the building and shouldering her way through the crowd.

A chill runs down my spine. It's like I've seen a ghost.

My mind must be playing tricks on me.

I squeeze my eyelids shut, rubbing the heel of my palms

into my eyes to the point of pain, but when I open them, she's still there.

Oh my God.

After all this time.

I start to walk toward her, my heart picking up speed, when Luca appears from the side of the lobby and grabs her by the arm, pulling her into the stairwell.

What the fuck?

I snake my way through the people gathered to watch the final match, my heart pounding like a drum. In the stairwell, I find the two of them standing a few feet apart, arguing. Luca is gesturing frantically, and I can only make out a few words as they shout over each other.

"—doing here with her—"

"—if you would just sign—"

"—left your phone at my—"

"—followed me here?"

I finally shout, "What the *fuck* is going on here?"

They look over at me and freeze.

It *is* her.

I look back and forth between them, trying to make sense of what I'm even looking at right now.

"Holly?" I say softly, breathlessly. I'm still not sure this is real. How is it possible?

"What did you just say?" Luca asks, his eyebrows furrowing.

"Willow," Holly says to me, her expression neutral. Somehow, she's not surprised at all to see me here. In fact, she looks smug, satisfied, as she crosses her arms and stands up straighter.

I cock my head to the side, trying to process all of this. "What the hell are you doing here? Where have you been all this time?"

Luca's face is ashen as he looks between us. "Do you..." His breathing picks up. "...do you two know each other?"

"She's my sister."

Luca's mouth falls open, and his hands grip the sides of his head.

God, she looks the same. Older, with more wrinkles, but it's still her. The same Holly I've always remembered. She looks so much like Mom—round face, green eyes, small nose—where I've always taken after our father.

I've thought about Holly every day since she left. Part of me wants to throw myself into her arms and hold on tight, squealing like I'm six years old again. Except...

"No," he says, shaking his head. "No, this is Sadie."

Sadie. I don't want to believe it, yet I know in my bones it's true.

"You're going by Sadie now?" I mirror my sister, crossing my arms. "Good to know. I'll be sure to address your Christmas card properly this year. Must be why I couldn't find you for the last twelve years."

I glance back over at Luca. He looks like he might pass out as he covers his gaping mouth with both hands. His eyes wide as saucers. "Holy...fucking...shit."

"Tell me, how do you know my sister?" I ask him. I already know the answer, but I have to hear him say the words, or I'll never really believe it. Because how could this be?

Holly shoots me a tight-lipped smile. The one I haven't seen since she abandoned me and my parents to go move around the country with some rich asshole. Never looking back.

Only ever thinking of herself.

"I think the better question, *Willow...*" Holly says, stepping close to Luca and linking her arm in his as bitterness fills my mouth. "...is how do you know my husband?"

53

WILLOW

Husband. Hearing her say it churns my stomach.

I shake my head. "You mean *ex*-husband."

Luca was married to my sister.

I still can't wrap my head around this.

Holly just stands there, arm in arm with my boyfriend. The man who loves me.

I'm waiting for Luca to correct her, but he's gone completely still.

Why isn't he saying anything?

Luca blinks like he's finally snapping out of a trance as he peels her off his arm. "Yes, ex-husband."

Holly laughs, and I feel it pierce my heart. "Sure, if you say so, Boo. Except I have unsigned papers that say otherwise. Papers you left on *my* coffee table last week."

There's a ringing in my ears as everything starts to blur.

"I signed them, why won't *you?*" he explodes.

Luca interlaces his hands over the top of his head and leans back against the wall, taking several deep breaths. I've never seen him like this. I think he might be having a panic attack.

"Why can't you just let me go?" His voice cracks.

"Wait, go back," I say evenly. "You went to see her in Greendale?"

Luca's head whips in my direction, his face dropping.

"And you really are still married?"

He hesitates, looking past me.

I step closer, and through clenched teeth, I force out, "*I need to hear you say it,*" returning his words from the other night, right before I let him fuck me without a condom. When I said I didn't want anything between us.

"We've been separated for over a year. But...yes, *technically* the divorce is not final. That's the only reason I went there: to get the papers signed. I swear."

"You said 'ex-wife.' That's what you said to me." Pain grips my chest. "You lied to me."

"I'm sorry."

"Were you ever going to tell me this?"

"Yes, I was going to tell you everything tonight after the tournament."

I scoff. "I don't believe you."

"Willow, I know I messed up. But there is nothing between me and Sa—Holly anymore. I should have told you sooner, but I promise you, nothing happened in Greendale."

Holly laughs again. "Oh please. You were practically begging for that kiss. Isn't that why you left your phone at my place, so you'd have an excuse to see me again?"

No.

I must have misheard her. I want this all to be some twisted joke. I need to wake up from this nightmare.

I start to back away, my hand covering my mouth as bile climbs up the back of my throat. I'm not sure I'm even in control of my own motions right now, just observing the worst moment of my life play out before me from outside my body.

Luca stops me with both hands on my arms. "Willow, no. Please let me explain."

I try to pull out of his grasp, but he only holds on tighter. "Let me go. God, I can't even look at you right now, you fucking liar." My eyes are burning. I need to get out of here.

"She kissed me, but I did not kiss her back. I stopped it immediately and left so fast that I forgot my phone there. That's the truth." His grip loosens, fingertips grazing my arms as he lets his hands fall.

"Fuck you," I say with a mirthless laugh, trying to hide the tremble in my voice. "Fuck you both." I turn and run back toward the courts as fast as I can.

"Willow, stop!" I hear Luca shout, his footsteps echoing off the walls of the stairwell. "We—we're playing in ten minutes!"

"Do *not* follow me!"

He stops, his hands up in surrender.

He can't possibly think I'll play with him now. I can't even be near him. After all that talk of honesty and trust and love, while he was still secretly married. As I worried about his well-being in Greendale, he was just busy kissing his wife.

Not ex-wife. Wife.

And the fact that Holly is *here*?

My big sister. After twelve years of silence. Dropping on me like a bomb, leaving everything in ruin. Again.

I'll never forgive them for this.

I knew he was hiding something. I knew something didn't add up about that trip. Everyone always has a secret. Everyone is always lying.

I just can't believe I let this happen again. That I let someone into my heart against all my better judgment. Letting myself be fooled again into thinking I could ever love someone for real. That this time could be different.

That we could be enough.

I reach the benches and sling my duffel bag over my shoulder. I can't let all these people see me fall apart. I'm sure they would just love that. People love to watch a trainwreck. They probably think I deserve it.

A commotion grows behind me, but I don't look back. I walk off the courts toward the front doors, ignoring the shouts and attempts to get my attention, as everyone starts to realize I'm leaving. Right before the final match.

They'll count this as a forfeit. I guess Jerry and Margaret win again.

We came so close too.

"Willow! Stop!" It's Angie. I don't slow down though, because I'm still in view of the crowd, which is now in pandemonium.

What was it all for? What was the fucking point?

Angie catches up to me and puts her arm around my shoulders, keeping pace with me as we step outside. She doesn't say anything, she just holds me as we walk to her car to get far away from here.

54

LUCA

"You need to leave," I tell Sadie, without looking at her.

"Oh, look who's finally starting to find his words," she mocks. "I kind of like this new side of you. You know, we could pick back up where we left off."

"What are you even doing here?" I finally turn to her. "What do you want from me?"

"I want to know what you're doing with my sister," she says as she pulls something out of her back pocket—my phone.

"So what, you went through my phone, and then you followed me here? Like some psycho stalker? What is wrong with you?"

"What was I supposed to do when I saw this?" She holds up my phone with a photo of Willow and me. I clench my fists. We took that photo in her bed after our make-up date and then hours of making love. Our hair is messy, and we're covered by a thin champagne-colored sheet, blissed out and smiling wide.

Sadie swipes forward a few times. There's a picture where we're smiling, one where we're making kissy faces, one where we're laughing, and another where we're looking into each other's eyes.

The one she stops on is where I'm kissing Willow's forehead and our eyes are closed. At the time, it felt silly to take these selfies, but I loved this one so much I made it the background on my phone.

Seeing Sadie hold that priceless memory is just too much to take.

I snatch the phone out of her hand before she can pull away, and I invade her personal space. "Leave me the fuck alone."

Walking out of the stairwell, I head toward the courts, but I know she's following me. The crowd noise crescendos ahead.

"How long have you been with my sister?" she asks.

I stop and whirl around on her.

"You don't get to ask me about my life. Before last week, I hadn't seen or talked to you in almost a year. It's over."

"You can't get rid of me that easily," she says, twirling her rich brown hair in her fingers.

God, they have the same hair.

That searing look Willow gave me at pickleball the morning after our first date reminded me so much of Sadie, but of course I didn't make the connection. What are the odds I would fall for two sisters in different cities?

No...I refuse to believe they are the same. I squeeze my eyes shut. Nothing about this woman can compare to Willow. Even if they share the same blood, they could not be more different.

Under that tough exterior, Willow is kind and protective. She cares about me. Or...cared.

But I ruined it.

"What are you doing with my little sister?" she repeats.

"Not that it's any of your business, but I didn't know she was your sister," I say quietly. "How could I possibly know that? You changed your name and abandoned her twelve years ago."

What am I going to do?

"You told me you were an only child too. What else have you lied to me about, huh? Your name isn't even Sadie, for fuck's sake."

I need to get out of here.

Everything Sadie touches, she destroys.

"Sign the goddamn papers."

I start to walk away when she says, "Did you never figure it out? Why I was with you?"

Squeezing my eyes shut, I tell myself not to take the bait.

"You think it was a coincidence that I couldn't follow you to Athens when you started working for Kevin McIntire? That prick would've ratted me out to Pres in a heartbeat."

That stops me dead in my tracks.

"Preston McIntire? Kevin's father? What does he have to do with anything?"

I hate the satisfied grin spreading across her face.

"Oh, Boo. You really didn't know." She pouts. "God, you are so naïve."

I should keep walking. I don't want to hear this.

"Everything I've done...is for that man. I've loved him for twelve years. He's my soulmate. He was scared of his feelings for me, so he pushed me away. But that's where you came in. I thought, surely he would realize his mistake after I moved on with some hot, younger guy. And I was right. It drove him crazy."

I feel the blood drain from my face. She's lying. She's always fucking lying.

"She moved in with some older rich guy, changed her name, and just left it all behind."

Oh my God.

"I thought for sure you would figure out that I was using you," she continues. "But you stayed so loyal. Never questioning, never standing up for yourself. Pathetic."

"So why not sign the papers? End this now and you can go be with your precious *Pres*."

"Oh, but it's so much more fun this way."

I let out a long breath. I can't stay here and listen to this. I can't even begin to process what this all means right now, but I will no longer allow her to have any power over me.

That power belongs to her sister.

Thankfully, Sadie doesn't follow me when I leave to get my gym bag.

But Willow is gone. We can't finish the tournament. Because of me, we have to forfeit.

The crowd is in an uproar, as it's evident that the championship game won't be played, and no one knows what to do next.

I can't even blame Sadie—or, Holly—for everything, because I never told Willow I was still married or about what happened in Greendale. If only I had been open and honest with her about my past, this never would have happened.

That's all she's ever wanted from me, or anyone in her life. Just honesty, and I couldn't even give her that.

This is all my fault.

55

WILLOW

Why, of all the people in the world, did it have to be Holly?

I think back to my last memories of her. Of my big sister. She never could sit still, always going from one place to another. At seventeen, she was bouncing around friends' houses every night, dating new guys every week, changing jobs the moment she got bored or felt inconvenienced. We were complete opposites.

I could never understand why she didn't just want to be still. To be...with me. I tried so many times to get her attention or to spend time together, but it always ended the same: with disappointment and loneliness.

I was turning fifteen, and I just wanted some kind of relationship with her. Any crumb or morsel she could spare for me.

Except when she *was* around, things had a way of ending in chaos. She would constantly lie to get her way. We all hoped she would grow out of that too, but instead, she just left.

Now I'm sitting here with my best friend, one of the only

people in the world I can trust. More than my own flesh and blood.

"What do you need?" she asks as I stare off in the distance from my living room couch. Henry's chin rests in my lap; he's no doubt sensing that something is wrong.

"I need...to lie down..." I hardly recognize my voice. Hollow, distant. "Or maybe a drink."

"Who says you can't do both?" she says from the kitchen, already opening my cabinets. "You just lay your pretty little head down, and I'm going to fix you up something nice and strong."

Luca has texted me no fewer than fifteen times already.

I haven't answered any of his calls or replied to any of his messages. No doubt this incoming message is from him too.

LUCA

Please let me explain. I'm coming over if you'll see me.

I love you

I toss my phone aside, hugging my knees to my chest. I feel like such an idiot. Somehow, I became the other woman in his marriage to my sister.

Holly has lived a whole life since I last saw her. She even had a life with Luca, however long that lasted. He said it was toxic, but at one point, they had to have been in love. What did he see in her? What memories did they share?

I can't help but picture them touching and kissing...and fucking.

A tear streams down my face when I squeeze my eyes shut.

Angie sits beside me, placing two pink drinks with salty rims on the coffee table. Wrapping me in her arms and rubbing small circles on my back, she gently rocks me back and forth.

That small, loving gesture is what does it for me, and the flood-gates finally burst open.

After about half an hour, the tears have subsided, and Angie has us watching some horror movie on Netflix. I'm barely watching it, barely absorbing anything, but am immensely grateful for the distraction, and for the endless strawberry margaritas she keeps putting in front of me. Not to mention the swirling crazy straw she found in one of my drawers so I don't even have to lift my head off the pillow to drink.

A sudden knock on my front door has me jolting upright. Angie presses a hand to my shoulder to lower me back down on my pillow. "I'll get rid of him."

I nod and go back to watching the movie. But I can't help but overhear her when she answers the door.

"She doesn't want to see you," Angie says in a low voice. Only allowing the door to open a few inches.

His voice is pleading, but I can't quite make out what he's saying.

"Not now, okay?" Her voice is more forceful this time.

Once again, he says something I can't hear, and she cuts him off.

"I swear to God, Luca, I am so close to punching you in the face right now. Just...give her some space, okay? Please?"

What would I do without her?

Angie has always been there for me, always supported me in every way she possibly could. She was always like a sister. What a true sister should be.

I rub at the watercolor heart tattooed on my wrist.

After shutting the door, she joins me back on the couch as I look up at her through tight, puffy eyes.

"He looks like shit, so that's something. If it were me, I'd want to hear what he has to say," she says before taking a long sip of her margarita. "But we're going to let him suffer a little first."

"Do you think there's any possible explanation that would make it okay that he lied about still being married? Or that he didn't tell me he went to see her last week?"

Her mouth twists to the side, and she shrugs. "I don't know. I've never been in this situation. You'll have to let me know how it all turns out."

56

LUCA

I didn't sleep at all last night, and I haven't eaten since our breakfast together yesterday morning before the tournament. The sauce I made for our romantic dinner sits ruined on my stove. I stand up from the table and start to run hot water in the sink.

I can't even imagine what she must think of me right now, but the longer she goes without hearing my side of things, the more I worry she'll decide to be done with me forever. If she isn't already.

Maybe I deserve it.

My phone buzzes, and I quickly shut off the water.

WILLOW

why don't you come over

My heart skips as I grab my keys and bolt out the front door, not even bothering to put on a jacket. I run five blocks until her white townhome appears in the distance and then sprint faster. I refuse to believe this is the end for us.

I'm ready to deliver my grand speech as I knock on her

front door, but the moment she opens it, every thought evaporates from my head.

Henry circles my legs, and I just stand there trying to catch my breath as I take in the sight of her. An oversized black sweatshirt hangs off one shoulder, barely covering the grey short shorts underneath. Her hair is up in a messy top bun, and her eyes are red and puffy. It breaks something deep within me.

"Can I come in?" I ask.

"I'd rather you not," she replies plainly, crossing her arms in front of her chest.

"I owe you an explanation," I start, but she scoffs, looking off to the side and dropping her hands.

"For how you're still married to my sister, or that she kissed you when you went to her house last week and never told me?"

Henry saunters back into the house as I take a deep, steadying breath.

"Both. Everything. I absolutely should've told you. But our marriage was over a long time ago. She and I never should have gotten married in the first place. We've been separated for a year, and I've been trying ever since I moved out here to get her to sign the divorce papers. That's the only reason I went to her house. I didn't want to bring that part of my past into what we had because—"

"You don't get to pick and choose what parts of yourself I'm allowed to know about. You can't just omit pieces of your past because you're afraid of how I'll react to them. You chose to withhold a huge part of your life from me—you lied to me— all the while, asking *me* to trust *you*. You made a conscious decision to keep it a secret."

I can barely think. Can barely breathe.

"And *that* is what I can never get over."

"No, wait—"

"Goodbye, Luca."

"Willow—"

She closes the door in my face without another word. The sound of the deadbolt locking into place may as well be a bullet fired directly into my heart.

57

WILLOW

I can't even bring myself to leave my house. The idea of running into him anywhere in this neighborhood or this city keeps me firmly pinned in place. Curled up under my warm covers.

I blocked his number the moment I shut the door in his face, before he could sweet-talk his way back into my heart.

No matter how much it hurt.

More than anything, I wish I could go back to how I felt weeks ago when he left: assuming the absolute worst in him and being totally fine with hating his guts. Even reminding myself of how he acted on our first date doesn't help. Knowing everything I do about him now, and the fact that Holly was the nightmare ex-wife he had been referring to, just serves to rationalize away what he did. And makes it harder to do what's necessary.

As I lie in bed and stare off in the distance, I'm still trying to come to terms with the fact that it was my sister who traumatized Luca and made it hard for him to speak up for himself. Who fueled his anxiety and tried to break his spirit.

I wouldn't have believed it if I didn't see him have a panic attack in that stairwell with my own eyes while Holly pushed and pushed.

I hate that he went through all that, but I refuse to be his emotional caretaker.

And in the end, I can't be with someone I cannot trust. Someone who hides things from me. I have to keep reminding myself of that. I refuse to compromise on my principles.

It's all I have left.

ANGIE

Let's play pb tonight

I shake my head as I type out my reply.

ME

No

I don't want to see him

ANGIE

Max said they won't be there

so we're in the clear

Well, that's certainly a relief. Maybe I should get out of the house and play. Lord knows I need the physical activity after being confined to my bed for the last three days. Is it possible for muscles to atrophy this quickly? I've probably undone about a month's worth of conditioning with how little I've moved since breaking things off with Luca.

ME

I don't know

Pickleball used to be the one place I could lose myself and have fun without thinking about anything or anyone else. Now there are just too many memories of playing with him. It's too hard.

Closing my eyes, I think about how well we played together. I had never played so well with anyone, not even with Angie or Faris. We were always so in sync.

ANGIE

haven't you punished yourself enough?

you're going

I'm on my way

Why do I miss the one person who shattered my heart, confirming all my worst fears about letting someone in? If this was the right thing to do, then why does it hurt so goddamn much? Why do I feel worse than I ever have before?

Henry looks up at me and licks the tears off my face as I scratch his belly. I usually don't let him up in the bed, but he hasn't wanted to leave my side since the last moment he saw Luca on my front porch.

For the past three days, he has stared toward the front door, as if Luca could just walk in at any moment. Sometimes I'm convinced I made the whole thing up in my head, and he's just out in the kitchen making us breakfast, or about to come strutting into my bedroom wearing those gray sweatpants.

I swear I can still feel his lips pressed to my temple.

I instinctively reach for that spot on my head, when I hear the front door burst open, and I startle.

"Come on, get up," Angie says, walking into my bedroom.

"I really can't play, okay? Please don't push me to go, I won't be able to concentrate. I'll play like shit, and it'll just piss me off."

She knows how much I hate losing and looking bad out there in front of other people.

"Then we go on a walk."

At that, Henry's head pops up.

I look up at Angie. My person. Her blue eyes filled with compassion.

"Just a walk?" Henry jumps off the bed in a fit of joy.

"Just a walk." She holds out her hand to help me to my feet before pulling me in for a hug.

I wrap my arms around her and immediately start sobbing, my head resting on top of hers as she squeezes me tighter. We stand there for a few minutes as I cry, until she pulls away and wipes my face with her sleeve.

With her hands on my forearms, she says, "Let's go. I want to tell you about an idea I have."

58

LUCA

A mysterious box randomly shows up on my doorstep. Confused, I pick it up and bring it inside, noticing there's no mailing label and that it's not even taped up. As I set it down on my dining room table, I have a startling and blinding realization.

Oh, no. Please no.

With shaky hands, I pull open the top flaps, and the moment I spot one of my T-shirts, my fears are confirmed. All my stuff I left at Willow's. I slump into the nearest chair and cover my face with my hands.

So that's it. It really is over.

Some T-shirts, deodorant, a toothbrush...my coffee mug. God, how I loved our mornings together, sipping coffee. Making her breakfast, talking and laughing.

Then I see the illustration I made of the two of us on the pickleball court. The one I made for her birthday. That's what breaks me, and I completely lose it.

My insides crumble like the aftermath of an inferno. A

forest after the wildfire has burned its way through and finally snuffed out.

Dead, lifeless, ash.

I think of the way her eyes lit up when she saw it. I tried so hard to make that birthday special for her, to undo a small part of what her sister did to her all those years ago.

Her sister.

God, how do I even process the fact that Sadie is involved with Preston McIntire? And has been since she left Willow all those years ago.

I knew impulsively marrying her was a mistake, but part of me did have feelings for her once.

Or, what I used to think was love before I met Willow.

I take a long, deep breath.

My therapist couldn't fit me in for an emergency session until tomorrow, so I go through all the calming and grounding techniques I've learned for when I start to spiral.

Eventually, after popping one of my anxiety meds, I pick up my phone to try calling Willow again, but with no luck. It's obvious now that she's blocked my number.

I just want to know she's okay. Even if we can't be together, I only want her to be okay.

But it fucking hurts.

It's been three days since she closed that door in my face. Seventy-two miserable hours since I felt our relationship sever for good.

Max has come over to check on me a few times, always commenting on how I need to take care of myself. As if it's that easy. He's brought over food that he and Kayla made for me, but I can barely eat. They've invited me over to get out of the house and take my mind off things, but I don't want the kids to see me like this.

The silence in this house roars in my ears.

The ache in my chest making it nearly impossible to get out of bed or even shower.

Sleep is even harder. I could never sleep well without her anyway. My mind refuses to shut off, constantly reminding me that this is all my fault. I let my fear of rejection hold me back from telling her my whole truth, and it became a self-fulfilling prophecy.

I look over at my TV, streaming some show I don't even know or care about. Clicking back to the main menu for something else to disassociate to, *Golden Daggers* pops up. The new episodes just dropped.

I can't watch them without her.

I sit there staring at the screen, as the memories come flooding back. It was the first night together we didn't have sex, but it was a different kind of intimacy. One I've longed for since I could remember. One I wouldn't trade for anything in the world.

It gave me a glimpse of a future with her. A future with favorite shows and inside jokes and snuggling on the couch.

Making a home together.

We never got around to discussing it, and I wasn't sure I'd ever even want kids after my own childhood experience, but that night I could see it all so clearly. If that was something she wanted.

I turn off my TV.

I need to get out of this house. Everything is a reminder of Willow.

This couch we picked out together. The bed, the TV.

Maybe it was foolish of me to have her pick out furniture with me so early on, as if I could will our relationship to endure out of sheer necessity.

I can practically hear my mom saying, "*Che cazzo*? What's the matter with you, huh?"

She would've handed me my ass for how badly I messed this up.

So what do I do?

Am I really going to let Willow go without a fight?

WILLOW

I pull my luggage out of the closet, dusting off the old beige suitcases and matching duffel bags. The musty smell reminds me I haven't gone anywhere in the three years since I moved here.

But now, Angie and I are going on a long-overdue vacation. We leave in a few days for England and will spend the next few weeks traveling through Europe. It's been a dream of ours since we first became best friends, and now we're finally doing it.

Her brother, Wesley, lives in London and works for a major hotel chain, so he's hooking us up with all the best places to stay for dirt cheap. Angie's consulting job is 100 percent remote, so she can do it anywhere in the world, and my current freelance projects can come with me too. Though, since technically I'm my own boss, I've decided not to accept any new gigs for a while so I can maximize my time away and unplug as much as possible.

Faris is upset that he can't come with us, but he is still in recovery, and traveling with crutches and a walking boot sounds like a huge pain in the ass. Plus, he has physical therapy twice a week that he cannot miss. Angie and I promised to take him and Simon somewhere fun when he's all healed up.

I just need to get away from all this and clear my head.

ANGIE

started packing!!!

ME

me too

ANGIE

omg it's starting to feel real!

I can't contain my growing smile as I open my luggage and start figuring out what to bring on this trip. I honestly don't even know where to start. What are we even going to do out there? I basically need to bring everything, since we don't know when we're even coming back.

Henry glares at me from the other side of the room.

"Oh stop, you're going to have so much fun with your sister up at Sandy's. I'll be back before you know it!"

Angie's mom will be down here tomorrow to pick up the dogs and take them back to her farm upstate. What would I do without Angie and her family?

Our upbringings and our families could not be more opposite. I wish things could have been different for me and my parents. I always wondered what it would have been like if she hadn't left. How different my life would be.

I know Holly's departure was difficult for them, but I shouldn't have had to assume the responsibility for caring for them when they couldn't face what happened. Not when I was still a child myself. She abandoned *me*, too.

And then I was left with no one.

Over time, I learned that things get a whole lot easier once you stop giving a shit about what other people do with their lives.

I dump my laundry on the bed, ready to get a handle on what to pack, when I spot the red shirt I made for the tournament. Goddammit, it's like this stupid shirt is haunting me. I throw it across the room, missing the garbage can by a foot, and I sigh.

Fucking hell.

I've tried so hard not to think about Luca, but it's impossible. Did he really feel like he couldn't trust me with the information about his past, that I would leave him if he told me the truth?

On the other hand, can I blame him? I've avoided getting close to people my entire life. Holding my cards close to my chest so no one would ever know what hurts me. So that when they did eventually leave, maybe it wouldn't be so painful.

My thoughts of him have gotten so muddled, like I keep wanting to rationalize away his behavior and what he's done. That's why I have to go on this trip. I need distance to remind myself of who I am and what I really believe.

Because he's everywhere.

He's all over this house and ingrained in my heart.

60

LUCA

Thirteen days.

I haven't seen her in thirteen days now, and it hasn't gotten any easier.

I've done everything I can think of to distract myself, but it feels like I'm walking around with a gaping hole in my chest.

Nothing has been able to pull me out of this, not even the news that the motion was granted to release all of Dad's assets. The funds have already been wired into my bank account, so I won't have to worry about money for a long time. At least I don't have to apply to any more soulless corporate jobs; I can take my time and come up with a solid plan.

Except now those plans no longer involve the woman I love.

Kayla found out through Simon that Willow and Angie got one-way tickets to Europe with no plans for when they might come back.

The fact that she felt like she had to cross an entire ocean to get away from me is hard to come to terms with. How quickly we went from what we had together to being alone on separate continents with no way of knowing if she's even okay. I suppose in a way it's karmic justice for how things went down when I left for Greendale without her.

Max gets in my Jeep, and we head out to another Saturday pickleball session.

"How great is this weather?" Max says, way too chipper. "We should take the top back down."

"Sure, why not."

At my lack of enthusiasm, he shoots me a pitying look, and I clench the steering wheel.

"Stop looking at me like that."

"Then stop acting like *that*."

I turn up my music so I don't have to talk and pretend that everything is okay.

He's been dragging me to the courts every chance he gets, trying to help get me out of the house and stop wallowing in self-pity. But every time I walk onto the neighborhood courts or step through those doors at Dink Shot, I let myself imagine for just one single moment that she's there.

Home from her trip, from wherever she escaped to.

Home.

Greendale used to be my home, once upon a time. I spent my entire life there, so technically it's still my hometown. But ever since Dad passed away, I realized there was nothing left for me there. I had simply outgrown it. All that remained were the ghosts of my past and an ex-wife who still can't seem to be exorcized.

I had been thinking these past few months that here in Athens is where I feel at home, but that's not quite right either. It was Willow. Because now her absence has made this place feel empty, too. It was only with her that I felt at peace. Truly at home.

I have to find a way back to her.

Max and I arrive at Dink Shot and set our stuff down by the side wall, beginning our usual stretches. Though I know she's not here, I still look around for familiar faces and immediately spot a father and his young son, who's maybe about eight years old, on the court together.

The father looks to be teaching his kid how to play, and they lob the ball back and forth to each other without a care in the world. With every hit, they both smile. It's such a beautiful moment.

Every kid should experience that.

And then it hits me.

An idea. A purpose.

"I'll be right back," I say to Max as I jog up to the front desk.

I find Darrell standing in the lobby talking to Carrie. I nearly turn back around, but he immediately takes notice and waves me over.

"Hey man, what's up?" Darrell says. "You remember Carrie?"

"Of course. How are you?" I ask.

"Pretty good. Still sour over this guy making me sit out of the tournament." She smacks Darrell's arm.

I look to Darrell with wide eyes. "Oh...I..."

"No, it's fine," she says with a smile, waving her hand around. "It was for a good cause. I'm gonna head out. I'll see you boys later." She walks out the front door, and I'm more confused than ever.

At my expression, Darrell says, "Don't worry. She's my cousin, I knew she could handle it. Plus, once I explained *why* she needed to drop out, she was totally on board." He elbows my side.

Then I finally understand.

With Carrie gone, he could pair me up with Willow.

"Oh, you didn't have to do that, man." I drop my chin. "But...thank you."

"I was sorry to hear about..."

"Yeah, no, don't worry about it." I clear my throat, desperate to change the subject.

"So what's on your mind, Luca?"

I let out a long breath. "Do you run any kind of youth programs here, like classes or camps?"

"You know, I've thought about it, but just never got around to it. Why, do you know someone who's interested?"

I scratch at the thick, unkempt hair on my cheek. "What would I have to do to help set it up?"

His head tilts ever so slightly, a smile playing on his lips. "Well, honestly it wouldn't be too difficult. I can pull all the paperwork, and then we would just decide on a date and get volunteers. Maybe someone to help with marketing and promotion to get the word out."

"How soon could we put it together? What's the schedule like around here?" I ask, bouncing on my toes.

Darrell angles his head for me to follow him to the front desk. He starts clicking around on one of the computers, then turns the monitor toward me so I can see the official schedule for the facility. It shows scheduled blocks for private lessons, group reservations, open play, and individual bookings.

"Quickest we could do it is *maybe* next month, but we would have to start planning everything right now. Actually... in a month it's Thanksgiving, so we'd need to do the week after."

I look closer, and my eyes catch on something blocked off two weeks from now. "Hey, what's this?" I point to the screen. "*The Kitchen Sink* is coming here to record a podcast?"

"Yep. You heard of 'em?"

"Yeah." I smile wide. "Yeah, I've heard of them."

61

WILLOW

2 months ago

He's twenty minutes late. No messages, nothing. I'm *actually* getting stood up by this guy.

Un-fucking-believable.

I didn't even want to do this, but I just had to go and listen to Faris and Angie and all their bullshit about putting myself out there again and finding "true love." After matching with Luca, though, I admit I felt a spark. Some shred of hope that maybe this wouldn't be so bad after all. We could have some fun and just see where it went. No pressure.

I let myself get excited about it.

But now I'm being stood up and have to live with the utter humiliation of a complete stranger hurting my feelings. It's bullshit.

Behind me, the restaurant is filled with couples and large groups, laughing and enjoying all the delicious food this trendy steakhouse has to offer. The pungent, almost cheesy aroma of dry-aged beef has my mouth watering. I was really looking forward to eating here too, and now I have to go find my own dinner.

I set down a ten-dollar bill to cover my drink and a tip as I turn in my bar stool, ready to get the fuck out of here. My feet hit the floor, and I think about the fact that I opted for flats instead of heels, just on the off chance he lied about being six foot, and his first impression of me is one where I'm towering over him.

Which is also bullshit.

I should be weeding out the insecure assholes from the start, so if they have a problem with me being tall, then I don't have to waste any more of my time. Not that I ever plan on dating again after this.

A gorgeous, dark-haired man stumbles in. I squint, because it *looks* like the guy from Luca's profile picture, but the lights are dim, and something is off about him.

He saunters over to me, nearly tripping over his own feet as he weaves between tables. "Willow?" he asks, breathing the word on me. I reel back from the stench of whiskey.

"Luca?" I look him up and down with a grimace. "You're late."

"Ooh, she's feisty!" He laughs, and it immediately grates on my nerves. Walking past me and taking the seat next to where I was just a moment ago, he eyes me and pats my stool to sit back down. I'm not quite sure what this guy's deal is, but he's nothing like what I imagined.

I decide not to leave just yet, but only because our messages back and forth these past few days have been so incredible. We had a real connection. But this doesn't even feel like the same person.

Maybe he's just nervous.

Or maybe he was faking everything to get me to agree to this date.

As I reluctantly sit back down on my stool, I notice he's staring at my legs. I snap my fingers in front of his face to get his attention and roll my eyes.

Instead of apologizing for it or for being late, he pulls out his phone and reads something for the next thirty seconds. He aggressively types out a reply, completely ignoring me. After another minute or so of this rude behavior, I place my elbow on the bar and rest my chin on my fist as I stare at him, forcing a smile.

"Everything okay there?" I say through gritted teeth, trying very hard to keep my composure.

"Hmm?" He's still not looking at me.

"Alright," I say, standing back up. "This has been the opposite of fun, so I hope you have a great rest of your night."

He quickly sets his phone down and stands, grabbing my wrist as I reach for my purse. Narrowing my eyes, I shoot him a look that very clearly states, *Get your fucking hand off me.*

Surprisingly, he picks up on it through his drunken haze, releasing me and raising both hands. "I'm sorry. Please don't leave."

I cross my arms over my chest, suddenly wishing I *was* towering over him in my heels. "I would love for you to give me one good reason why I should stay. You showed up late, drunk, and now that you're here, you've barely said two words to me, all while you're busy texting someone else."

I have never been so let down by my own expectations. This guy just sucks. He emotionally catfished me.

He scrubs a hand down his annoyingly handsome face. "I'm having a really bad day, okay?"

"Oh man, I'm so sorry, you're the first person to ever have one of those."

He huffs a laugh, shaking his head. "Look, I'm sure you're used to people just falling all over themselves for you, doing whatever you want, looking the way you do," he says, waving a hand up and down at me, his lip curled. Eyes staying on my legs just a little too long. "But you could be a little nicer too, you know."

"*Nice?* Why the hell should I be nice to you?"

"I think you'll find that people aren't going to stick around very long if you treat them like shit."

The words cut like a knife, and I flinch. "You don't know the first thing about me."

"And you don't know *me*. You don't know what I've been through." His breath hitches. "You're yelling at me, and we haven't even started our date yet."

He then brings his hand to his eyes, squeezing them shut. When he opens them, they're brimming with tears.

Oh, what the fuck?

"Are you...Are you crying? Seriously?"

"I'm just going through a lot right now," he says between sobs. "Not that you care."

This is insane. What am I, his mother?

I look around the restaurant and notice a few heads peering our way. I need to get out of here.

"I'm leaving." I snatch my purse from the bar and start heading toward the entrance. I don't need this shit.

"Typical," he calls after me, like *I'm* the irrational one here. "You didn't get your way, so you blame me for all your problems and just walk away. Super classy!"

I give him the middle finger as I walk through the glass doors and out onto the sidewalk. My phone is already out as I delete Tinder off my phone, and any trace of Luca Giordano from my life.

62

___

WILLOW

I'm in love.

The UK is absolutely stunning.

I can't believe I've gone my entire life without coming here.

My family never went on big vacations, aside from a few road trips to the beach or the mountains—before Holly left, of course. I got my first passport a few years ago so Angie and I could spend a week in Canada, but I've never experienced anything quite like this.

We started in London, getting familiar with the city and the surrounding areas. Sightseeing, visiting all the major attractions like the Tower of London, Westminster Abbey, and Madame Tussauds. We learned where to have afternoon tea, and that the best curry was at Brick Lane. But we also found some hidden gems like Neal's Yard, a colorful little street full of bookstores and cafes, as well as a garden rooftop with the most spectacular views and secret underground bars.

We've been having the time of our lives, not even pretending we aren't obnoxious tourists.

At night, the vibrant, bustling city is so full of life that we found ourselves closing out nightclubs and making friends with locals wherever we went. Well, Angie at least. I just lost myself in many, many drinks while she ran the social agenda.

After about a week and a half, we took the train up to Edinburgh and spent a few days exploring old castles, cathedrals, museums, underground vaults, and botanical gardens. We walked the cobbled streets, enjoying the stunning landscapes and sampling the local cuisine.

Next was Glasgow for a day, hiking through the Scottish Highlands to take in the breathtaking views, and at night, enjoying several different music venues. I can't wait to come back again one day.

We spent the final three days in Dublin. Our hotel was right on the River Liffey next to several orange brick buildings that housed tiny bakeries, cafés, and taverns. We toured more castles, hiked the Cliffs of Moher, and visited museums and the Guinness Storehouse. Even a quiet, withdrawn American like me felt welcome.

I could've stayed here another week, easily.

Traveling with Angie has brought us even closer too, which I didn't think was possible. After all this time together, we are still learning new things about each other, and I realize how grateful I am to have her as a friend.

"I can't believe it's time to go back to London already," Angie says as she sits in the seat next to me, settling in for the ninety-minute flight. Initially, we had planned on taking the train all the way back to enjoy the scenery, but as soon as somebody explained to us that it would take all day and include a three-and-a-half-hour ferry ride, we opted for the plane.

"I know, right? Thoughts on what we want to do next?"

"Whatever we want, babe! If you're tired and you've had enough, we can head back to the states," she says as I scrunch up my face. "Okay, or we can rest up in London and then get back out and see more amazing shit."

"Fuck yeah."

We've barely scratched the surface out here, and now that I've gotten a taste of it, I want more. I want to see everything. Experience everything.

All my problems feel so small out here. I've been so focused on myself and looking inward, I hadn't even thought about the big world around me. It's really helped me gain some perspective and finally feel more like myself again. It's about time.

After arriving back in London and taking a much-needed nap, we start getting ready for a night out with Angie's brother. He's treating us to some fancy restaurant, and then it's on to one of the trendiest clubs in the city. I'm really looking forward to letting loose tonight.

While we get dressed and ready, Angie pulls up the new *Kitchen Sink* episode on her laptop and places it between us on the desk. I couldn't believe it when I heard they were going to be recording at Dink Shot to talk about the Pickle Bowl. I only wish we could've been in town to meet them and watch the episode get filmed live.

Though my initial excitement of my favorite podcasters visiting my favorite pickleball place quickly gave way to panic when I realized they were going to bring up the fact that I walked away from the final match, ending the entire tournament in the most anti-climactic—and chaotic—way possible. Handing the trophy to Jerry and Margaret Feldman yet again, and this time without them even having to face us.

As if I want to relive one of the worst moments of my entire life.

It's been over three weeks since I walked away from the tournament and from Luca Giordano, but somehow it feels like a lifetime ago. Maybe I was a fool for getting in so deep so quickly with him, making myself believe he was any different from every single person I've ever known. Other than Angie, Faris, and Simon, of course.

Can you even love someone after knowing them for only a few months?

Coming out here with Angie is just what I needed to move on.

"How long until it drops?" I ask, taking out the heatless curling headband and letting my long hair bounce free.

"Any minute now," Angie replies from the other side of the room. "Talked with Darrell after they recorded it the other day, and he said it went really well." A slow, devious smile spreads across her face.

My eyes narrow as I sit on the bed to put my high heels on. "What's that look for?"

"What look?" she asks.

Now I'm definitely suspicious.

"Bitch, why are you acting so w—"

"Shh, it's up!" She cuts me off and hits play on her laptop, shooting me another weird glance before walking over to the full-length mirror to start putting on her makeup.

"Hey everyone, welcome to *The Kitchen Sink*, talking all things pickleball. I'm Bradley..."

"And I'm Larissa, and today we have a very special episode. We are coming to you from Dink Shot in Athens, Illinois, home of the big annual pickleball tournament, the Pickle Bowl!"

"Well, let's get right into it, shall we? This year's tournament was off...the...rails!"

My stomach drops.

I jump to my feet to shut the laptop. Not tonight. We're supposed to be getting ready for a night on the town, and this is just going to put me in a sour mood. I'll listen to it later when I'm by myself and no one can see me spiral into a pit of despair.

Angie runs over and swats my hand away. "What are you doing?" She presses the spacebar to pause the video.

"I changed my mind, I'm not up for this. I don't really feel like watching my favorite podcast rip into me and embarrass me about one of the lowest moments of my life. Exposing my failures to thousands of people online? No thanks, I'd rather die."

"That's not going to happen," she says as I roll my eyes. "I already talked to Darrell, and he assured me when they recorded it that he wasn't going to let them embarrass you."

"He can't promise that. They can edit it however they want. They don't answer to Darrell."

"Just sit down and shut the fuck up," she says with an amused smile.

I cross my arms and plop back down on the bed, scowling. I don't see how it's possible to come out of this not sounding batshit crazy, but I guess we're about to find out.

She hits the spacebar again to continue playing the video.

"And here to tell us more about it," Bradley says, extending his hand, "we have Luca Giordano joining us. Welcome, Luca."

My arms fall to my sides.

The video cuts to Luca wearing headphones, sitting next to them on a white armchair. As he greets the hosts and they all make small talk, I look closer and realize the red shirt he's wearing is the one I made him for the tournament. One ankle is propped over his knee, and a large microphone is angled toward his face.

The same handsome face that haunts my dreams every night, the one I've tried to convince myself I don't need in my life, it's suddenly right there on the laptop screen in front of me. And I can't breathe.

He looks gorgeous as always, but at the same time, he looks…awful. Miserable. That warmth and spark behind his eyes has dulled, his face sullen. No hint of that devastating smile, the one that could bring me to my knees in a flash.

And I know it's because of me.

"A lot of people want to know what happened at this tournament," Larissa starts. "It caused a huge stir. You and your partner, Willow Blackburn, worked your way up the ranks against some pretty tough opponents, making it all the way to the final match, which never actually took place, forfeiting at the last minute and awarding the other pair their second championship title. Can you tell us what happened?"

"Well, Larissa, first off, I take full responsibility for what happened that day. I have no doubt we would have won and taken home that trophy had we played. And that's on me."

"So, what did happen?" Bradley asks.

Luca scratches at the hair on his cheek nervously.

His beard has grown so much longer since the last time I saw him. It makes him look older.

"I made a mistake...one that I can never take back. One that cost me everything, and that I'll regret for the rest of my life. You see, Willow and I were...more than just partners."

"So, you two were dating," Larissa guesses.

Luca chuckles softly. "Sure, if you want to call it that. Though the word 'dating' hardly does justice to what we had or what I feel for her still. We were together only a short time, but...she is the love of my life."

63

WILLOW

I snatch the laptop off the table and prop it on my lap, pressing the spacebar to pause the video. I clasp my hands over my mouth as if I could swallow the feelings I've been shoving down since I arrived here. Buried, so I don't have to feel anything or acknowledge the truth staring me in the face.

Angie studies me as she leans back against the wall, her fingers fidgeting.

My lip trembles as I suck in a deep, steadying breath, suddenly craving the sound of his voice, needing to hear the rest of this. I shouldn't *want* to hear what he has to say, shouldn't care. But of course I do. So I push play.

"If she were watching or listening right now, what would you want to say to her?" Bradley asks.

Luca uncrosses his legs and sits up, wiping his hands on his pants as he looks into the camera.

Angie walks over and hands me a tissue.

"I...I've spent most of my life on the sidelines. Going with the flow, allowing others to make decisions for me, and just staying quiet and out of the way. It's been hard for me to stand up for myself sometimes or to say what I really wanted or needed. Until you. Willow, I've known from the first—well, okay maybe second—time I saw you..."

I can't help but huff out a wet laugh.

"...I knew what I wanted. Even though you hated me in the beginning, I knew you were worth fighting for."

"That certainly sounds like an interesting story," Bradley says.

Luca blinks, as if remembering he's not alone on this podcast. "We'll have to save that for another time."

Larissa smacks Bradley and says, "Don't interrupt him! God, you always ruin the moment." She motions to Luca to continue.

"Look, I know I'm not perfect...but you make me want to try. I am so, so sorry that I let the fear of my past prevent me from starting my future with you. For the rest of my life, I will regret not being honest with you from the start. If there's any part of you that would consider giving me another chance, there would be nothing off-limits between us. I will lay every mistake I've ever made out on the table for you."

"Such as?" Larissa asks with a curious smile.

She's making him say it all, and I'm reminded why I like her so much.

"Like…the time I texted my best friend in high school after losing my virginity but accidentally sent the text to my mom instead."

I shake my head and smile against my will.

"Or the time I accidentally taught my neighbor's six-year-old kids the term 'shit-stain.' Sorry, Max."

A full-throated laugh escapes me. The memory of how sweet he was with Gabe at the bookstore flashes through my mind. And when I panicked that it was his own son, before Max swooped in.

"Willow. You *are* the love of my life. I am so sorry for what happened. And if this was all the time you and I ever had together, then I will be forever grateful for those moments. You made me feel safe and loved. I knew I could show you all the different parts of me without feeling judged. You have to know how much that matters to me."

I wipe my eyes with the tissue I've been clinging to, and it's smeared with makeup.

"You asked me once if I was lucky, and I know now that I truly am. I am lucky to have met you. I'm lucky to have experienced life with you. You showed me how important it is to speak up for what I want. And what I want... is you. All the highs, all the lows, and every shade in between. Now and forever. If you'll have me."

"Wow," Larissa says after a beat of silence. "I'm getting teary-eyed over here."

Bradley adds, "That was so beautiful, man. I hope the two of you can work things out."

Luca smiles wistfully.

"So what's next for you?" Larissa asks. "You're still going to keep playing pickleball, right?"

"I'm not sure I could ever quit, but I might take a break. Go back home for a while and try to sort some things out."

"Well, best of luck to you. You'll have to keep us all updated," Bradley says, shaking Luca's hand and turning back to the camera. "Next up, we're going to be speaking to Darrell Frink, the owner of Dink Shot, after we take a quick break to thank our sponsors—"

I close the laptop and toss it next to me on the bed. Letting my head fall into my hands, I can't help but weep like a child. Every possible emotion rolling through me, everything I've tried to deny. It's almost too much to bear.

Angie wraps her arm around my shoulders as the spot next

to me on the bed sinks down. "What are you thinking right now? Tell me."

I sniffle and swipe at the tears flowing down my cheek. "I don't know. I've been trying so hard to get over him and move on, but...I do miss him. And I'm terrified."

"Of what?"

"This feeling." I press a hand into my sternum. "I...tried not to let myself fall for him so I wouldn't get hurt, but it didn't work. It didn't stop the pain. And being away from him has only hurt that much more."

"So, what are you going to do? What do *you* want?"

"I...I want to be with him, I do. But...if he breaks my heart again..."

"What if you break his?" she says. "Or what if *this*, what if *that*? Babe, you can't control any of that. You can't live in a state of 'what if.' You will drive yourself crazy. All you can do is listen to your heart and try your best. That's all any of us can do."

I nod. "You're right."

"So...?"

"I should call him. I should...book a flight home." I sit up straighter. "Wait, he said he was going home. Does that mean he's leaving Athens to go back to Greendale?"

Where Holly is.

"Hold that thought, I have an idea. I'll be right back," Angie says with a huge grin as she grabs her shoes and her purse and...flees our hotel room. What is she doing? Why did she take her stuff with her?

I stand to look at myself in the mirror. My face is a complete mess from crying, but I don't even care. I scroll through my phone to Luca's contact info to unblock his number, when there's a knock at the door.

"Angie, did you forget your key a—"

But when I open the door, it's not Angie standing there. It's Luca.

64

LUCA

I'm pacing my extravagant hotel room when I finally hear the knock at my door, the specific one Angie and I agreed upon earlier to be the all-clear signal.

Okay, here we go.

Opening the door, I give Angie a thumbs-up. She mouths *"good luck"* before skipping barefoot down the hallway toward the elevators, her shoes and purse dangling from her fingers.

I take a slow, deep breath as I smooth down the front of my suit jacket with one hand, a bouquet of red and orange flowers in the other, similar to the ones I gave her on our first *proper* date.

My stomach does flips as I walk the ten paces down the hallway, stopping in front of her hotel room door. I run my hand through my hair and then knock.

Willow's voice drifts from the other side of the door. When it opens, she freezes like a deer in headlights. My breath catches at the sight of her. Of *her*. Not just an image I conjured in my head. Her.

"Hello, gorgeous," I say as steadily as I can.

"Hey," she says on a soft breath, her amber eyes almost comically wide, and I can't help but smile. "What are you doing here?"

I hand her the flowers. "I missed you."

She slowly takes them from me and closes her eyes on an exhale. Tears begin to fall beneath her long lashes, and I step closer to wrap my arms around her, pulling her to my chest. The flowers drop to her side as she buries her face into the crook of my neck, and her free hand fists my dress shirt. I hold her tighter, stroking her soft hair as I inhale her familiar lavender and coconut scent.

She's really here. This isn't just a dream.

I could stand like this with her forever. I've missed her so much. Her presence, her voice, her touch.

I brush a strand of curled hair away from her wet face, tucking it behind her ear before kissing her temple.

"I heard what you said," she says with a sniffle. "I thought you were going back home."

"I did, that's why I'm here."

She blinks a few times as I wipe away a stray tear with my thumb.

Cradling her face in my hands, I add, "I'm here because, Willow, *you* are my home."

She looks into my eyes with such intensity...

"What, too cheesy?" I ask, my voice nearly cracking.

She shakes her head. "Nothing wrong with cheesy."

My grin widens as she angles her head back up and captures my lips with hers, and it truly does feel like home. I deepen our kiss, letting my hand drift up into her hair, pulling her closer and closer. I can't get close enough.

The flowers fall to the floor as her hands move up to my face. At some point, we break the kiss, pressing our foreheads together. Both of us fighting to catch our breath.

"Luca...I need you to know something." She pauses, and I watch as her throat bobs.

"What is it?"

Those radiant eyes hold my gaze as she says, "I...I love you."

My mouth falls open. This is the moment my heart explodes. It feels like I'm floating. "God, I love you too. I love you so much."

I crush my lips to hers. I have been suffocating these past few weeks without her, but now I can finally breathe again.

Her hands snake around my torso, holding me tighter. And it's all I've ever needed.

Amore mio.

The love of my goddamn life.

Here in my arms.

I'm never letting her go again.

She finally says, "I can't believe you're really here. How did you even know where I was?"

"Hah, take a wild guess," I say, leaning to kiss her neck.

"Angie." She shakes her head. "Of course."

"So, are we just going to stand here in the doorway all night, or are you going to invite me in?" I nibble at her earlobe as she gasps softly and arches her back.

"What about Angie? What if she comes back?"

"We're meeting her and her brother downstairs in one hour." I pull away and casually pick the flowers up off the floor, walking past her into her hotel room and setting them on the table along with my key card.

"We are?" she asks as she closes the door. "Wait, what else have you two been scheming?"

I shrug off my suit coat and casually lay it on the bed. My nerves are now gone, and my slumbering courage roars back to life.

Slowly, so slowly, I remove my cufflinks and roll up my sleeves, watching as she takes me in from head to toe. Her back presses up against the wall as she bites her lower lip, and I swear she squeezes her thighs together. That alone nearly breaks my composure.

She's dressed in a sparkly, royal blue cocktail dress that stops just above the knees. Matching high heels put her at eye level with me. Her long hair is down and curled, her face a little red and puffy with hardly any makeup on, but she's never looked more beautiful. So real.

I start walking toward her. "You're in charge, gorgeous. Where do you want me?"

She goes still. "What?"

"You...are the one running this show. You...are in control." I drop to my knees in front of her, running my hands up her smooth, voluptuous thighs. "Boss me around. Tell me what you want."

A slow, feline grin spreads across her face, and in that moment, I know I'm done for. She caresses my cheek as I stare up at her.

"I want you, my love...all over this hotel room."

My dick twitches, and I hum in agreement, pulling up the hem of her dress a few inches, kissing high up on her thigh. "What else?"

"I want your naked body on top of mine. Need to feel the weight of you on me."

I kiss her other thigh, higher this time, until I reach that sensitive skin right at the edge of her panties. "What else?"

She takes my head in both hands, tugging at my hair and directing my attention up to her face. "Most of all, I want... what you want. So here's what we're going to do."

She steps away from me as she slowly reaches back and unzips her dress, never taking her eyes off mine.

"I'm going to tell you every...single...thing I want you to do to me, and when to do it. You do as I say. When I say it."

The shiny blue dress falls gracefully down her body in a puddle at her feet, leaving her in just a black lacy bra and thong, and those sky-high stilettos.

"And then...it's your turn. I want to hear every filthy, salacious word that comes into your mind. Every command. Unfiltered. *Unleashed.*"

Her hands go behind her back again, unhooking her bra before dropping it in front of me. My eyes closely following its descent before landing back on those perfect, round breasts.

"Is that clear?"

Swallowing around the lump in my throat, I reply, "Yes, ma'am."

She steps closer to me as I stare up into her eyes, still on my knees. "Take off my underwear." Her husky voice is like fire licking down my spine.

Hooking my index fingers into the top of her thong, she grabs my wrists. "With your teeth."

Dear God.

I run my hands around the curves of her ass, squeezing as much as I can fit in my grasp. I lean in and bite down on the fabric just above her pussy, breathing in the scent of her arousal. With my teeth, I pull the black thong down her thighs past her knees, until I'm practically bowing down on the floor as she steps out one foot at a time.

"Up," she commands, and I obey.

My heart is pounding, and I'm already so fucking hard. My breaths come faster and faster, making me light-headed. I stand there, patiently awaiting her next instructions. She's tormenting me in the most sensual way.

She sits down on the end of the bed and scoots herself back, letting her legs fall open, baring everything to me. "Now, take off your clothes." When I rush to unbuckle my belt, she adds, "Slowly."

Taking a deep breath, I pull the belt through the loops with a snap and unbutton my dress pants as slowly as I possibly can. I have to close my eyes as I unbutton my shirt, because the sight of her open and bare like this is almost too much to take. I really want to get through this without having to name any more dead presidents in my head.

Does she know how much she affects me?

After every piece of my clothing is on the floor, I open my eyes to find her pleasuring herself on the bed. My breath hitches at the sight. Her slender fingers slide into her dripping wet entrance then rub circles over her swollen clit. Her long hair fanned out beneath her head.

"Touch yourself while you watch me," she commands.

Goddamn.

I do as she says, my hand gripping my rock-hard cock as she masturbates on the bed, torturing me. "Fuck, I'm dying over here, gorgeous. Please," I beg. I don't even care if I sound pathetic. I'm ready to worship every inch of this ravishing goddess in front of me.

My goddess of fire.

That slow grin forms on her face again as she pulls her hand away from her glistening pussy and raises herself on her elbows. "Then come over here and fuck me like you mean it."

Lowering my head, I growl, "If you say so."

65

WILLOW

"Before we go downstairs," Luca says as he buttons up his black fitted shirt, "I need to show you something."

On wobbly legs, I glance at him, confused, pulling my new favorite blue dress back up my thighs and the straps over my shoulders. "Okay...?"

"It's in my room, I'll be right back."

"Wait, your *room*? You have a room here?" I guess I haven't had much time to think about the logistics of when he got here and where he's been this whole time.

"Just a few doors down. But I only checked in a couple hours ago," he says, tucking the shirt into his suit pants.

"Okay, this is so surreal. I'm going to need more details about what you've cooked up here with Angie."

"All in due time, my love," he says as he cups my cheek and kisses my temple. "Be back in a sec."

I stand there dumbfounded, watching as he grabs a key card off the table and leaves my hotel room. So many questions are swirling in my mind right now. I can't believe he's even here.

My reflection in the mirror catches my eye, and I realize I should probably fix my makeup. And my hair. But I don't really care at this point.

He's *here*. In London. He came here for me.

He professed his love for me to the world and then made sure he was here when I heard it.

For the past forty-five minutes, we've been making up for lost time, taking turns being in charge and speaking our deepest desires for one another out loud, making love on nearly every surface of this room. But now we are left with only a few minutes to get ready and meet Angie and her brother downstairs.

And that's another thing. Was *he* in on this whole scheme, too? He's the one who even made this trip possible for us. How long have they all been planning this?

I've only met Wesley a handful of times before, but I want to be sure to thank him for everything he's done for us. This trip has been life-changing in so many ways.

As I reapply my foundation, the door opens, and Luca enters with a large manila envelope, his eyes sparkling.

"What is that?" It reminds me of the envelope I opened on my birthday, with his illustration of the two of us inside. The one I gave back to him in a cardboard box, carelessly tossed on his front porch in an act of extreme pettiness. I know that must have crushed him, and I wish I could take it back.

He holds out a hand and says, "Come sit with me."

I let him lead me to the edge of one of the beds. He sits down, and I take the spot next to him, his thigh warm against mine.

"While you've been gone, I've spent a lot of time thinking. Thinking...and working to get this." He holds up the folder, and my heart picks up. "I knew we couldn't move forward until we had this, and I'm sorry I couldn't get it done sooner."

He places it in my lap, his arm wrapping around my waist. I look into his warm brown eyes as he lifts his chin toward it for me to open. Pulling out a stack of documents, the first words I read are "PETITION FOR SEPARATION DIVORCE."

My eyes widen as I look back over at him for some kind of assurance that this is what I think it is. He nods and leans his head on mine.

I flip to the last page to see it with my own eyes, the two signatures: Luca's and...a judge's? "Wait...but she didn't sign it."

"She didn't have to," he says with a reassuring smile.

I narrow my eyes. "What do you mean?"

"My lawyer was able to file for a no-fault separation-based divorce. Basically, she and I lived apart for over a year, and at that point, only one party needed to consent to it." He takes the papers out of my hands and puts them aside on the bed. "It wasn't easy, and it didn't happen overnight. But it was necessary."

I squeeze his hand. I know this must have been hard for him to face.

"My lawyer had warned that this kind of thing is not always cut and dry, and Sadie—I mean, Holly—was legally able to object to it, which she did, of course. So it moved to a court hearing. It was the second time I've had to stand in front of that same judge in a month."

She puts her hand on my arm. "Wait. Your dad's case. Did you hear back yet?"

I smile. "I did. It's done. Just like this one." I point to the papers. "Look, I'm happy to give you as many or as few details as you want to hear, but in the end, it was clear that the marriage was irreparably and decidedly *over*. And he granted the divorce on the spot."

I let loose a sigh of relief. "When did you even do all this?"

"I had my divorce lawyer get the paperwork in motion a few days after we…" he clears his throat, the struggle evident on his face. "After I last saw you."

Meaning after we broke up and I shut the door in his face.

"But then the objection was filed soon after, and I had to appear for the court hearing on Tuesday."

"Wait, so you went back to Greendale *three days ago*?"

"Well, technically I drove there Monday night, had the hearing and got all the paperwork done Tuesday, drove back to Athens to record the podcast Wednesday, and then caught the first flight out this morning."

My mind is spinning. I can't believe he did all that in just three days, and now he's here.

"You're…incredible." I hold up our interlaced hands and kiss his knuckles. "So…it's really over."

"Willow, it's *been* over, but yes, now officially…legally…it's done." He gently brushes his thumb along my cheek. "It's just you. It's only ever been *you*."

"I love you," I say again, the words still unfamiliar on my tongue, yet so true. So right.

"I love you too." He leans in and captures my lips. Softly at first. Loving, tender. A promise of his love and his devotion, poured into me with every breath we share. But just like every other time, it quickly turns hungry and intense. His freshly-trimmed beard scratching at my raw chin.

Pulling away, he lets out a quick breath. "*Cara mia.* We really should go downstairs. They're expecting us."

"Hm." I continue kissing him, ignoring his suggestion and running my hands through his thick black hair and tugging gently.

He laughs as he kisses me back but soon stops again with his hands on my forearms. "I thought you wanted to hear all about my scheming with Angie, and how I came all the way to London to see you."

I look up at him with a pout. "Ugh…I really do."

Standing up, he holds out a hand to me. When I take it, he pulls me close to him, his other hand finding the small of my back, as if we were slow dancing. The two of us sharing the same breath. The only two people left in the universe.

Holding our interlaced hands between us pressed over our hearts, he says, "We may need to alter the plan a little though, because this was actually supposed to be Angie's room. I was instructed to bring your things to *my* room, but I got a little distracted."

We look around at the mess we've made. Both beds are a complete wreck, pillows and blankets strewn about all over the floor.

"Oh…yeah…she may not want to sleep in here," I say with a laugh.

We just stand there locked in each other's embrace, swaying gently from side to side. Feeling another shift between us, our future together unwritten and suddenly wide open for us. Knowing what we have is so special and rare, I can't imagine my life without him now. He's already a part of me.

I feel my heart expand for him, letting him in once and for all. Allowing every part of him to intertwine with every part of me. And for the first time in my life, I'm not scared.

66

LUCA

Willow and I have spent the last few days traveling around England together, just the two of us, while Angie spent some quality time with her brother. I wanted to stay out here a little longer before having to return to Athens, but I promised Darrell I would be back in time to get the youth pickleball clinic set up.

Once I told Willow about it, she insisted we both go home at the end of the week so she could help out, too. We agreed to make it a priority to travel the world together one day, now that our future together is full of endless possibilities.

I also told her about Holly and Preston McIntire, which seemed to throw her for a loop. But she said in some strange way, it gave her some much-needed closure.

The four of us get seated for our final dinner together at a beautiful, tiny Italian restaurant with framed photos and all kinds of tchotchkes on the walls. A chaotic, yet comforting reminder of my Nani's old house, where we would all come together for family dinners every weekend.

Suddenly, a tall man with auburn hair steps up behind

Wesley's chair and plants his hands on his shoulders. "There he is!" the stranger proclaims.

Wesley looks up at him and immediately jumps to his feet, hugging the red-haired man. "Asher? Oh my God, what are you doing here?"

They pull apart with huge smiles on their faces. "In town for work. What about you? I can't believe I'm running into you here!" He looks around our table and raises his hand. "Hello, sorry to interrupt."

I stand, extending my hand to him as Wesley makes the introductions. "Asher Hayes, this is Luca, Willow...and you remember my sister, Angie?"

Willow shakes his hand too, and we all look to Angie, who is still sitting down. Her eyes are wide, and I worry she might be having some kind of medical emergency. She's not blinking, not reacting.

"Of course," Asher says softly. "Hi, Angie. It's good to see you again."

"Asher," she finally says. "Wow, it's been a while. You look great—I mean, how are you?"

Angie's freckled face is bright red. I look at Willow, but she shrugs.

Wesley pulls up a chair from another table and places it between him and Angie. "Join us, please. I want to hear what you've been up to."

"I'd love to."

As Asher takes a seat, I notice a silent conversation happening between Willow and Angie. Raised eyebrows and heads shaking. Something is definitely going on here, but I know Willow will get to the bottom of it and fill me in soon enough.

For now, I just want to enjoy the company of her and her

friends. I am beyond grateful to Angie and Wesley for their help in reuniting me with Willow.

Thank God I got that all-clear knock.

I don't plan on letting Willow out of my sight any time soon.

We both have things from our past we still need to work through—both together and separately—to show up and be the best version of ourselves we can be for each other. It won't always be easy, but it will be worth it. It's always going to be worth it with her.

To completely open yourself up to another person is truly a gift. It's terrifying and can be painful, but still a gift. One that I will never take for granted for as long as I live.

The conversation between Wesley and Asher continues, Angie still suspiciously quiet and never taking her eyes off Asher.

I put an arm around the back of Willow's chair and lean in close, my nose brushing softly against her ear. "You ready to go back tomorrow?"

"I am," she says with an easy smile. "I've really missed—" I bring her face to mine for a kiss before she can finish, but when we pull apart, she says, "pickleball."

The laughter that escapes us is pure joy and elation, and I kiss her again, trying to swallow the sound and have it live inside my heart forever.

After we land in Athens the next day, I hold her hand on the way to the parking garage. I spot something small on the hood of my Jeep and start laughing.

"What's so funny?"

"Look what someone left for us." I point to the front of my car, where a single rubber duck is awaiting our arrival.

She shakes her head, but I don't miss the half smile on her lips.

After loading our suitcases in the back, I take our new friend off the hood and open the driver's side door, placing him on the crowded dashboard next to the other ducks.

"Admit it, you think it's fun *and* nice," I say as I back out of the parking spot. "I'll even let you name him."

Rolling her eyes, she says, "Fine. What's the Italian word for 'cheese?'"

"Formaggio."

"Okay, that's actually pretty cute. I like it."

"Me too," I say as I take her hand and interlace our fingers. We drive home in comfortable silence, my classic rock music playing low through the speakers.

A text comes in on Willow's phone, and her mouth drops as she reads it, extracting her fingers from mine to type out a reply.

"What is it?"

"Just something Asher told Angie," she says with a half smile.

Last night, Angie told her all the details of her history with Asher. Willow relayed everything back to me, but she lost me during the part about someone named Ernest.

"I'm happy for her. Childhood friends, brother's best friend, second-chance romance? That's the making of a great rom-com."

She gasps. "How many of those books have you read?"

"Everything from your list."

"Impressive," she says with a raised eyebrow. She finishes typing on her phone, setting it in her lap and lacing our fingers together again.

When we pull into the neighborhood, she asks, "Want to play pickleball tonight?"

"Sure. Is anyone else from the group coming?"

"I don't care. Let's play just the two of us."

I bring her hand to my lips and kiss her knuckles. "Just the two of us then."

A sense of calm washes over me, my mind and body finally at peace. I may not know what the future holds, but with Willow by my side, I feel invincible. Empowered. She has given me the strength and the courage to chase the life I want and deserve.

A life of truth and love, full of laughter and adventure, alongside my partner.

EPILOGUE
WILLOW

11 months later

Sweat glides down my burning hot skin. My heart pounds wildly against my ribs as I squeeze my eyes shut, trying to control my ragged breaths. Readying myself for this.

God, we are so close.

I look to Luca. My partner. My love.

We are so close now.

Just one more point and we will win this year's Pickle Bowl.

Dressed in our new matching purple athletic shirts that read *If you want a soft serve, go get ice cream*, Luca and I are more than ready. We've been counting down to this day for months.

Max and Angie paired up again this year, climbing the ranks alongside us and doing us the favor of defeating Jerry and Margaret in the second round. In a stunning and nail-biting turn of events, the four of us managed to come together in the finals to compete for the championship title.

I know I said I would be happy for Angie if she and Max won, but I really, really want to win.

But I also know that no matter what happens here today, I'm going home with the man I love. And that means more than any trophy ever could.

"Fourteen thirteen on one!" I shout before serving the ball across to Angie. She returns it to Luca, who lets it bounce before hitting it back over the net, the sound echoing off the tall ceiling.

Max hits the ball toward Luca and strikes him in the shoulder. *Shit.* Hopefully getting body-bagged by his best friend is enough to light a fire under him. My sweet, lucky golden boy needs to step it up if we're going to pull out this victory.

I walk over to him as he massages the sore spot where he was hit. "You good?"

He nods, taking a deep breath.

"Hey." I tap him playfully on the ass with my paddle, lowering my voice. "Unleashed."

A slow, wicked grin spreads across his face as he nods again and winks.

There he is.

Luca bounces the ball in front of him as he walks back to the baseline, readying himself for his serve. We just need this one last point. The crowd is collectively holding its breath, waiting to see who gets crowned as champions. The space is so quiet you could hear a pin drop.

"Fourteen thirteen on two!" he shouts before hitting it over the net to Angie's square. After the bounce, she returns it to me. It all happens so fast. The back and forth, the firefight at the net. Both sides are desperate for any advantage. All four of us grunting and panting with every hit.

At some point, the ball flies high above me and I fake a swing, letting it bounce one time before slamming the bright yellow ball past them both, and we all watch—in what feels like slow motion—as it heads toward the baseline. I pray to all the gods that it stays in.

Max and Angie are too far forward to get to it in time as it lands just inside the line and bounces off the court.

It was in.

We won.

Holy shit.

Luca and I scream at the same time as I jump into his arms, my legs wrapping around his waist. The crowd around us erupts into cheers as he spins me around and pulls my head down for a crushing kiss. I get lost in the feel of him, smiling against his lips as the rest of the world falls away.

After a moment, finally remembering where we are, I pull away from him slightly, and he lowers me to my feet. Angie hands something to Luca, or maybe she shakes his hand? I can barely process anything happening around me right now as confetti falls all around us.

I clink paddles with her and Max before she pulls me in for a full-body hug. She extracts the paddle from my hand and leans away, fiddling with my hair as I swat at her hands.

"What are you doing, you maniac?" I ask, but she's all smiles and pursed lips before taking me by the shoulders and spinning me around, nudging me away from the net.

Darrell approaches us with the giant golden trophy in one arm, and says into his microphone, "Give it up for this year's Pickle Bowl champions...Willow and Luca!" He extends the trophy, and we take it together, raising it over our heads. The commotion around us is overwhelming.

The part of me who normally hates being the center of attention is steady, elated even. Because I'm not alone out here. I'm surrounded by the people I love, and who love me, too.

I meet Luca's gaze, his smile so wide the skin around his eyes crinkles. He then lets go of the trophy, leaving me to hold the heavy monstrosity alone.

Darrell hands him the microphone, and Luca turns back to me with mischief in those reddish-brown eyes as he drops to one knee.

From behind his back, he produces a small black velvet box. The crowd murmurs around us.

Oh my God.

My heart is in my throat.

I lower the trophy to the ground as he gently takes my hand. "Willow," he says into the microphone, the sound of my name echoing off the walls of the building. "My partner. My love. We've been through so much this past year. You hated me for the first few weeks or so, but that's okay, I deserved it."

I bark out a laugh, tears already blurring my vision.

"We've grown together, we've laughed, we've cried. You taught me to stand up for myself and fight for what I want. You've shown me what true love is. We've made a home together. Waking up with you every morning has brought me more joy than I could have ever imagined. Will you do me the honor of letting me wake up next to you every day, for the rest of our lives? A life full of partnership and...dog hair, and binge-watching shows, and bookstore shopping, and pickleball, and love. Willow Blackburn...*amore mio*...you are my family. You are my home. Will you marry me?"

He opens the box, and I stare at the silver princess-cut diamond ring inside. I recognize it immediately from the photo at Luca's house. His mother's wedding ring.

I cover my mouth as I nod furiously. Tears streaming down my face. "Yes. Hell yes. Of course I'll marry you."

He sets down the microphone to slip the ring on my finger,

our hands shaking. When he stands, he grabs my face to kiss me fiercely, and the crowd goes wild.

This feels like a dream.

This magnificent man before me.

He is *mine*. And I am his.

He wasn't lying when he said we've been through a lot this year. After the success of the initial kids' camp Luca set up at Dink Shot last year, he and I launched our youth pickleball program as an after-school class for various age groups.

We were not prepared for how popular it would become, and before too long, the demand was so high that Darrell decided he would open a second Dink Shot location, which would serve as the home for an official youth league that Luca and I would run together.

We became certified pickleball instructors and have been busy building the league to reach as many kids in the community as we can—which now sits at six teams in the county—as well as hiring new part-time coaches, including Max and Faris.

I convinced him that coming back to coach might spark his love of the sport again, and I was right. Seeing the joy on those kids' faces brought it all back for him, and now he can't stay away. He and Simon became investors too, after learning that Luca put a bunch of the money from his dad's estate into getting the league off the ground. We couldn't have done any of this without the help and support of all our friends. Our family.

Of course, I designed our logos and all the marketing materials, while Luca has been focused more on growing the business. He even found a way to partner with mental health experts, who now attend sessions once a month, and are available to all the kids and their families at no cost to them.

It's been incredible for us to see these kids play, learning about teamwork and friendship, building their confidence and nurturing their mental health. All while instilling in them a love for pickleball.

And now, after winning this tournament, Luca and I finally get to go down to Florida to see the US Pickleball Open. Together.

I'm not sure when any of this is going to feel real.

After a few celebratory drinks upstairs in the bar with Faris, Simon, Max, Kayla, Angie, and Angie's boyfriend, Asher, we politely excuse ourselves to go home for the night, not bothering to fake any illnesses to leave early this time.

I carry our trophy while Luca lugs our duffel bags over his shoulders, and we walk through the parking lot to my car, hand in hand.

He looks over at me as I lean in and hug his bicep, appreciating this incredible man—my *fiancé*—and everything we've been through together.

We toss our stuff in the back of my Jeep, barely fitting it all with this big-ass gaudy trophy. I climb into the driver's seat, my eyes catching on the little rubber duck I have dangling from my rearview mirror. The only duck I've ever allowed in this Jeep.

A few months ago, Luca painted over Herbert's tennis racquet to be a pickleball paddle, and now it's a constant reminder of what brought us together.

Luca leans across the center console for a tender kiss. "I love you so much," he says on a soft breath.

"I love you too," I reply, smiling so wide it hurts my face. "I cannot wait to marry you."

"I can't wait to call you my *wife*."

"Ooh, I like the sound of that."

The drive home is quiet and content, our fingers interlaced while his thumb rubs the sensitive spot on my wrist. The diamond ring on my other hand feels strange and heavy.

That's definitely going to take some getting used to.

My mouth waters thinking about the sauce he's had simmering on the stove all day for the celebratory dinner he insisted we have tonight. We do have so much to celebrate. Our future together is wide open, and I've never felt so hopeful. I commit this feeling to memory as I pull into the driveway of our new home.

The two-story home in the newer section of West Brook at the end of the running trail. The house with a crimson-red door and colorful flower boxes under the windows.

The one we moved into just last week on my birthday.

Stay tuned for Angie and Asher's story...

Want more of Willow and Luca?
Sign up for my newsletter to receive a special bonus chapter!

ACKNOWLEDGMENTS

This book would not be possible without the support of my incredible family, who always believes in me and puts up with me when I'm in gremlin work-mode. A special shoutout to my husband, who really tore his Achilles playing pickleball. That was the opposite of fun, let's never do it again.

My beta readers, who showed me so much enthusiasm and love at the start. It really encouraged me to keep going.

My fellow writers on Threads and Instagram, I have enjoyed building a community with you. Thank you for all your advice and support!

Victoria, my editor, for giving me the tools to turn this story into the best it could possibly be.

Emilie for fitting me in for a final proofread at the last minute!

And all my friends and family who don't even know I've written this. I love you, but most of you shant find out.